ANGELO'S VENGEANCE

A DARK MAFIA ROMANCE

THE COMMISSION SERIES
BOOK 3

HAVEN FOX

BLURB

He was the man she was promised to. Now he's the last one she wants... and the only one she can't live without.

————

Theodosia:

I have loved Angelo Santelli since I was twelve.
I was meant to be his—bound by a blood oath our fathers signed before we understood it.
Once, I would have given anything to be his wife. Now?
I wouldn't marry him if he paid me.
I've always loved beautiful things—fabric, design, control over chaos. Nothing about

Angelo Santelli qualifies as *safe*, but damn if he isn't beautiful in his own dark way.

———

Angelo:

I built my empire with blood and steel.
Loyalty is currency in my world, and betrayal earns a bullet. I don't trust easily, and I don't love.
Theodosia Anthakos has been a thorn in my side since the night she caught me with another girl.
She's hated me ever since, going out of her way to make my life hell, wrecking my car, pushing every one of my buttons.
And yet, I can't stop wanting her.
Now we're tangled in something dangerous —something bigger than both of us. My enemies are closing in. My mother wants me dead. And the only thing more explosive than the war outside these walls… is her.
And I'll burn the world to keep her.

COPYRIGHT

CONTENT WARNINGS

Dear Reader:

This is a work of fiction. Names, characters, businesses, places, events, and incidents are either products of the author's imagination or are used in a fictitious manner.

This book features themes that are suited to the mafia romance genre. Please read responsibly.

———

Also be prepared for:

* Hyphens & em dashes … I love them. If this triggers you, please be aware of this in advance. I also love short, choppy sentences #sorrynotsorry

TRANSLATIONS

Translations:

Italian:

Cazzo: Fuck

Fratello: Brother

Sorella: Sister

Picolla: Baby / Babe

Famiglia: Family

Hai Capito: Do you understand?

Amore Mio: My love

————

Greek:

Yamas: To our health (a toast)

ABOUT THE AUTHOR

Haven Fox writes spicy romance novels featuring alpha men, strong female protagonists, and loyal friends. All of her books can be enjoyed through Kindle Unlimited.

Please don't forget to leave a review after reading. Each one makes a huge difference!

―――――

The Commission Novel Series (this series)
Maxim's Promise | Conall's Reign | Angelo's
Vengeance | Belonging to Ilias

Iron Brotherhood Motorcycle Club
Saving Helena | Sheltering Hollis | Pike's
Redemption | Claiming Veronica

―――――

Join Haven's Newsletter List for exclusive
news: HERE

to all those who love us even when we're crazy

CHAPTER 1
ANGELO
AGE 11

I HUNCHED OVER MY EGGS, shoveling them in as quickly as I could, ignoring the look from our housekeeper, Renata, who valued better manners. I knew my mother was already on the stairs, and once she came down, I wouldn't be able to eat in peace.

My mother, Carlotta Santelli, never cared much about anyone's feelings except her own. She felt better when she made others feel worse, especially if they were her kids.

My little brother Remo was only five, and my sister was three, so they had a nanny, but that never stopped her from poking them. The nanny was clever, though, and had already begun moving them out of the kitchen, their jammy fingers leaving smudges on the doorframe, before my mother reached the bottom step. Her disapproving glare met mine just as I shoved the last bite of egg into my mouth.

"What are you doing here? I thought you had to go to that meeting with your father?" Her mouth pinched with displeasure, as if my lingering in her presence was offensive.

I pushed my chair back, the scrape of wood against marble sharp in the quiet room. "I was eating." It was obvious what I was doing, but this was what she excelled at: making you feel small, tearing you down to nothing.

Her eyes narrowed. "You should be in the car by now. Don't keep your father waiting."

I wanted to roll my eyes, but I knew better. Rolling my eyes only earned me a smack across the face. She preferred that I stay out of sight, waiting in the car for hours instead of her having to look at me. She thought I was stupid. Well, I wouldn't play her games.

I brushed past her before she could say another word, but the second I stepped into the hallway, I heard heavy footsteps approaching. My father appeared, filling the doorway, his dark eyes locking onto me with a silent command.

"Get in the car." His voice was low, the

growl of impatience promising violence if I didn't hurry.

My father was old-school mafia—one of those guys who believed that if you didn't jump when he said to, he should knock you around until you learned better. He wasn't shy about it either, and never cared who was around. He had kids so he could train them the way he wanted. He wasn't winning any father-of-the-year awards, if you catch my drift.

My hands clenched at my sides. "I don't want to go." The words sounded petulant even to my ears, but I couldn't help it.

His expression hardened. "It's not up for discussion."

I glanced toward the front door, measuring the distance, but he saw it before I even twitched.

"You run, and I'll make sure you regret it, *stronzo*. We don't have time for any of that."

A surge of anger rushed through me, hot and defiant. I hated him. I hated all of this, but I also knew there was no escaping it. Not today. I took a step, but not toward the car. He blocked me easily, his hand snapping out to grip my arm in an iron hold, tight enough to leave marks.

"I'm not in the mood," he muttered under his breath.

I twisted, jerking back, but he tightened his grip. It wasn't hard enough to hurt, just enough to remind me who was stronger. Who was in control.

For now.

I lifted my chin, my heart hammering. "One day, you won't be able to make me go."

Something flickered in his gaze, something unreadable. Then he smirked, the kind of knowing look that made my stomach twist on itself.

"We'll see about that. Today, I can. Tomorrow, I still have your little brother and your little sister, don't I?" His lips curled into that cruel smile that told me he wouldn't mind playing dirty. "You care about them. Maybe you don't care about yourself so much." He bent closer to me so his jowly face was close to mine. "But having weaknesses isn't a good idea, Angelo. You'll need to learn that."

He was heavy and obviously Italian, with his dark, greying hair swept back in a widow's peak. Me? I didn't look like him at all. My hair and eyes were light colored. He said I was his son, but I wasn't convinced. My father was the worst kind of man. His children were just tools in his arsenal, meant to be used. If he broke one, he'd get another.

And just like that, he dragged me outside, shoving me toward the waiting car. The door was already open. Our driver, Uberto, didn't even look at me as I slid into the leather seat.

The door slammed shut, locking me in.

The engine hummed to life, and as we pulled away from the house, I felt the tightening grip of a future I didn't want settling around me like a noose.

CHAPTER 2
ANGELO

AGE: 11

EVEN THOUGH I was only eleven, my father loved taking me around with him on all sorts of his Santelli mafia crap. Training, he said.

I had learned not to interfere with what he and his men did. I was supposed to learn the business so I could one day take over and keep the Santelli name alive. That meant when my father introduced me to people, I was supposed to nod and keep my mouth shut. On a good day, I had problems with that.

"This meeting we're going to is important." His fingers drummed on the leather seat, ignoring Umberto, who pulled away from our house in silence. Staff knew that my father preferred no conversation or interaction from them unless asked specifically. Umberto's job was to drive, protect, and, if necessary, die. In the Santelli mafia, the soldiers were disposable toys to my father. Their value was negligible.

"Now, this meeting we're going to is important," his fingers drummed on the leather seat. "You can't fuck this up for me Angelo. *Hai capito*?"

"I understand." It was the only response that could shut him up.

Once I was a don, I wasn't going to drive around in a crappy Lincoln Towncar, and I sure as hell wasn't going to have a driver like I was helpless. My father had no sense of style when it came to cars. When I grew up, I'd make sure my cars reflected who I was—a badass. No more of this bullshit. It would be Ferraris for me.

"The meetings are all important." The reply sounded robotic as I stared out the window while Umberto navigated through the Bronx toward the club where this point-less meeting was supposed to take place. My father grunted in agreement, satisfied with my response, as he scrolled through his emails.

He had already filled me in on most of what would happen at this meeting. It had been planned for months. The Santelli mafia *famiglia* was going to sign an agreement with the Volkov Bratva, the O'Kelly mob family, and the Anthakos… not sure what the fuck they did. Shipping, maybe? Smuggling of some kind? My father was all hot for the agreement because it would give him better and safer trade routes for his shady deals. He wanted to move up in the hierarchy of the organized crime families, and the Italian mob life wasn't cutting it.

I tried to keep occupied by watching the cars pass and imagining the ordinary lives of the people in them. Sometimes, I wished for a normal life for myself and my siblings— maybe without guns and deals with the devil, but maybe that's all my life would ever be.

The club was a dump.

A neon sign flickered weakly above the entrance, half the letters burned out, making it read more like "LUB" than anything else. The smell of cigarette smoke and beer clung to the air, thick and unshakable even outside. A bouncer leaned against the doorframe, barely glancing at us as Umberto pulled up to the curb.

I slid out behind my father, wrinkling my nose. "This is where we're meeting them?"

"It's neutral territory," he replied without

looking at me, already adjusting his suit jacket as he strode toward the entrance. "That's what matters." He glanced at me briefly. "If you can't meet someone on your own turf, then you meet them on neutral ground. You check your shit."

My father liked to drop these pearls of wisdom as part of his training. That was when I was expected to nod and keep my mouth shut. I didn't understand why neutrality had to mean meeting at a shithole, but I didn't bother wasting any energy on arguing. Instead, I followed him inside, where the lighting was so dim it took my eyes a second to adjust. The place was half-empty, with a few drunks slouched in booths, ignoring us. A woman was working the pole in some half-hearted attempt at dancing, though she looked drugged even to me.

In the back was a full table of men, and the area around them had been cleared. That was obviously where we were headed. My father moved toward them, and I studied each one as we approached. My stomach did somersaults as I noticed that each of them had kids with them. It wasn't unusual for mafia bosses to bring their sons with them, but this felt strange, and all my senses began to tingle.

The O'Kelly boss, Cormac O'Kelly, looked

like he had just come from working under a car. His red hair was a mess, and a grease stain smeared across the front of his white button-down shirt. He had the build of a man who had thrown plenty of punches and taken just as many to the face. His son, who was perhaps a few years older than me, was the exact opposite of his father. He was dressed as neatly as a pin in a suit that didn't quite fit his large frame, with his freckled face set in bored defiance.

The Russians, on the other hand, seemed to take pride in their professional appearance. You could probably cut yourself on the pleat of Alexei Volkov's slacks. He sat rigidly, his suit crisp and flawless despite the grungy setting. His face was sharp and severe, the type that appeared to have never smiled.

"Santelli." He nodded, his thick Russian accent dripping from his few words, while his dark eyes flicked in my direction once before wholly dismissing me. His son sat beside him, mirroring his father's cold composure. He didn't slouch or fidget. He was like ice.

Then there was the Greek—Yianni Anthakos. He was large, his belly straining against the buttons of his expensive silk shirt, and he was already drunk. Distaste coated my throat. My mother was a drinker, and it made her even meaner. Alcohol changed people, and it was rarely for the better.

His thick fingers drummed against a glass half-filled with what looked like whiskey. I had tried it — it was terrible. His kid was the youngest of us, and I already felt kind of sorry for him. Every time his father laughed or got too close, he flinched. He seemed unsure of himself, too thin, with eyes darting as if he were waiting for someone to give him a reason to run. I could have told him that there was nowhere to go and that no one in this world would save him. I had learned that lesson already.

My father took the last empty seat, gesturing for me to sit beside him. I crossed my arms, glaring at the table, already knowing whatever was about to happen was going to suck. Nothing my father did was sunshine and rainbows, but this already reeked to high heaven.

"Let's get this done," Alexei said, his Russian accent clipping his words. His lips curled slightly, and I could tell that he found the club as distasteful as I did.

"Volkov, calm down. The lawyer isn't even here yet. Let's have a drink first and relax," Yianni laughed, leaning back with his glass. "Let the boys get to know each other. This is my son, Ilias." He placed a heavy hand on the poor kid's shoulder and nearly pushed him face-first into the tabletop.

The kid twisted to glare at Yianni with unfiltered hate, flinching away from him even while his father grinned like a maniac.

"Just getting him used to the business. He's spent too much time with his mother," Yianni added. "Try some of this." Yianni thrust his glass toward the boy and poured himself another generous serving.

Ilias was clearly familiar with his father's habits since he didn't bother refusing the glass, but he didn't drink it either. Yianni had already moved on to animatedly talking with the O'Kelly boss, who was equally unpleasant —no wonder these men had gone into business together. My father and the Volkov pakhan had begun a stilted conversation about an operation on the East River.

I tuned them out and tried not to worry about what would happen when the lawyer arrived. I didn't know the other boys' names, but I didn't care much. The small consolation was that they weren't happy to be here either. The O'Kelly boy looked distinctly uncomfortable, and that pleased me.

Not fifteen minutes later, a man who looked like he'd blow away in a strong breeze rushed up to the table. "Apologies, apologies."

He must have been the lawyer everyone was waiting for. The guy looked like a fucking mouse in his outdated suit with his little briefcase. It was hard to believe he was working with the mafia and hadn't gotten popped yet.

"You're late," Alexei Volkov snapped.

The guy turned beet red and bowed several times, repeatedly apologizing as he explained there had been traffic. It was fucking New York. When wasn't there traffic? If I were the don, I would have told him that he should have planned ahead and arrived on time, but my father said nothing.

Finally, he got the show on the road and opened his briefcase to distribute copies of the contract that everyone would sign. I saw my father's forehead wrinkle as he read it line by line. One of his rules was always to know what he was signing. My father was a slimy dickwad, but he wasn't stupid — and a lot of times his advice was solid. This was one time that I thought it wasn't wrong. I noticed Yianni Anthakos didn't even bother to glance at the document. Fool.

"Give it here. The Volkovs will go first."

Alexei rudely gestured impatiently to the little man.

"Of course, of course. You'll need to sign and then press your thumb next to your signature." The lawyer put a little wooden box in the center of the table, flicked the lid open, and revealed an old-fashioned tack.

I watched in rabid fascination as Alexei signed with a flourish, then savagely pressed his forefinger to the tack and sealed the bloody print next to his signature.

"Maxim," Alexei commanded. The Russian shoved the contract and the box at his son, who looked like he was anything but willing. Maxim looked as if he were going to revolt.

Everything in me went still. My father hadn't mentioned anything about me signing a contract. Would I have to? I knew some of what this was about, but why were we signing? Maxim Volkov frowned but picked up the pen—hesitated until his father growled out something in Russian that obviously provided the needed motivating factor. He read the document, frowning at it, but signed his name carefully and then slashed his thumb, repeating the motion his father had made before pushing it away from him.

"Feck, he's a bloodthirsty one," Cormac

O'Kelly boomed like it was all a big joke. "Best keep an eye on him, Conall."

The red-haired boy, Conall, didn't respond to the taunt. After his father signed, he methodically reviewed the document but didn't hesitate to pass it to my father after he signed himself. I felt sick, and I could sense the little Anthakos boy trembling next to me. I hadn't read it and didn't know what I was agreeing to.

"Here, boy." My father shoved the papers at me, reminding me more than ever that I was somewhere I shouldn't be. The fact that I was in a moldy club at eleven instead of sitting in elementary school like a normal kid made me furious.

Sometimes, I loved the thought of the mafioso life —the danger and the excitement —but most of the time, it made me feel resentful. I'd watch my brother and sister and know deep in my gut that they were missing out on a real family. The only person they had who really loved them was me, and wasn't that fucked up? That their parents didn't love them?

Anger rose in me, hot and furious, as I struggled to focus on the words. It was a good thing I wasn't stupid. I had always been quick, partly because I had no choice. I read carefully, even when my father grumbled at me to hurry up. I kept my finger on the document, noticing all the sections where these idiots spoke about forming a group called the Commission and the part where they guaranteed each other specific things for their nastier businesses. Guns, drugs, human trafficking— you name it, these bastards did it. They rolled in the mud like the pigs they were. They had no class.

Then my breath hitched. That rage inside me exploded. My father was such a fucker.

"I won't do it, you asshole!" I cursed in Italian. *"Non lo farò, stronzo!"*

The dickface wanted me to marry one of these assholes' daughters when I was older? That's what I was signing? I shouldn't have been surprised by the stuff my father did, but somehow he still managed it. He wanted me to agree to an arranged marriage when I was older, and he was selling my little sister on top of it. She was part of this sick agreement. It wasn't even enough that he trafficked other people. His own children weren't safe from his schemes. My emotions surged and swirled too intensely for me to manage as my eyes flicked from the contract to the crime bosses at the table, then to the other boys who hadn't had much choice either. Even as I attempted to scramble away from the table, my father yanked me back into my chair with a sharp slap that jerked my head to the side.

"You're embarrassing me, you little fuck. Sign it." My father shot me a look that would have had most men pissing themselves. I didn't care if his patience had snapped; mine had too. "Angelo!"

He wrenched me forward as I screamed and fought, pulling my limbs together against his as he jabbed my finger onto the tack. I bared my teeth as he smeared my blood onto the page while cursing his name three ways to the Madonna.

"Sign it, or Remo gets sent away." His eyes narrowed, and I realized he meant it. He would do it. He'd throw my little brother to the slavers if I didn't comply. Although I wasn't sure it was any better that I would be signing Francesca's life away, but that was a problem for another day. Narrowing my eyes at him, I scrawled my name next to the messy blood marker, ensuring he saw the anger behind it. He'd made an enemy out of me today.

The last person to sign was Yianni's son. His hand was steady as he pressed the pen down to the paper, and his mouth remained closed against any comments. His father was jovial, making crass jokes around the table even as his son's eyes screamed promises of revenge. Maybe Yianni wasn't catching on, but I certainly had.

After it was over, the lawyer folded the paper and tucked it back into the wooden box, as if we hadn't just signed away our futures.

I rubbed my bleeding finger against my pants and muttered under my breath in Italian, swearing and spitting out every curse I knew.

My father just smirked. "Good. It's done."

I glared at the table, thinking about my name written in blood.

No, my father was wrong. This was just the beginning.

CHAPTER 3
THEODOSIA

THEODOSIA - AGE 15.
ANGELO - AGE 22

FRANCESCA SANTELLI HAD BEEN my best friend since I was six, and our brothers ran around like gangsters together. We had naturally become friends because we always ended up in the same places, our brothers dragging us along since they were too afraid to leave us at home with our asshole parents.

I'd admit freely that my dad had scared the crap out of me. Yianni Anthakos was a mean drunk, but he was even meaner when sober. He also unnerved my brothers, so they kept my little sister and me as far away as possible. I learned to be careful around our house at a young age, staying in the shadows and peeking around corners to avoid confrontations. When I was twelve, my father died of a heart attack right at the dinner table. Nobody was sad. My brother, Ilias, spat right on his body at the table and told him he hoped he was going to hell.

Like Frankie, I have lived with my brothers ever since. They took care of me and my little sister, Polina, even though they were still hoodlums. They were involved in some shady business together, but I didn't mind. Our house was happy and safe, and I knew my brothers loved me. Plus, I could go to Frankie's for sleepovers, which was the best. We were allowed to go to the same school together, and sometimes, we crashed at each other's houses.

Frankie and I went together like peanut butter and jelly, Cheetos and pickles, and buttered popcorn sprinkled with sugar.

We had supported each other through the deaths of our fathers (neither of whom we liked or cared about), and I had thrown her a little party just the two of us when her mother left. We were there for tears and secrets. We had promised each other that we would tell each other everything.

The house was quiet, except for the gentle ticking of the clock on the nightstand. We were having a sleepover at her house, the kind she had to beg her brother for. Now that her father was dead and her mother had left them, she lived with her oldest brother, Angelo, and her little brother, Remo.

I could wake Frankie up, but she was out cold, breathing deep and steady, curled up in her blankets like she didn't have a single care in the world. I should've been asleep too, but something had woken me—a sound, low and sharp.

I turned onto my back, staring at the ceiling, my pulse quickening as I strained to listen. Another muffled but distinct noise drifted up from the garage beneath the bedroom.

I sat up, my heartbeat hammering.

It was stupid, but my mind went straight to danger. What if someone was in trouble? What if something was wrong? What if—Angelo was hurt?

I knew he was down there. He'd come home late, the rumble of his latest car rolling into the driveway just before midnight. He was always nice to me, teasing sometimes, but never mean, never dismissive. And he looked at me, really looked at me, as if I mattered. Sometimes, he'd watch movies with me, Frankie, and Remo. He'd share popcorn with us, dipping his hand into the bucket next to me, casually brushing his hand against mine as if it were nothing. Probably, it was nothing to him, but it meant everything to me.

Being around Angelo made me feel all gooey inside — hot and a little sick at the same time. I knew that he didn't see me as anything other than a little kid, but that wasn't how I saw him. Angelo was all hard edges except with us. He was protective and strong — everything that I admired.

So if he was in trouble if someone was hurting him—

Careful not to wake Frankie, I slid out of bed and tiptoed to the window. The garage door was cracked open, the light spilling onto the driveway in a hazy golden glow. Another sound—deeper this time, a husky murmur—sent a shiver down my spine.

I shouldn't go down there.

But I couldn't help myself. Angelo could probably take care of himself. I knew he was in the mafia, so he had a gun and everything. He didn't even bother hiding it when he came to our house, and he had his capos with him. I'd heard him talk about them. Capos were soldiers in his little mafia army. My brothers liked to think I didn't know anything, but I wasn't an idiot. Still, if he got hurt and I could have helped, I would never forgive myself.

There were guards on duty here, too. Maybe that's who was making the noise, but it didn't hurt to make sure.

Barefoot, heart racing, I crept down the stairs and across the cool hallway tile, my pulse a wild staccato in my ears. The closer I got, the clearer the voices became. His voice, deep and rough-edged, sent a thrill through me, but the other voice made me want to throw up. It wasn't threatening. It was cajoling and feminine. He'd brought a woman home. It was soft, breathy, almost a whimper.

My stomach twisted.

I stopped just outside the garage, my fingers hovering near the doorframe. One step closer, just one, and I could see inside.

I shouldn't look.

Angelo was there, leaning against one of his cars, his hands gripping the edge of the hood. His head was tipped back, eyes half-lidded, lips parted. And between his thighs— a woman.

She was kneeling on the concrete, her hands gripping his thighs, her mouth moving along his … holy shit. I wasn't sure where to look, but *there*. He had his long fingers threaded through her blond hair, guiding her, pumping into her mouth, holding her there like she belonged to him.

Heat crawled up my neck, and my stomach twisted into something ugly and unfamiliar. Feelings rose in me that I didn't understand.

He wasn't in trouble. He wasn't hurt.

He was enjoying himself.

I'd rushed down here to *rescue* him … and …

I pressed a hand to my chest, trying to calm the frantic thudding of my heart, but it didn't help. I felt ridiculous and humiliated, as if I had been punched in the gut. Warring with those feelings was something else I didn't want to name, and trailing after them was shame.

Of course, he wasn't in danger. Of course, he was fine. He was Angelo Santelli—gorgeous, untouchable, and seven years older than me.

And I was just a stupid fifteen-year-old girl who had had a crush. That's all it was. I wasn't in love with him.

A crush that I vowed then and there to leave behind in that garage. Sniffling a little, I hunched in on myself and hurried through the living room and back to the part of the house I should be in. I had been stupid.

"Theo, wait! I want to talk to you." A door slammed behind me.

I didn't even want to turn around at the sound of his voice. Had he seen me watching? I could already feel my cheeks getting red with embarrassment, and I wanted to die on the spot at the thought of him actually talking to me. I thought about running, but I didn't want to have this conversation where anyone else could hear it. Making myself stop moving was an effort, but turning around was even harder.

"Why are you down here?" His eyes were narrowed at me, suspicious in a way that was unfamiliar to me. Normally, he was kind and smiling. "You were spying on me," he accused flatly.

"I didn't mean to," I managed to get out, tears threatening to spill over. "I'm sorry." I thought about telling him I was worried he was in trouble, but now it seemed stupid.

"That was private. You should have been upstairs."

His face twisted as he regarded me, and I imagined how I must appear to him: my long hair frizzed from spending most of the day with Frankie in bed watching movies, dressed in pajamas that were far from grown-up. There was even a zit patch on my face, and I wore my bright pink flannel pajama bottoms with orange crocodiles with my Supergirl t-shirt. I wasn't fooling anyone that I was grown up … not that I was trying.

"Look, you need to stop," he said, running a hand through his hair.

I had clearly reached a new level of hell. I didn't misunderstand his meaning, but I would deny it as long as I breathed.

"I'm a man. You're…" He waved dismissively, sending a rush of embarrassment coursing through me. "Whatever this is, I will never be interested in you. Would never be interested in you, even if we were the same age. Got it? Is it crystal clear? Stop embarrassing yourself. That's all you're doing right now. Being an absolute embarrassment. If you don't stop, I'm going to have to keep you from coming over." His lips pinched together. "Maybe I should do that anyway."

"Wait." The word was desperate, pleading as tears spilled over not just with humiliation now, but with the thought that he might ban me from spending time with Frankie. He had the power to do that, but I hadn't even considered it. It hadn't even been on my radar as a possibility. "This was a mistake. I'm sorry."

"No, just stop."

With that parting shot, he disappeared

back into the garage, leaving me with the weight of his words.

Never.

Embarrassing.

Crystal.

The roar of an engine shook the door down the hall, and the screech of tires echoed as I crept back up toward the bedroom where Frankie slept. Before I got there, I sat on the stairs, slumping against the banister, letting my face rest against my knees, and allowing the tears to flow as I sobbed.

CHAPTER 4
ANGELO

PRESENT - ANGELO - AGE 36

FORTUNE SMELLED like new money and old power. The scent of paint, whiskey, and the faintest trace of sawdust still lingered in the air. The club had been rebuilt—bigger and better—ours. As I sat in the new VIP lounge, I couldn't help but admire my own damn work. It was like a fucking phoenix rising from the ashes. I chuckled, recalling it had been reborn twice now.

I stood near the bar, taking it all in—the expanded VIP lounges, the second floor overlooking the club, the bulletproof glass. It was a fortress designed to print money. I had designed the bar with a Prohibition gangster theme. It looked kickass. Even my brother Remo thought it was cool, and he was hard to impress. Every inch of the club had been designed perfectly. We hadn't even had the grand opening yet, but I was sure it would be a hit.

"Not bad," I muttered, rolling the scotch in my glass.

"Not bad?" Conall O'Kelly scoffed from his place on the leather couch, shaking his head like I had personally insulted him. "Say it properly, ye stubborn bastard. This place is a *fucking masterpiece*. I hate to say it, but I'm glad it burned down. It's even better than before. Maybe ye needed a bit of practice." He waggled his eyebrows at me. "Hell of an expansion," Conall continued, stretching out like he owned the place. The Irish bastard probably thought he did, but I let it slide. After all, he owned part of it—he could stretch a little. "Ye finally got tired of hiding that you're the most ambitious fucker at this table?"

I smirked, flicking the cap off the scotch bottle. "Took a page from your book, O'Kelly. Turns out, thinking bigger pays off."

Maxim Volkov lounged to my right, looking absurdly relaxed for a man with a newborn in his arms. The baby, tiny, swaddled, and blissfully unaware that he was in a den of criminals, rested against his chest while Maxim sipped his drink like this was a typical Tuesday. Of course, baby Vasily should have been relaxed—the world would drip in blood before we let anything touch him.

Ilias Anthakos leaned back with an amused snort, watching the baby as if it were napalm. "Cora, let you bring the kid?" He raised an eyebrow that indicated he knew the answer already.

Maxim shrugged, adjusting Vasily in one arm. "Cora needed sleep. It's the same thing. Here or there. What's the difference?"

Conall coughed into his fist. "You mean you were supposed to watch him at the townhouse while she napped? She didn't give you permission to take off with the baby."

Maxim only grinned, the smug, satisfied kind that we were used to right about now from him. "Believe what you want. I was doing her a favor." This was him at his finest — trying to convince himself that he did a good thing until Cora rained hell down on him for making her life harder. "She'll be glad for a nice nap."

"Sure, you eejit. I'll bet my sister will be screaming bloody murder when she wakes up and finds you and the baby gone. Just warning you that I'm not taking the fall."

I was pretty sure we all agreed with Conall on that.

We had already experienced a few incidents like these, so I didn't doubt Conall was right. Cora hadn't liked Maxim taking the baby in the past, and I didn't think she would this time, either. Maxim shrugged, snuggled his son a bit tighter, and gave him a gentle poke through his blankets. It was unsettling seeing him like this—all gooey. I had been used to Maxim being an unfeeling icicle, and seeing him have actual human feelings made me want to simultaneously hurl.

"I left a note this time," he said defensively as if that made up for it.

I tapped my glass against the table. "We talkin' business first, or are we just here to bust Maxim's balls for being a glorified babysitter?"

Ilias smirked. "Why choose?"

Maxim sighed and rubbed his hand down his face. "You're all just bitter. When it's your turn, I'm going to bust your chops. When's your wife going to give you one, Con?"

Conall shrugged. "When she thinks the time is right, or maybe we'll just cuddle on this one and offer to babysit. It'll be the best of both worlds. We'll get to love on a baby and then give it back."

I could fill in the blanks, but I didn't say anything. My sister had complicated feelings about her childhood and our mother. She always said she didn't want to marry or be a wife. Unfortunately, she didn't have any real choice regarding the wife part. The blood oath we'd had to sign years ago sealed her fate. Thankfully, Conall was a good man, and they seemed happy together. I knew that Conall would love nothing more than a house full of children, but he would let her decide if she wanted them.

So far, of the four of us, it has been nice to see Maxim and Conall happily married. I wouldn't go so far as to admit that the blood promise our fathers insisted on sealing their unholy alliance with was a good thing, but the four of us became friends because of it. It was also the motivation we needed to ensure our fathers died because of it... so maybe some good things had come from it. I also knew Cora and Francesca wouldn't change anything. It helped me knowing that — marginally.

The words barely left his mouth before Ilias and I side-eyed him at the same time. "You are married, O'Kelly," Ilias drawled. "You need to study some 'Art of War' or some shit. Wage a campaign or something. You want kids, right?"

Conall scowled, rolling his eyes. "I'm not going to war with my wife, you dipshit, and you have no room to talk. You're not even married yet, you know jack shit."

The Irishman growled something under his breath about Greek bastards, but I waved him off, steering us back to the reason we were here. I didn't want to get into a talk about wives or women. That was a quagmire of a topic for all sorts of reasons, and one I didn't want to think about either. It brought up thoughts that were better left in the dark.

"Speaking of war and hostile takeovers, can we get to business? Take care of some issues? That's why I drove over here to meet with you, arsewipes."

"Sure, sure. Let's not admire the majesty of the club," I sulked, though I didn't truly mean it. I knew they appreciated all the work done here, twice.

Fortune had always held significant meaning for all of us. First, it was where our fathers had made us take the blood oath. We burned that rundown piece of trash to the ground, howling like crazed maniacs the entire time, the heat of the flames on our backs and the thrill of rebellion slamming through our veins like the best drug in the world. Then, when we had established ourselves, we bought the property and eventually built *Fortune*, transforming it into a refuge for ourselves. Unfortunately, it was burned to the ground in an almost ironic twist that I doubted the man who did it even understood. Looking back on it now, it was nearly funny. Dante Caruso had no idea when he did it that we had burnt the original club.

Maxim cooed, "Uncle Angelo did great, didn't he, Vasily?" He smirked. "Even though he had a practice run."

"Fucker. Give me my nephew. I want to hold him." I reached for the baby but lost to Conall after a bitter tug-of-war with Maxim.

"You guys suck. This is supposed to be daddy time," Maxim whined.

"Well, you bring him here and have to share." Conall shrugged. "Not our problem if you don't like it. Let's hit the highlights before Cora shows up and wants your balls."

"I hate you all." He peered over at his son, tucked into Conall's arms as if contemplating snatching him back, but I knew that it gave him endless satisfaction to have his child so loved, even if he had to sacrifice a little bit of his bonding time. He reached over and tossed a few peanuts in his mouth.

"Business then," he said sternly. "I am seeing gains and strong profits from our business on the West Coast. Cartels are pushing products, but you guys know that. We encountered some trouble recently with our trucking supply in Arizona, but I had Maddox and Pike take care of that," Maxim shrugged.

The Volkov Bratva operated on both coasts, greatly benefiting the Commission because we could leverage Maxim's connections. When we agreed to collaborate, we arranged to protect each other and share in profits whenever possible. Naturally, we each had our own territory, some of which remained distinct. Ilias, in particular, was like his own little island and was as rich as Croesus.

Pike Walters was married to Maxim's cousin, Natasha Petrova Walters, managed a one-percenter motorcycle club in Arizona, and had a connection to another MC. This had proven useful more than once. Pike's brother, Eli, now worked exclusively for Maxim in his operations in California, although the guy was such a wildcard that I was surprised Maxim allowed it.

"I also heard from a bratva in Moscow, the Antonovs, that they're looking for territory in

Jersey. They're aiming to... collaborate," Maxim added.

"Color me intrigued," Ilias leaned in. "Why would they be interested in Jersey, of all places?"

"Apparently, they want to work with the Volkovs, which would give them a foothold in America. I'm researching them myself, but I wouldn't mind if everyone else looked into them and shared their opinions. I'm uncertain how much influence we can exert. If I discover they aren't the type of people we want to do business with, we can make their lives pretty miserable if they come anyway. That might be fun," he added with a smirk.

"I'll check it out. I've heard of them, but I'll dig deeper," Ilias said, pulling out his phone to start a text thread.

I had no doubt he was texting one of his brothers to look into it. The Anthakos family was large. Ilias had two brothers and two sisters—one of whom was a pain in my ass. Both brothers were heavily involved in the Anthakos smuggling and shipping empire, with connections everywhere. Typically, if there was information out there, Ilias's brother Kostas could find it. However, I'd be surprised if Maxim's contact couldn't uncover everything on her own. Veronica Walters was a hacking superstar, and while I didn't mention it to Maxim, I relied on her all the time. He'd be a little pissed off to know I was contacting her—not that I gave a shit.

"Not that you're not great ... but why are they eager to work with you?" Conall asked. He had been occupied with little Vasily, and I must admit the guy was a natural with babies.

"They want to work with *us*, actually. We're making a name for ourselves in certain circles, according to Matvey Antonov. Efficient at business, brutal, loyal, and anti traf ficking."

I didn't mind how that sounded, and I could tell from how everyone shifted that it didn't bother anyone. Our reputations in business were solid, and we stood firm against trafficking. Our fathers had been pieces of shit, but we didn't have to be. We'd been born into the business, but we all agreed that we'd dismantle that part of what they'd built. If we were proud of anything, it was that we'd made progress in that area.

Maxim rubbed a hand over his jaw, looking more than a little tired—one of the joys of having a baby in the house. Still, the little guy was pretty cute with his tiny fingers and toes. Even the eyelashes were intriguing, fanning out from each eyelid perfectly, just like a doll.

"The Antonovs value loyalty," he shrugged. Conall frowned, and we all immediately thought of Cosimo Oliveto. He had blown smoke up our asses about how impressed he was with our loyalty to each other. In the end, all he wanted was information about his brother's death, which meant he had been looking for Francesca and Theo. Not good. "They have a big family. We'll look into them. See what we find. I just wanted to let you know about the contact so we're all on the same page. We don't want to be surprised again."

Ilias took a sip of his drink, rolling the glass in his palm as he watched the baby with what looked like cautious amusement. "I'll have Kostas dig in. If they're solid, it could be useful. If not—" He shrugged, leaving the rest unsaid. We all knew what would happen if they weren't useful.

"Speaking of problems that need to be handled," I said, setting my glass down with more force than necessary. "The fucking Scarpato family is sticking their nose where it doesn't belong again. Construction sites in the Bronx. They're trying to muscle in. I caught some of their guys snooping, trying to bribe my foremen. That makes it twice now."

Conall exhaled sharply, shaking his head. "They really that stupid?"

"Or that desperate," Ilias reflected. "Dino Scarpato isn't the sharpest tool in the shed, but he's vicious. If he's testing you, he thinks he's got a shot at getting some of that territory."

"He doesn't," I growled. "I already sent a message. Two of his guys were escorted off-site and dumped back into his territory, missing a few appendages. But that was just a warning. If he keeps pushing, I'll have to handle it more permanently."

Maxim watched me, his expression thoughtful. "You got eyes on him?"

"I do," I confirmed. "And I have a meeting with someone from the Cardoni family. It might be connected. They've been neutral until now, but if they consider backing Scarpato, I need to shut that down fast."

The Five Families in the New York area had been stable for years, but the upheaval caused by the Olivetos had recently made things shaky. The Scarpato and Cardoni mafia were scrambling for any scraps of territory like dogs over a bone. None of them liked that the four of us had united in an alliance that went beyond the traditional rules of organized crime. Now, we had a new player in the game coming in and grabbing up pieces of the board that the Olivetos had left. Claimed he was some long-lost cousin or some shit. Salvatore Renzetti. We hadn't even met yet, but he was making a reputation.

The Commission kept things fluid, but we tended to specialize in specific areas. Conall ran our booze and gambling venues, Maxim ran our guns, and I laundered our money. We all dabbled in the drug trade, but we typically left that to the Yakuza and the cartels. Ilias, on the other hand, seemed to dabble in everything while running a conglomerate of shipping that we benefited from for our ventures. He had the broadest reach of all of us.

Ilias tapped his fingers against his glass, considering. "You want one of us there?"

I smirked. "I appreciate the offer, but I think I'll go solo. It's more of a conversation than a threat."

"And if it turns into a threat?" Maxim asked, his tone mild, but the meaning was clear.

I shrugged. "Then maybe you'll lose that five pounds you gained in the last few months. You'll get some exercise."

"Fuck off."

There was a brief silence, and we all discussed the implications of another family getting involved in our business. We had built a careful balance between us, but outside threats never stopped coming.

Then Conall shifted, his usual smirk becoming sharper. "Since we're discussing threats and deals... I heard an intriguing rumor." He leaned forward, focusing directly on Ilias and me. "There's been some chatter about the blood oath. Some other organizations are curious if you two will honor your bargains—or if your brides are up for the taking."

"What?" I ground out.

The air in the room shifted. The casual camaraderie dissipated, replaced by a tension ready to ignite into something explosive. Ilias's hands clenched into fists, his knuckles turning white.

Conall didn't flinch, but I saw the tension in his shoulders. "You heard me. People are sniffing around. Makes sense. We are successful. That means alliances. People are starting to wonder if you and Ilias will follow through —or if it is open season. There are other matches to be made with our families." He cleared his throat awkwardly. "Nico Balestra even asked. Maybe he's thinking he can gather enough support to build his own mafia, although I'm not sure that will fly with Renzetti muscling in."

"The blood oath isn't something that others can intrude upon," Maxim scoffed. "Amateurs. It's already been decided that Angelo will be tied to the Anthakos, and Ilias to the Volkovs. Someone else can't change an oath. It was decided decades ago."

"Well, I suppose people are realizing that the sister's name wasn't specified exactly," Conall mentioned so casually that I didn't even catch on at first.

Ilias had two sisters, Theodosia and Polina, but Polina had never been considered as a match for one of us. Theo would have scratched our eyes out for mentioning her. The Anthakos siblings were fiercely protective of their youngest for reasons the rest of us never really talked about. Polina had always been sheltered from the mafia life, to the point that I rarely remembered that Ilias even had another sister.

"That greedy bastard," I muttered. "He thinks he can talk about Theo like she's some unclaimed asset?"

I wasn't sure why I felt so angry. Theo had made it clear how she felt about me. She wasn't a fan. At one point in her life, she couldn't get enough of me, but that was when hero worship was still a factor.

Now that she was a fully formed human, she'd realized I wasn't that great of a guy. Nobody could say Theodosia Anthakos wasn't smart. Hell, a few years ago, she helped my sister cover up a murder. They kept it secret for years. Frankie told us that Theo was the mastermind behind hiding the whole thing, so I had no doubt in my mind that she was clever enough to see I was a losing bet, which was why she put an ocean between us.

Of course, she was still harboring a significant grudge. After that night, she had never been the same with me. I had crushed her teenage dream under my heel with a ruthlessness that even my mother would have approved of. The irony, of course, was that she was signed, sealed, and delivered to be one of our wives. I hadn't been about to tell her that, especially when she was fifteen and wearing pajamas with orange crocodiles. She didn't know that I still felt bad about it, the way her eyes had sparkled with tears. At the time, I had wanted her to stop mooning after me. It made me feel weird—the age difference, and the intimate knowledge I had of the situation. I felt guilty and ashamed. There had also been an anger in me, both on my behalf and hers... that she was already sold off.

Conall shrugged. "I don't think he was saying it to me personally. More like putting feelers out, seeing if there's any room to maneuver."

Ilias let out a slow, controlled breath, but his fury was evident. "Nico Balestra is a corpse walking if he even thinks about touching either one of my sisters."

I slammed my glass on the table hard enough to make the liquid slosh over the rim. "Let me be very fucking clear right now—Theodosia isn't 'up for grabs.' If anyone wants to test that, I'll put a bullet in their goddamn skull myself."

"Then maybe lock that down," Conall suggested, not unkindly. "Before someone gets stupid."

Maxim finally spoke up. "You two knew this was coming. We all did. The blood oath binds us. If you don't take care of it, someone else will try to muscle in. At the heart of these things they are business arrangements. We might not like how that sounds, but ..." he shrugged.

He wasn't wrong, but I ground my teeth. "It's my decision. My business. I've told you all that before. *If* I marry, I'll do it in my own time."

They glared at me. We had gone over this more than once in the last year and a half, going round and round in circles until our voices were raised. My father might have forced my hand, but I wasn't eleven anymore. They claimed it was about honor, but I wasn't so sure I was ready to buy that line of bullshit. When they said it might affect our business, that meant a bit more to me, but I had yet to see anyone mention it, and I wasn't sure that would sway me. Maxim, Conall, and Ilias were just as much my brothers as Remo, and I would never intentionally hurt them. Sure, I was supposed to marry into the Anthakos family, but it didn't say *when*. Theo didn't want me. She was off doing her thing anyway.

"Your business might be turning into everyone's business," Conall said, calm but firm. "It's time to decide, Angelo. Either you claim Theo, or you risk someone else thinking they can. She's running around in Europe right now unguarded. At least to my knowledge." He arched a brow at Ilias.

Last year, when we'd drawn names, and the Anthakos name had unfurled on the slip, something hot and forbidden had slid through me. Theodosia had become a beautiful woman, but more importantly, she was interesting and loyal to the bone. That would be important to me.

If.

Still, just because I wasn't going to marry her didn't mean anyone else could.

My hands clenched, and the idea of anyone laying a fucking finger on her made my vision go red. Ilias was just as tense, his jaw working as he stared at his drink. The room was heavy with expectation.

"She's not unprotected. She might think she is, but they're nearby. My sister can roam Europe as much as she wants. My intended," he said with derision, "I suppose I need to look into that. Your point is taken."

"Nobody is going to touch Theo," I said, my voice like steel.

Maxim pointed at Ilias. "You and I will have words if you disrespect my sister."

Ilias shrugged at Maxim's threat, his face impassive. I was somewhat surprised by the mention of the elusive Galena Volkova, the illegitimate and mysterious offspring of Alexei Volkov. Ilias felt similarly to me regarding the blood oath. It hadn't been our choice, so we weren't in any rush for the yoke of marriage and all it came with, regardless of how fast our friends had fallen into their matches.

Just as things were about to get serious, I saw Cora stomping across the club floor in her trademark rain boots and torn jeans. I couldn't see her t-shirt yet, but I'd bet a hundred dollars there was a zombie movie saying on it.

"Uh oh." Conall had obviously spotted his sister because he was passing Vasily off like a game of hot potato. "Here you go." He dumped the baby back into Maxim's arms. "Good luck."

"Maxim Volkov, give me my baby!" Cora rounded the landing of the stairs, with Lev and Kolya following her, grins spreading across their faces as if they couldn't wait for the show.

"*Zayka*, look," Maxim started. She stomped over and peered at Vasily, who was still fast asleep despite being transferred again to his father's arms and all the noise. "He's fine. I had to go to a meeting. Didn't I?" He looked to us for support. "I'm working. Aren't I?"

"We didn't need him," I shrugged. "Maxim came uninvited. He should have stayed at the townhouse, Cora," I said with a grin. "Sorry, *fratello*."

47

"He should have listened." Conall shook his head as if disgusted with Maxim. "Vasily is too tiny to be out in places like this. He could get sick. It's not suitable for babies." He wrinkled his nose at me.

I would have laughed at the expression on Maxim's face, but that would have drawn Cora's attention directly to me, and even I wasn't that stupid. Or that good of a friend.

"Alrighty. We'll see you later." Conall brushed a kiss over his sister's cheek. "Maxim, I hope you show better judgment next time. Come on, Ilias, I'll walk you to your car."

It seemed like a good time to abandon ship, so I figured I'd check out one of my construction offices and ensure everything was in order. Laundering money was a full-time gig. I chuckled to myself, leaving Maxim to get torn a new asshole for taking the baby from the house. He just couldn't help himself. No way I'd ever be that crazy.

CHAPTER 5
THEODOSIA

THEODOSIA - PRESENT - 29

I TWIRLED A MEASURING tape around my fingers as I strutted through my so-called atelier—if you could even call it that. It was more of an underground fashion den, a vibrant, chaotic blend of neon lights, mismatched furniture, and racks of daring one-of-a-kind designs. A year ago, I'd arrived in Europe on a whim, chasing a dream I wasn't entirely sure was mine. Now, I thrived among the misfits, dressing the rule-breakers who thrived outside the mainstream.

My ever-exasperated but devoted assistant, Vivienne, appeared in the doorway, arms crossed. "You've got a message, Theo."

Mid-spin with a glittery swatch of fabric that I was considering for a lemon yellow top with puff sleeves, I raised a brow. "Ooh, is it a love letter? Finally, someone appreciates me."

Vivienne smirked. "Probably more like a threat, but sure, let's call it romance if you want."

Vivienne had been my steadfast friend here in Italy, ensuring that I wasn't lonely in my pursuit of fashion domination. We bonded in Milan during fashion week in what I would describe as one of my more interesting adventures. There was a perfect opportunity to catch a glimpse backstage at the Chanel show, and I couldn't resist. How was I to know that they'd mistake me for one of the models? I was curvy, to say the least, and busty, but the stylist had insisted. To say that one of the models took offense is an understatement. Chaos ensued. Hijinks unfolded, and security was called, but they were slow to respond. In the end, it was more than a little comical, and Vivienne, who was working as a stylist, played an instrumental role in my escape. Later, we met up and shared a good laugh about it. Good times. She decided that we were destined for great things, and we've been together ever since.

She tossed a sleek white envelope onto the worktable. I plucked it up with dramatic flair, tearing it open. My playful expression faltered as I read the single line inside.

Your groom is waiting. It's time to go home.

Clicking my tongue, I shook my head. "Well, that's ominous. Very 'mysterious stranger in the shadows' vibes. I kinda love it."

Vivienne leaned over and examined the note, frowning before shooting me a pointed look. "You still don't think anything at home is connected to your business mysteriously falling apart? The suppliers backing out, the clients ghosting you?"

I had been vague with Vivienne about the entire situation concerning my brothers' criminal activities and my anticipated role as a mafia bride. Those weren't exactly things that the average person could understand. Vivienne was awesome, and I considered her a good friend, but she had no point of reference for the world I grew up in. You couldn't just lay that on someone all of a sudden, and trust wasn't something that came easily in our world. Lately, I increasingly appreciated Frankie and how we had grown up together. My best friend came built-in with knowledge of all my secrets, so there was no tiptoeing around the murky waters of the illegal nature of my family business. Having relationships outside the underworld was difficult. You had to watch your words and actions, and you never knew when others were taking advantage of you.

And sure, we had faced some unexpected difficulties with the business. Things had been growing at first. I'd had clients and everything. It was hard to pinpoint the cause when we couldn't get anyone to return our calls. Things had been going well, and then suddenly, everything came to a screeching halt. I considered asking my brothers for help, but that was a whole mess of its own, and part of me worried that Ilias would mention coming home. That he would encourage it. I wasn't sure if I could take that. It was something I didn't want to do. Even though I missed Frankie and our little apartment in New York, I knew she was happy with Conall. My best friend was finally settled, and that made my heart glad. It was the only way I felt good about coming to Europe and pursuing the piece of myself that I'd wanted to explore for years to see if I had what it took to survive in the industry.

As I eyed the message, I chewed on my thumbnail. I knew my family wouldn't have sent it. Certainly, it wasn't from Angelo

Santelli. The dick. He didn't want me. Even I knew that, no matter how much it hurt.

But …

Your groom is waiting.

The groom could only be Angelo Santelli. According to the blood oath, that was who I had to marry. The entire New York organized crime world knew it.

I sighed and flopped onto a velvet-upholstered chair, kicking up my boots. "Viv, I was hoping for sabotage from a rival designer, not creepy cryptic messages. I mean, at least that's industry drama. This? This is personal. It might be from someone back in New York," I admitted.

The criminal underworld resembled a spider web, even at its best, but one filled with cannibal spiders constantly devouring each other. It was smart never to trust anyone except your family. Naturally, I included Francesca in that group. She was different. But everyone else — no. Everyone was always trying to outdo each other, seize territory, push in, and kill one another. This is why the break in Europe had been so refreshing. Nobody here belonged to that world.

Oblivious to my dark thoughts, Vivienne continued, "Speaking of industry drama—Bassiano Torsiello wants to meet tonight."

"Tonight?" I sat up, suddenly intrigued, turning the note upside down and pushing it under the corner of a fabric swatch. If I couldn't see it, then it didn't exist. Bassiano was a big deal, the kind of designer who oozed exclusivity. I would *love* to meet with him. "The Bassiano Torsiello? Mr. 'I Only Work with Legends'?"

"That one. If people see you meeting with him …" she trailed off, her eyebrows lifting hopefully.

"They'll stop treating me like a fashion outcast?" I grinned. "Fantastic! What are the details?" I clapped my hands together and tried to feel re-energized. Maybe I could wear my cute jumpsuit I'd just finished. This downturn in business affected not just me but also Vivienne. If I couldn't make things work for *Mythos Designs*, it could be the end of things here in Florence for me, for us.

Vivienne arched a brow. "You're not even a little worried about the message?"

I waved a hand dismissively. "Please. If someone wants me home so badly, they'll need to put in more effort than just a little note. This isn't first grade. Until then, I have a date with destiny. And possibly Bassiano Torsiello." I waggled my eyebrows.

Jumping to my feet, I spun in a blur of silk

and sequins. The note still lingered in my mind, but I was nothing if not a performer. If someone thought they could rattle me, they were about to be very, very disappointed.

"I need something fabulous to wear!"

And I would not think about Angelo Santelli.

I would not think about home.

CHAPTER 6
THEODOSIA

BESTIE *Chat*

> Frankie: What'cha doing?

> Me: Getting ready to go to a meeting. Check out my outfit. It's amazing.

I sent her a picture of my adorable jumpsuit.

> Frankie: Oooh. Jumpsuit. I like it! How's business?

> Me: Decent, still slow. I'm not exactly sure what's going on, but I'll figure it out. How are things in NY? Is that man of yours still treating you right?

Frankie: Can I help at all?

Me: Not yet.

Frankie: K. You call — I'll answer. Things with the husband are good. Better than. Haven't told him yet, but I'm going to the doctor tomorrow to have the implant taken out.

Me: No way! I might get to be an Auntie Theo?!

Frankie: SHHHHHHHHHHHHHHH. I haven't told him yet.

Me: Bitch he can't hear me, and I'm so excited. I'll come home for that shit.

Frankie: Really? LOL. I'd have gotten knocked up sooner if I had known that. Text me after your meeting. Let me know how it goes.

Me: Will do. Love you, babe.

Frankie: Love you back.

I was thrilled for Frankie. She had been

twisted up about marriage and the idea of having kids, but she had found her groove now. I was excited for her and about the prospect of becoming Auntie Theo. I would be making baby clothes galore! She might think I was joking about coming home, but the thought wasn't unappealing. It might take me a few months to wrap things up here, but with business on the downturn, it wasn't so hard to imagine closing up shop and going home. I definitely wouldn't want to miss out on a baby Frankie. Maybe moving *Mythos* to NYC and regrouping was what needed to happen, but either way, I would be there if Frankie was going to be preggars.

CHAPTER 7
ANGELO

ASSHOLE CHAT

> Ilias: Heads up. I've got reliable intel that your lovely mother has been poking around. She's been seen having lunch here in the city.

> Me: Fucking great. Just what I need right now.

> Ilias: You want me to put a pin on her? We lost sight of her, but we can start tracking her when she pops back up again.

'Put a pin on her' was Ilias's way of having Kostas and his crew mark someone for surveillance.

> Me: I think that's a good idea. I'm not sure what she's up to, but whatever it is, I'm sure I won't like it. Thanks, man.

> Ilias: No problem.

It worried me that my mother had been spotted. She left New York just before my father's death twenty years ago. I had always assumed she'd become fed up with old Stefano and given it all up. She left him and abandoned the three of us. Carlotta was a cold fish with no maternal bone in her body, and none of us felt sad she was gone or surprised that she didn't take us with her. Still, after I took over the Santelli *famiglia* and all it entailed, she never crawled back for a penny. You'd think she would have. If there was anything I was sure of, it was that Carlotta was only out for one thing — herself.

Of course, we had recently learned that another mafia don was my sister's biological father, which meant our mother might have had other sources of income we were unaware of. I wouldn't be holding it against her if she'd made any sort of financial arrangements to give birth to us, but knowing her, they were all strategic. She probably made all kinds of deals that we didn't know about. All three of us were illegitimate. At one point, she took great delight in telling me that Don Santelli couldn't father children and that I was a bastard. It later became clearer to me why we were so disposable to him, or perhaps it made it easier to accept. Remo and I still didn't know who fathered us. I wasn't sure I cared, but Remo did.

Deep in my bones, the one thing I knew about Carlotta Santelli was that she was trouble. If she were back, it didn't bode well for us. She was mean to her core. Something inside her had festered and rotted to black long before my father had gotten hold of her. There were many things I could have forgiven in a person given the right circumstances, but nothing redeemable about her remained. I had no soft memory of her, not even a tender moment when she held my hand or my siblings' hands. Neither of my parents deserved to have children in their custody, let alone care for them. The best thing my mother did was hire a nanny. At least then, sometimes my siblings were fed and sent to bed on time. I had seen movies where the parent comforted their kids or loved on them, but that wasn't her.

She'd been cruel on her best days and evil on her worst. The day of the blood oath, she'd looked over my father's copy with satisfaction, telling Stefano he'd done a good job. She'd ignored my split and bleeding lip as if a beat-up eleven-year-old was no big deal. She hadn't cared that my sister and I had been bartered away like sacks of potatoes on the altar of greed.

I hated her. She had been right not to ask me for a fucking penny because she wouldn't get anything from me.

CHAPTER 8
THEODOSIA

I KNEW something was off when I entered the dimly lit, ultra-exclusive lounge. Not in a 'this-place-has-no-sparkle' way, but in a 'this-place-feels-like-a-trap' way. Which, honestly, was kind of exciting. Aside from the mysterious messages and collapsing business, my life had felt too routine lately. But a little mystery kept things interesting, right?

I adjusted the oversized vintage glasses perched on my nose, which I didn't need since I had perfect eyesight. They were tinted, but I loved them. The lighting was so moody that it was practically a whisper, and even I had to admit it was a bit hard to see, but fashion was a commitment. So was looking untouchable, especially when walking into a business meeting with one of the most powerful names in Italian couture.

Except it wasn't Bassiano Torsiello waiting for me.

Instead, lounging like a cat that had just eaten a particularly plump canary was Carlotta Santelli. Geez, what were the odds that she was here by accident? Zero.

Angelo and Frankie's mother. The woman I had heard whispered about in dark corners. Ruthless. Manipulative. Cold as ice. My pulse spiked, and my fingers instinctively curled around my folio and tablet as if they might shield me. Suddenly, my cute jumpsuit felt too snug across my breasts, and my confidence started to wilt. Had I just gained a few pounds? I wished I'd used some kind of tamer on my hair. Immediately, I stopped myself. Those weren't thoughts I indulged in anymore. Counterproductive. I was fierce. I was all-powerful.

What on earth was she doing here?

There had only been one time when I'd actually met her in person. It had been at a fundraiser that my father insisted we all attend. My mother bought me a princess dress with gold chiffon and tiny crystals at the hem. When I moved, it looked like I sparkled. When Frankie told me she was going, we were both so excited. We snuck off behind the marble pillars at the party and spun in circles until we nearly threw up. Then Carlotta found us. I had only been six, maybe, at the time, but she looked down her nose at me and frowned as if I smelled.

The memory was seared in my brain, her bitchy words something I'd never forget.

"I should have known you couldn't follow directions and that you'd already have dirt on your dress. I told your father we shouldn't have brought you. You're useless." She'd grabbed at Frankie's arm, holding her hard enough to bruise as she wrenched her away. Frankie sniffled as she tried hard not to cry. *"And you,"* she sneered. *"Your nanny needs to do something with your hair. And you should be on a diet."*

I stopped mid-step, one stiletto-clad foot hovering next to the table. "Huh. Either Bassiano Torsiello got a dramatic makeover, or I just entered a scene from one of those old mafia movies. You know, the kind where the unsuspecting protagonist realizes she's been lured into an ambush?"

Carlotta smiled, a vision of polished elegance and quiet menace, her lips curling around her teeth like a shark. "Theodosia, darling, I knew you were sharp. Come, sit. Let's talk." She patted the seat beside her.

Oh, I *did* not like that. Not one bit. My instincts screamed at me to turn on my heel and walk right back out, but that wasn't my style. No, no, no—I was the kind of girl who walked straight into the fire to see if she could make it look good. It grated on me that she acted like this was normal, but I was nothing if not capable of rising to the occasion. I was not afraid of her. I wouldn't give her the satisfaction of knowing how much it grated that the designer I had admired for so long wasn't the one who had called the meeting.

"Someone contacted my assistant about an opportunity that was too good to pass up. I didn't expect an 'elaborate intimidation setup.' You could have just asked me to coffee like a normal person. I know this great place that serves an oat milk cappuccino with edible gold flakes. Super chic." I was laying it on pretty thick, but there was no way I would give her an inch. If she were someone I liked, I'd take her for an affogato at my favorite spot, but this bitch would definitely be the oat milk sort. No affogato for her.

I slid into the chair, my movements deliberately slow. If I had to walk into the lion's den, I would do it as if I didn't have a care in the world. Frankie would have a fit about this, although I wasn't sure whether I should tell her. Carlotta had run out on them decades ago, and I didn't think that Angelo or Remo even knew where she was. Frankie certainly hadn't kept tabs. I wondered if Carlotta knew the latest gossip about her daughter. If she knew that Frankie had discovered her biological father was a supervillain.

Carlotta let out a small sigh as if she were handling a particularly unruly child rather than a fully grown woman who had built her own underground fashion empire through sheer stubbornness and questionable decision-making skills. "This is more important than coffee, Theodosia. This is about your future … and my son's future."

My eyes nearly popped out of my head. Since when did she care about her children, and who was she to interfere with my life? Carlotta had washed her hands of her children years ago when she abandoned them. It seemed a bit rich for her to pretend to care now. So, she was here about the blood oath — what was her angle? I couldn't begin to imagine how it would benefit her if Angelo and I were hitched. What would she gain from it? I took off my glasses and folded them neatly beside the place setting, trying to control my anger.

"Oh, honey, my future involves me

designing absurdly expensive clothes while sipping champagne and laughing at those who doubted me. I'm pretty sure I don't need your help with that. I'm not certain what I do or when I do it is any of your business."

"Since you and Angelo are dragging your feet," Carlotta began, leaning forward, her meticulously manicured nails tapping against the rim of her untouched martini glass. "Salvatore Renzetti has decided to express an interest in you. He's a new player in New York; maybe you've heard of him?" I hadn't and couldn't care less about 'new players' since I had plenty of mafiosos to keep track of. "He's related to the Olivetos," she added. "But he should not be trifled with."

Well, that was an *unexpected* plot twist. The *famiglia* that wouldn't go away.

I blinked. "Salvatore Renzetti? I don't even know who that is, Carlotta." I put on a bored expression, but it shook me a little.

I wouldn't admit that to her. The last thing I needed was more drama in the mafia world regarding the whole dumb marriage issue. While I might have accepted long ago the transactional nature of women in the criminal underworld, that didn't mean I would be okay with being exchanged for another arrangement as if I were some kind of inter-changeable spare part.

She nodded, her beady eyes fixed on mine. I didn't dare look away in case she thought I was losing my nerve. "He wants you, or the connections you bring. And he always gets what he wants."

A laugh bubbled out of me before I could stop it. *Oh, this was rich.* "Okay, hold on—let me make sure I understand. You lured me here. In *Italy*," I emphasized because it was funny to me that she'd come all this way. "You made up this whole thing with Bassimo to tell me that some mobster wants to collect me like I'm a limited-edition handbag? Don't get me wrong —I *am* limited edition, but I don't exactly come with a gift receipt."

Carlotta's expression didn't change. "You should take this seriously. Salvatore doesn't offer choices—he takes them away. Marriage or leverage. That's all he sees you as. Angelo might indulge this nonsense of yours, but Salvatore won't. This whole droll sideline you have going on? It's got to stop. You're getting up there in age, you know. Your usefulness is coming to an end."

The laughter dried up in my throat. She did look serious. Carlotta Santelli had a history of knowing dangerous men and seemed to play the game somehow. Either she married them or ended up having their babies. Carlotta knew how to leverage, there was no denying that. I wasn't 'getting up there' — I was only twenty-nine. There was still plenty of time for babies. Right?

There it was. The weight of those words, the ugly reality behind them. I'd been playing a game I thought I understood—flitting around Europe, building something mine, separate from my family's world, Ilias and his empire of shadows. Separate from Angelo Santelli and the stupid blood oath my father had signed.

But I was wrong.

Because in the end, I was still a piece to be moved. A prize. A bargaining chip.

And I *hated* that. I wanted nothing more in the world than to be truly loved and cherished for real, and it was soul-crushing to realize that it wouldn't ever happen. When I was still a teen, I had big dreams. Romantic ones. Sure, they all centered around a certain someone, but even after he shattered my heart, a part of me was more pragmatic. I'd figured I'd find love— someone who could see the real me even if he couldn't. The other part of me? Well, that other part still clung to

Angelo Santelli and the love he'd never be able to reciprocate.

Then there was that fateful day of Frankie's eighteenth birthday when we discovered the blood oath in Angelo's office. Its weight poured over me like wet concrete. Then I reasoned that maybe Angelo wasn't the one I'd be matched with. Perhaps I'd find love with Maxim or Conall, but I always knew somehow my fate was tied to Angelo. It was inescapable. He'd never love me the way I wanted.

I crossed my arms, the humor gone. "You do realize that the arrangement has already been made for me. I'm essentially already bought." The words tasted bitter in my mouth.

"That's true, I suppose, but you have a sister, don't you?" she shrugged. "The oath didn't specify which one." Her expression was coy, but it was clearly malicious.

Polina, the aforementioned sister, had just celebrated her twenty-first birthday. She was delicate, made of spun sugar and dreams rather than blood and steel. As a family, we had all agreed years ago that she wasn't cut out for any part of the criminal underworld. She wasn't allowed around our friends, my brothers' men, or their businesses. I never even had her near Frankie or her husband — ever. She attended a private school and then a private college. Polina was completely unaware of our world, and it would stay that way. She'd marry a dentist or something equally mundane and raise a few children in the suburbs if we had our way.

"My sister is off-limits. You know that."

My brothers would kill anyone who tried to push Polina into anything. I would help. I wouldn't fight the blood oath forever. I might run, but I knew better than to believe the Anthakos family could decline politely. That just wasn't done in the world we inhabited. Blood promises anchored the underbelly of the criminal world. If your family signed in blood, your word meant something, and other families would hold you to it. With so few rules, they had to be followed. It was brutal, but I understood. So, if I didn't follow through, then Polina really would be on the hook, and I'd never do that. "And what do you hope to gain from this, Carlotta? Because I don't believe for a second that you're just here out of the goodness of your heart." If there was one thing I knew for sure, it was that she wasn't here for my benefit or Angelo's.

She tilted her head, considering me. "It

seems like people aren't keeping you in the loop. I'm giving you the information you should have already had: alternatives."

I let out a slow breath. "Let me guess—this alternative involves a brooding Italian don who doesn't want me but would rather die than let Renzetti have me?"

Carlotta smiled just a little. "Angelo is many things, but he understands the value of protecting what's his."

As if she knew anything about Angelo and his motives. I wasn't sure she was wrong, but I couldn't be certain she was right either. When it came to the blood oath, Angelo was completely twisted up. He'd also made his disdain for me clear. There was also a part of me that knew Angelo was too proud to allow another man to take a woman who was set to marry him.

I snorted. "I do not belong to him. And if you think I'm going to allow you to maneuver me into some absurd chess match among criminals, you haven't been paying attention, but then you haven't been around. Have you?"

Carlotta's expression remained unchanged, but I saw something in her eyes—something calculating as if she were evaluating whether I was playing dumb or genuinely naive enough to believe I could walk away from this.

"I still don't get why you're here. Why you're involving yourself? I know you haven't even been in New York for years." I was suddenly thankful we were in this dark corner where the servers ignored us. "It seems like you wouldn't care if the blood oath was honored or not," I pressed.

"Let's just say that it's in our best interests to ensure everything gets finalized."

That was vague. I considered her for a minute, but she didn't seem inclined to offer me anything else, and I was honestly bored with the whole set-up. The only reason I'd come was the lure of a possible meeting with Bassiano Torsiello, and now that I knew that was all a fake-out, the energy had drained out of me.

I pushed back from the table, the scrape of my chair against the floor sharp and final. "Well, this has been fun. Truly. But I have a life to get back to, a job that doesn't include being some mobster's trophy wife. So, if you'll excuse me—"

Before I could turn, the door behind me swung open. I had noticed it but thought it was a back entrance or a side kitchen.

Two men stepped inside, and I pin-balled

between them and Carlotta, trying to piece together what was going on.

They were big. Broad. Unsmiling.

Oh, you had to be kidding me.

I shot a look at Carlotta. "Really? Really? The whole 'send in the goons' routine? That's so predictable." I aimed for joking, but fear was beginning to creep in.

Carlotta didn't blink. "I told you, Theodosia. Salvatore always gets what he wants."

One of the men moved quickly for someone his size. I twisted, reaching for the nearest weapon available—which, unfortunately, was a cocktail stirrer.

Not ideal.

A hand clamped around my arm. I jerked back, kicking out, my heel colliding with someone's shin. There was a grunt of pain, but it didn't matter—I was already being hauled toward the door, my feet barely skimming the floor.

Panic clawed up my throat, but I shoved it down. No. No, no, no. I was *not* some damsel in distress. I was Theodosia Anthakos, and if these idiots thought they could just *take* me, they were in for a very unpleasant surprise.

I twisted hard, slamming my elbow into the guy's ribs. He grunted, loosening his grip just enough for me to plant my feet and—

A sharp sting exploded at the back of my head. The pain violent and intense.

The room spun. My vision blurred. My body went *wrong*, legs folding beneath me.

Distantly, I heard Carlotta's voice, smooth as silk. "Tell Salvatore he owes me for this."

And then—

Darkness.

CHAPTER 9
ANGELO

WHEN I RECEIVED the call from Ilias, I was face down in my bed, the cool cotton of my sheets a blissful reprieve against my split cheek. My body ached, my knuckles still raw from the night before—a business dispute that had turned bloody. Sleep barely began to sink its claws into me when my phone started buzzing—a shrill, insistent vibration against the nightstand cut through the silence of my bedroom.

I initially ignored it, groaning as I buried my face in the pillow. But it kept ringing. Persistent. Demanding. My instincts, honed by years in this life, sent a shot of adrenaline through me. Ilias didn't call just for shits and giggles.

I reached for the phone, swiping it off the

nightstand and putting it on speaker as I rolled onto my back. My ribs protested the movement. "What's up?" My voice was thick with exhaustion, my brain still sluggish from too little sleep and too much scotch.

"Theo's been snatched."

That did it.

I bolted upright, the words hitting me like a freight train. My breath rushed out of my lungs, and my fingers tightened around the phone. My mind raced, shaking off the last remnants of sleep.

"I thought you had eyes? You said you had people there?" I shoved the sheets aside and swung my legs over the edge of the bed, pressing the heel of my hand to my temple to force myself fully awake. I hit the speaker button and tossed the phone onto the dresser as I yanked open a drawer, searching for clean clothes.

"We did," Ilias snapped, frustration evident in his voice. "It hasn't been close protection. They've always watched from a distance." I yanked on a pair of black slacks, my mind racing a thousand miles an hour. I wanted to interject and complain about his security, but I kept my mouth shut. "She was supposed to be meeting a designer. The place was poorly lit, with no cameras."

"What do we know? *Anything?*" I pulled a black shirt over my head, not bothering to check for wrinkles.

"They had transpo outside. They knew what they were doing, in and out, in under two minutes. My guy outside barely caught a glimpse before they vanished."

"Who the fuck is responsible? What about the designer she was meeting?" My voice rising.

Silence. A beat too long.

"Kostas is on it, but he's already contacted Theo's assistant to find out what she knows." A feeling rose up in me that I didn't like — unfamiliar and conflicted. "Bassimo something or other, but he's been in the States working in California on some movie. It was a set-up. I don't know," Ilias admitted, and the fury in his voice mirrored my own. "She met a woman, but the servers didn't get a good look. I'll find out more."

"No," I snapped, shoving my feet into my shoes. "I'll find out."

Theo was mine to deal with. Mine to bring back. My stomach twisted at the thought of her in some bastard's hands, scared, alone, or worse—no, I wouldn't go there.

"I'm getting on a plane," I said, grabbing

my keys and sliding my gun into its holster. "I'll call you when I land."

Ilias exhaled sharply but didn't argue. "I'm coming with you."

I was already on the move, firing off texts to my men, Maxim, and Conall. "Meet me at the airstrip then."

———

CHAPTER 10
ANGELO

ANGELO

The private jet hummed with restrained tension as I stepped inside, my jaw clenched so tightly it ached. The bruises along my ribs protested every movement, but I ignored the discomfort. Ilias was already there, sitting at the round table in the main cabin, a whiskey glass untouched before him. His dark eyes flicked up when I entered, filled with an emotion I recognized all too well—rage restrained by necessity.

Theodosia's brothers, Kostas and Vaso, were already seated, both statues of barely contained aggression. Their presence alone made it clear just how serious this was. The plane was already stacked with men—soldiers from each of our respective organizations, who sat in stony silence, waiting for the actual discussion to begin.

My brother Remo and my consigliere, Bacco, climbed the stairs behind me. We'd driven straight here, quickly gathering what we thought we'd need, although I was certain Ilias was setting us up on the ground once we arrived.

"The captain said we'll be airborne in five minutes, sir," a flight attendant remarked as she secured the door. Ilias nodded in response.

Slumping in the chair, I exhaled, "What do we have?"

Ilias leaned forward, his hands clasped together. "Not enough. Kostas has been working leads, but whoever took Theo was precise. There were no unnecessary moves and no witnesses who saw anything useful. The people at the restaurant who saw Theo seemed more focused on her than on who she was meeting. This wasn't some random grab —it was calculated."

That wasn't surprising to me. Theo was someone who grabbed your attention. A hurricane wrapped in silk, spinning through life without a care for the wreckage she left behind. Not only did she tend to dress herself like she either farted a rainbow or was colorblind, but she radiated joy. It made it so you couldn't look away. Still, she was an Anthakos. Theo had connections that were undeniable. There was no way this was random, and we all knew it.

Bacco scoffed as he crossed his arms. "There has to be something. There is always something. I can't believe your men on the ground let her get kidnapped."

Bacco was old-school. He hadn't thought much about my decision not to marry right away, but he was wise enough to keep his mouth shut, or I would have shut it for him. Bacco had been my consigliere/enforcer long enough to understand my views on specific hot topics. We had talked about it until I told him to shut his trap. He had also advised me against letting Theo wander off to Europe without protection. Technically, she was to be my wife — the wife of the Santelli Don — and she shouldn't go anywhere without a ring on her finger or a detail. Bacco mentioned during the ride over that it would never have happened if we'd been on top of this. He wasn't wrong, and that pissed me off. I didn't like being told that I fucked up.

Guilt didn't feel good. Theo might be a hurricane, but she was *my* damn hurricane, and she was my responsibility — something I had obviously forgotten. My feelings about the blood oath might be conflicted, but that didn't mean I was a monster. Theo was Ilias's sister and Frankie's friend. I didn't want anything to happen to her.

"She's been there a year and has been protected. They've been doing their jobs," Vaso ground out, his face reddening in anger at Bacco's implication that they hadn't protected her. "Like you did anything to help," he sneered.

Bacco rolled his eyes but didn't take the bait. It was one of the things I appreciated about him and why he worked well with me. I tended to be quick-tempered, while Bacco wasn't bothered by much. He never felt the need to justify himself. We balanced each other out, which was good for business. Good for the Santelli *famiglia*. Sometimes, I'd send Bacco to meetings I knew would annoy me. He was more even-tempered than I was.

"They knew her schedule and realized she wouldn't have much security. That suggests either a mole or someone who's been watching closely. Did you talk to the people at her business?" Remo asked.

Kostas, silent until now, let out a low, dangerous laugh. "You think we haven't already considered that? The woman she was supposed to meet doesn't exist. The assistant confirmed Theo received the invitation through a verified channel, but it was bullshit. The people behind this went to great lengths to ensure she walked into that trap."

Remo frowned. He looked rough around the edges, and I wondered whose bed I'd pulled him out of. The one thing about Remo, though, was that he was reliable. He was an excellent capo and an even better brother. I'd love to say he'd make a great underboss, but I wasn't sure he wanted that. Not to mention, I had a great underboss. Carlo was more than competent in running everything. He knew the ins and outs of the operation and could run it blindfolded for me. He was a family man from Queens and more of an accountant than a fighter, but that worked since mine was a laundering operation. He was a good underboss when paired with a heavy enforcer, and he'd watch out for the business while I was off in Italy.

Vaso, his fist clenched, growled, "And when we find them, we will make them regret it."

I understood that fury all too well. The thought of Theo being in the hands of an unknown enemy made my blood boil, and my fingers itch to wrap around someone's throat and squeeze until they provided me with answers. It was an effort to remember that anger wouldn't benefit us at all.

"I'm assuming you tracked her phone?" I asked, my voice tight, trying to sift through the information we had, which was jack shit, as the plane took off. "No good?"

"Nothing," Kostas confirmed. "Dropped with her shit behind the lounge. We had a tracker on it."

I nodded. I had already confirmed it with Veronica on the way here, but there was no guarantee they had a backup. I would never admit to having prayed that it was the case. It didn't sound like it, though.

"Any word on the vehicle?" Bacco tapped his pen on his notebook as he wrote his list of thoughts. I'd grown accustomed to his habits; he was a prolific doodler and list maker, even when there was no information to speak of. I'd told him before that if the Feds got ahold of his little notebooks we were fucked.

Kostas nodded and straightened in his seat. "They used a black Mercedes van, no plates. My contact pulled some traffic camera footage. Florence operates something like CCTV cameras. They have traffic-restricted zones that track the plates of vehicles coming in and out, but they switched vehicles a few blocks away. After that, nothing. Whoever they are, they're smart."

"Smart," I muttered, rolling the word around in my mouth like venom. "She met with a woman, but that was probably just the bait. If they took her on purpose, knowing who she was, they'll know what's coming for them."

Silence stretched for a moment before Kostas spoke again, his voice low and controlled. "We need to narrow down who would dare do this. Someone targeting Theo isn't just making a play against her—they're making a play against our families. It could be against both of us, or it could be against one of us. Either the Anthakos or the Santellis." He gave me a pointed look. It was no secret that I'd been dragging my feet, but I was happy he didn't belabor the point.

Bacco nodded. "Agreed, that's a good place to start. Let's list out potential suspects." With his pen poised, he looked at us.

I exhaled, rubbing my jaw. "Dino Scarpato is interfering with my construction projects. He's been a thorn in my side, but this would be a drastic escalation, and I'm not sure he could pull it off. If it's him, he's looking for something big. Or leverage," I added darkly.

"Scarpato isn't clever enough for an international play." Ilias ground his teeth. "There's also the possibility of an old enemy looking to settle a score. We've left bodies in the ground, and some wounds don't heal."

"We have other players in New York. There's Cardoni, but I think this would be out of character. I have that meeting set up, and their *famiglia* would be making huge moves. Valentino isn't an idiot like Scarpato. He runs a tight ship. I'm fairly certain he is busy with his kid after his wife passed away. It would be a big play."

"What about Vallone? He's been calm, yeah?" Remo accepted a drink from the stewardess, who was practically bending over his lap, showing her tits. He gave her a wink.

"I texted Conall about it, but he's sure he wouldn't gain anything from it, and he's been very pro-Frankie lately. He seems to be trying to develop that relationship." Ilias didn't sound convinced, though, even to my ears, and Bacco picked up on it too.

"So, he's on the list," Bacco scribbled furiously. "Vallone, Scarpato, Cardoni. None of them sound likely, but all have something to gain, right?"

"Truth," Kostas nodded.

"Renzetti should be on the list. He's at the

top, but I'm not sure if he has the money or the connections to pull something like this off. As far as I know, he's nobody. He claims to have connections to Olivetto territory, but I haven't found anything more than him being a second cousin, which wouldn't give him any claim over Nico." Renzetti was an anomaly to all of us, but that was where my chips would be bet.

Vaso drummed his fingers against the arm of his chair. His eyes locked on his brother. "And let's not ignore the possibility that this isn't about the families at all. Maybe it's about Theo personally."

That thought settled like lead in my stomach. Theodosia had a wild streak and a penchant for chaos, but had she angered the wrong person? Or had she been dating? My mind rejected the idea even as I considered it. No, this couldn't be just about her. Granted, Theo was reckless and tended to be a little wild. She was also willing to do things like burn a body — so, was it possible? Sure. But at the heart of Theo, she radiated sunshine and goodness. No one could meet her and not absolutely adore her.

"It's a theory." Kostas seemed to be weighing Vaso's hypothesis. "The men on her detail haven't given any indication that she's had anyone who would do something like this. She has attended some functions, but all related to her work. Her business had been going well until recently, but there has been a lull in her commissions. I think this is more about one of our families than anything else."

I agreed. Part of me had hoped that there would be a ransom demand or a clear direction that we could follow.

"We need to work fast," Ilias said. "Every hour that passes makes it harder to track them. Kostas and I will push our network in Greece and see if anyone's been asking the wrong questions. Vaso, you dig into our U.S. connections."

"I'll have my men hit the streets in the Bronx and Queens." Trying to keep any sense of worry from my voice. "Conall and Maxim are working their territories, and I have Veronica monitoring the dark web for me." That part made me sick, and I could tell that thought had crossed everyone's mind. Trafficking wasn't outside the realm of possibilities either.

Ilias leaned back, his expression sharp, calculating. "I'm calling in a couple of favors."

Kostas narrowed his eyes. "From whom?"

"A man who owes me more than one."

His lips curled into a humorless smile. "And he's very good at finding things people want to keep hidden."

I nodded once. "Good. We hit every angle until we have something solid."

No one doubted what would happen when we did. There would be no negotiations, no compromises, only fire and blood. We would come home with Theodosia. Period.

As the jet sped through the night toward our destination, I stared out the window, my mind playing out every possible scenario. No matter how this ended, I knew one thing for sure—whoever had taken Theo was about to learn they had made a mistake of biblical proportions.

My stomach twisted at the thought that she might have been vulnerable because we had allowed this entire marriage to twist in the wind. I knew she didn't want it either, but maybe it was time to reconsider our positions. Maybe our lives didn't need to change for a piece of paper. Maybe if it was the protection of a name, I could give her that.

I leaned back against the leather seat and closed my eyes, knowing that sleep would be hard to find in the coming days. I just hoped we'd find her quickly and unharmed. We didn't speak of them, but I knew that her brothers held some of the same fears I did. Unspeakable things could be happening. Minutes were critical. Hours? Fuck … anything could happen.

CHAPTER 11
THEODOSIA

DARKNESS PRESSED against the edges of my mind, thick and suffocating, a heavy fog that refused to lift. My head pounded, a dull throb pulsing behind my temples, and my tongue felt like sandpaper in my mouth. I inhaled sharply, expecting the familiar scent of expensive perfume and leather upholstery, but instead, the air was damp, thick with mildew, and something earthier—dirt.

My eyes flew open, panic surging through me like an electric current. My pulse thundered in my ears as I tried to move, but my limbs were sluggish, my body refusing to cooperate. I squeezed my eyes shut and forced myself to take a slow, measured breath. Think, Theo. What was the last thing I remembered?

I had been at that restaurant meeting with Carlotta Santelli, and she had set me up. The realization hit me like a gut punch, leaving a bitter taste in my mouth. I had walked into that meeting with my usual bravado, decked out in a perfectly tailored jumpsuit and heels that cost more than most people's rent, thinking I was meeting with Bassiano Torsiello. Instead, I got Carlotta. Admittedly, I'd been cocky, believing I could handle whatever she threw at me. I'd thought it was a public place. What was the worst that could happen? I should have known better. After growing up the way I had, with the father I had? I felt like an absolute idiot. Women weren't ever safe. I knew that.

It felt like I'd been drugged. I tried to do a quick inventory. My clothes were intact, buttoned, and fastened. A giant plus. Okay. Things could be way worse. I tried to shake off the fog that permeated the edges of my consciousness, wrapping everything in cotton.

And then there was that name. Salvatore Renzetti.

The moment she mentioned him, something inside me tensed. Carlotta had smiled— a cold, knowing smile—and told me he wanted me. That wasn't a good sign. New players in New York signaled someone seeking leverage, which didn't bode well for me. Women were chess pieces in the under-belly of the criminal world. Alliances needed to be made and forged. My brother and his friends might like to think that they'd turned the Commission into something better, but I was still bitter about the part I had to play. Angelo felt the same, and so I felt safe knowing that he hated the shackles of the blood oath as much as I did. It was a commonality that we had — one of the few.

Men like Renzetti didn't want women the way normal men did. If Renzetti was new to the New York scene, he was coming in empty-handed. He was desperate, which wasn't good news. If this was his idea of wanting me, then it meant possession, control, and worse, if this cell was anything to go by.

I struggled to sit up, wincing as my palms pressed against the rough ground. A cold, damp sensation spread through my fingers, and I recoiled, staring down at my hands in horror. My manicured nails were caked with dirt. My clothes—my gorgeous, custom-designed jumpsuit—was stained and wrin-kled, the once-crisp fabric now tainted by grime.

A strangled noise escaped my throat, caught between a whimper and a growl.

"Of all the goddamn things," I muttered, brushing frantically at the fabric as if that would somehow erase the filth. "Kidnap me, threaten me, whatever, but ruin my outfit? Unforgivable."

The absurdity of my own words nearly made me laugh. Nearly. Because beneath the irritation, beneath the dramatic outrage, fear coiled tight in my stomach. It was easier to focus on the state of my clothes than on the fact that I had no idea where I was or what Renzetti had planned for me.

I forced myself to take in my surroundings, setting my fashion crisis aside for the moment. The room was small, barely large enough for me to stretch fully. The walls were rough, composed of crumbling concrete, streaked with moisture and patches of sediment. The floor was uneven, made of packed dirt, and the scent of damp earth lingered in the air. There were no windows, only a heavy metal door reinforced with iron bars, reminiscent of an old prison cell. Italy was big on old architecture, so I could still be somewhere in Florence, but the dampness was throwing me off. The Mediterranean was drier than this moldy dampness that filled my nose.

I exhaled slowly, willing my heartbeat to steady.

I pushed myself upright, brushing off more dirt from my outfit with a huff. "Absolutely unacceptable," I muttered under my breath before turning my attention to the door. I staggered to my feet, my legs shaky, and took a step toward it. The moment I did, I caught movement on the other side.

A shadow shifted, then settled, as if whoever was there had been waiting for me to notice them.

My stomach twisted. I squared my shoulders, running a hand through my hair, even though I was sure it looked like a disaster. Presentation was everything, even in a damp prison cell — especially in a damp prison cell.

"Hey," I called out, my voice only slightly shaky. "Not that I don't appreciate the hospitality, but this room could really use a serious makeover. Have you ever heard of interior decorating? Maybe some throw pillows or a rug?" Silence. "No? Okay. Tough crowd."

I stepped closer, peering through the bars. The dim lighting outside the cell barely illuminated my captor, but I could discern the broad shape of a man standing just beyond reach, arms crossed. I felt his gaze, even if I couldn't see his face clearly.

"Well, this is awkward," I said, shifting my weight onto one hip. "Usually, when a lady finds herself locked in a cell, her captor at least has the decency to introduce himself. Do you have a name, big guy?"

Nothing.

I huffed out a breath. "Silent type, huh? I bet you're great at parties."

The lack of response sent a fresh wave of unease through me. Not that I would let him see it. I had spent years perfecting the art of deflection, masking my fear with humor and attitude. It had always been my shield, my armor. I wasn't about to abandon it now. I had honed it around my father and learned it well. The mafia world was, to me, a terrifying place to be avoided at all costs. Not that I had a choice, of course. I'd tried hard to learn everything I could and adopt a devil-may-care attitude instead. I learned some self-defense and kept my nightmares to myself. I googled. Bestie needed a body disposal? Sure. I could do that. I might have had nightmares, but I was capable. I was strong.

"Look, I don't suppose you'd be willing to tell me why I'm here?" I tried again, injecting just the right amount of casual boredom into my voice, as if being kidnapped were merely an inconvenience rather than a terrifying reality. "Because if this is Salvatore Renzetti's idea of courtship, he has a really twisted sense of romance."

Still no response.

"Not in an awesome dark romance way, either." I pressed my forehead against the peeling metal bars, frustration bubbling to the surface. "Fine. Be mysterious. I'll just sit here and talk to myself, then. It's not like I need conversation to stay entertained."

Silence.

I sighed, stepping away from the door, my fingers flexing at my sides. If I stayed still too long, I would start thinking about everything that could go wrong, about all the ways this could end. That wasn't an option. I had things to look forward to, things I wanted to do in my life. Frankie said she was going to get preggars. My throat tightened. No way was I missing out on that.

Carlotta had made it clear—Salvatore Renzetti wanted me.

The question was, for what? A wife?

My stomach churned at the thought. If he had me now and had gone to the trouble of orchestrating my kidnapping, then he wasn't going to let me go easily. The good news was that I knew Ilias had men watching me the whole time I was in Italy. They would have known I never made it out of the restaurant. It was only a matter of time before my brothers came for me, and they'd bring backup. I wasn't sure where this little hole in the ground was, but they'd find me. Somehow. It was just a matter of how long it'd take.

I clenched my jaw, shoving down the creeping tendrils of fear. No. I would not allow myself to slide down that slope. I would find a way out of this.

I turned back to the guard, placing my hands on my hips. "Alright, strong and silent, have it your way. But just so you know, if I don't get out of here soon, you're going to have to deal with one very cranky, very vengeful Greek woman. And trust me, that's not something you want."

I sighed dramatically and sank back onto the dirt floor, grimacing as the filth clung to my already-ruined clothes. "Hope you're ready for a long night, buddy. I can talk for hours."

The guard didn't react, but I swore his shoulders stiffened just slightly.

Good. Let him underestimate me. Let them all think I was just some spoiled mafia princess who would sit here and wait to be rescued.

They had no idea who they were dealing

with. There would inevitably come a time when they would enter this cell, and I'd be ready. I had ... dirt and hairpins. Well, I could work with that. And stilettos.

Yeah, they were stupid. They should have taken the heels.

CHAPTER 12
ANGELO

THE LOW HUM of the jet's engines did little to help me sleep. All I could think about was Theodosia being in the hands of monsters, their hands on her. Thoughts swirled in my head like angry bees — dark ones that I struggled to keep in check.

My fingers curled into fists on the armrests, my knuckles still raw from the last fight, and my cheek throbbed. The cabin lights had been dimmed, with gun oil mingling in the recycled air as our men worked on some of the weapons we'd brought, ensuring they were ready for the fighting we were bound to face. Outside the windows, the dark sky stretched endlessly, but all I could see was red.

Theodosia was gone. Taken. And I was going to carve through whoever had touched her.

The last time I'd seen her had been outside Conall's penthouse, right after my sister had been married. Theo had been all full of spit and fire about Conall marrying Frankie without either of us there. I had been studiously avoiding Theo for years, and then she had been right up in my face, grown up and beautiful. I hadn't even known what to do with myself, or where to look. All I'd known was that I'd had to get away from her before I pushed her up against the wall and fucked her raw. Apparently, she'd been just as horrified as I was because she'd darted away from me like I was hot lava, and then immediately moved out of the country.

Sighing, I scrubbed a hand over my face and looked out over the plane.

The Anthakos brothers were carbon copies of one another: giant brutes well over six feet tall and hulking. All had the quintessential Greek nose and hooded dark eyes. It was amusing to recall how small Ilias had been when I met him so many years ago in that smoky lounge my father dragged me to. He had been so wiry and short. Sure, he had only been ten, but I would have never guessed he would become such a giant. He'd been a nervous thing, too—twitchy as a rabbit. That had made Conall instantly protective of him while Maxim remained suspicious for years. Their youngest sister, Polina, looked nothing like them. She was waifish and blonde, unlike any Anthakos at all. It made you wonder if she was even related to them, though I didn't care. Polina was the fairy princess of their little clan.

On the other hand, Theodosia was lush and beautiful, dark like her brothers, with smooth Mediterranean skin that glowed in the sunshine like burnished copper. Once, she'd been embarrassed by her figure, but she'd grown into her curves, and now she was all woman with an ass that wouldn't quit and tits that I would give my left arm to bury myself in. She had dark hair like her brothers, but hers was long and curly. She embraced that, too, sometimes leaving it long and fluffing it out into a giant dark halo that resonated with her outfit, burying glittering beads or tiny colored combs in it. Other times, she piled it on her head into little buns.

"You okay there, boss?" Bacco asked, sitting beside me and flipping his butterfly knife between his fingers as if that steady rhythm would prevent him from losing his mind. He wasn't a fan of flying, but he wouldn't let me go alone. Bacco always claimed that being in an airplane made no sense to him. He insisted that the idea of two engines keeping a metal cylinder full of people in the air was ridiculous. While he doubted the physics of our transportation, there was sure to be fighting, and he wouldn't miss out on that.

"Not really," I admitted, adjusting and readjusting my grip on the brass knuckles I had brought. My head was all messed up, and it was hard to think clearly. Sitting still wasn't my forte.

We were heading to where we thought she was—but every second wasted felt like another cut, bleeding me dry. It was a weird thought. I didn't think I would care this much. Was it because I'd known her for so long? I didn't want to think about the little girl I had known, the way she'd grown up before my eyes. It had always made me uncomfortable because I knew all about the piece of paper burning a hole in my desk drawer. Looking at her back then made me feel ashamed that I knew she wouldn't have a choice—that she'd be saddled with one of us as a husband. It had felt weird and wrong. Now I wondered if I should feel bad that it felt right.

I'd set my father up to be killed in a drive-by shooting when I was seventeen. Made sure I'd be there to take the final shot so I could look the fucker in the eyes when it happened. I'd been happy as fuck when I did. Celebrated afterwards.

Frankie had only been nine, and Theo had been ten. They were just kids. At that time, I felt physically disgusted by what the blood oath represented. It made me irrationally angry to think that the mafia world had trapped us.

Trapped <u>me</u>.

I had never told anyone, but I had strongly considered taking my siblings and leaving New York —leaving <u>everything</u> behind. I imagined being a fisherman or something like that. Go somewhere where nobody knew who Angelo Santelli was... because who was I, really? Carlotta's biological son, yes. What the fuck did that matter in the end? She was a hateful bitch. I was half-Italian, I suppose. I definitely wasn't Stefano's son. Everyone could tell just by looking at me. I didn't even look Italian. I had learned Italian for Stefano's sake, but my skin was too pale, my eyes nearly green, and my hair so light brown it was almost blonde. Fuck, Conall looked more like my brother than Remo did. When I was younger, it had bothered me when the other dons of the Five Families had turned their noses up at me for not being Italian enough. Now I didn't give a shit what they thought. I had clawed my way up the ladder the old-fashioned way. Hard work, blood, and instilling enough fear in them that they would have to kill me to take the Santelli famiglia away from me.

My phone buzzed, dragging me out of my thoughts, ringing through on the special line — the one for which only a handful of people had the number. I snatched it up, barely glancing at the name before answering. A call meant information, and that was what I craved right now.

"Talk."

"Angelo," Veronica's voice was sharp and urgent. "I've found her."

I snapped my fingers and switched the phone to speaker mode. "Veronica found her." The entire cabin went silent. Every head turned toward me. "Where?" My fingers tightened around the phone as I hoped the news was good.

"Not Italy. She's in the United States. Louisiana, New Orleans, specifically."

My eyes were already scanning the cabin when I noticed that Kostas was up and moving toward the front of the plane. Good, I thought — he was going to get us on the right flight path. Still, my heart lurched into my throat. Jesus, we had been in the air for hours, heading in the wrong direction. We could have been there by now. Mentally, I calculated the math. This wasn't good. We had lost hours flying toward Italy, believing she was there. I tried to take a deep breath, clutching the steel of the knuckles to ground myself.

"*Cazzo.*" More to myself than anyone, I swore under my breath. "How the fuck did she end up there?"

"Salvatore Renzetti." Her words were precise, each one landing like a blade. "He took her to some kind of plantation there, and there's more."

My entire body went still. "Tell me."

"There's going to be an auction. A private, high-stakes one. She's listed as one of the top prizes."

The silence that followed was suffocating. Something cold and violent uncoiled inside me. My fingers itched for my gun, yearning for the sensation of my blade sliding into flesh. Auction. As if Theodosia were some fucking object. Some possession to be bought and sold. I forced myself to breathe steadily, but my vision was already darkening at the edges.

"Veronica." My voice was quiet, deadly. "Tell me you have something else."

"I've hacked into their encrypted communications. It's happening tonight. Only verified guests can enter. The bidding list is made up of traffickers, slavers, and other degenerates who think they're untouchable. Typical," she snorted.

They thought wrong.

"Renzetti doesn't plan to sell her immediately. He wants to make a spectacle. Show her off like a trophy before the bidding begins. This is his sort of crowd, and he's made sure that this group knows he's got her."

I swallowed back the urge to vomit. "Tell me Maxim knows."

"He does. He and Conall have already left for New Orleans with a crew. They're currently on the ground, gathering intel. A helicopter will be waiting for you. This place is far enough from the city center that you'll want one."

I looked at the men around me. Every face was locked in fury. "We're changing course," I said. "Get me whatever else you can, Veronica. Security measures, guards, the property layout—I want it all."

"You'll have it," she confirmed. "And Angelo—"

"What?" I ground out.

"Burn him," she said. "Make him suffer."

I hung up and made to stand when Kostas returned just as the plane banked.

"Changing course," he confirmed grimly. "Can you catch me up?"

I took a slow breath, gripping the back of a seat as I forced the words out. "Renzetti has her. He's planning a private auction."

"What?" His jaw clenched so hard I wondered if he'd break a tooth.

I cut him a look that made him pause, but I could see the same storm in his eyes that I felt in my chest. "Veronica hacked into their system. We have forty-eight hours before it happens." I turned to Bacco. "Contact one of the families in New Orleans that we know. I want everything they know about this operation of Renzetti's that he has there." He nodded, already pulling out his phone.

"Maxim and Conall are already there, so we'll have backup. I say we go in hard." I scanned each of them for confirmation. "We can check the intel first. There will be heavy security. I'm guessing that precautions will be taken if this is that sort of event. Firepower." Still, the idea of going in and sneaking around just to bring Theo out didn't sit right. She was the priority, but Renzetti needed to pay for this. I wouldn't feel comfortable with him walking around, breathing, after this.

Ilias ran a hand through his hair, his jaw tight. "I want that asshole fucking dead. I want blood."

"You'll get it," I promised. "I want it too, but we need a plan. We can't just take Renzetti. We wipe his entire fucking operation off the map. No survivors. No mercy. But Theo is the priority," I added. "If we can't get Renzetti, then we'll cut our losses and take what we can." I clenched my fists, digging my nails into my palms at the thought of not exacting the vengeance I craved, but I had a responsibility to Theodosia first.

Remo, who had remained silent until now, finally spoke. "What about the auction guests? If they're coming to buy—"

"Then they'll die alongside him," I said flatly. "Every last one, but Theo first. If other women are held, we'll try to get them too."

"Any thoughts about the why?" Bacco asked. "Renzetti grabbed her because?"

It bothered me, too. If he had grabbed her

111

and married her, maybe it would have made a little more sense—forcing an alliance with the Anthakos. They would form a powerful partnership to leverage their smuggling and shipping enterprises if he lived long enough. If he could actually pull it off, he might think that he could also secure a seat with the Commission. Perhaps he would have thought he'd be doing me a favor, and I'd thank him for it. But auctioning her off? That was stupid.

"We must be missing something. This feels like a fuck you. He has to know that treating her this way would be utterly insulting." Bacco had his knife back out, swirling around his knuckles, and I wanted to smack him in the face

"Who is this guy? I mean, yeah, we killed his cousin or whatever, but he deserved it." Vaso rubbed the back of his neck. "Are we missing the connection?"

"I'll get on it and see if I can find anything that Veronica has missed. I'm sure that she is looking as we speak." Kostas reached for his computer.

"You're right, Bacco. This grab is personal. Whatever the reason was behind it. He's going to pay for it."

Silence fell. The kind that came with understanding. I knew everyone felt the same

— off-kilter and unsure, with a sick sense of rage building behind it. Normally, our world existed in shades of grey. The Commission had clear lines within which we operated, doing some bad things to bad people, but for the most part, we kept that to those who deserved it. We definitely didn't go around kidnapping innocent women.

I pulled out my gun, checking the magazine before snapping it back into place. I glanced over my shoulder at the soldiers we'd brought along, wondering if we brought enough. Hopefully, Maxim and Conall came through for us.

"We do this fast," I continued. "We do it loud. And when it's done, there won't be enough left of Renzetti to fill a fucking shoebox."

Kostas exhaled sharply, his eyes gleaming with vengeance. "I like the sound of that."

I met Ilias's gaze. "We will get her back. We'll put him in the ground. And we'll make sure everyone knows what happens when they touch what's ours."

His throat bobbed as he swallowed, his fists flexing. "Damn right."

The cabin fell into a grim, focused silence. Weapons were checked, plans were made, and by the time the pilot confirmed our descent into New Orleans, one thing was certain.

Renzetti had made a mistake.

And I was going to make damn sure it was his last.

CHAPTER 13
THEODOSIA

THEODOSIA

The walls were sweating.

Okay, maybe not literally, but that's how it felt. The dampness soaked through the fabric of my jumpsuit—the one I had carefully paired with black suede Santoni heels that morning. A morning that now felt like it belonged to another life. Back when I still had clean clothes, breathable air, and an intact sense of self-preservation. Back before, Carlotta Santelli smiled sweetly over tea and handed me over like a party favor.

"God, I knew she was a nightmare," I muttered to myself, pacing the six-by-eight cell like a caged animal in couture. If you could even call it couture anymore. My jumpsuit was streaked with dirt, my heels were stained beyond redemption, and I was pretty sure something had died in the far corner of the room. It smelled like damp despair and rat droppings.

"Hey! Mustache!" I called out for the eighth time today. "You know, you could at least pretend I'm a person. Say hi. Offer me a drink. Maybe a snack? I'd murder someone for an espresso." Neither was a lie. I was starving and thirsty.

Silence. As usual.

I flopped down onto the grimy cot with a groan, kicking off one shoe to inspect it—my poor baby. Scuffed suede and some of the little rhinestones had come off. Santino would weep. These were the Sibille pumps, and I loved them with their shiny little constellations of stones. They made my feet sparkle. When I wore them, they brought me joy.

Of all the things I could focus on right now, I was furious about my clothes and shoes. It was easier to rage about fashion than to confront the dread curling in my stomach. The only thing I knew for sure? If this were Salvatore Renzetti's version of wooing, I'd rather date a sewer rat.

He hadn't revealed himself yet, but the air reeked of evil. Carlotta had spoken his name with the kind of smirk typically reserved for someone you didn't particularly care for. She'd set me up—smiling all the while—and now I was the one trapped in some horror-movie version of a prison cell.

I put my ruined pump back on and stood, pacing once more. I had searched the room a hundred times, tracing every crack in the wall and checking every loose piece of wood or rusted metal. Nothing. No window, no tools, no leverage.

But I still had pins in my hair.

And I had grit, even if it was currently stuck in my bra.

The sound of boots on the wooden stairs outside made me tense. I froze mid-step, my eyes fixed on the cell door. Metal scraped as the barred door was opened.

"Time to clean up," a voice barked. Male. Gruff.

"Excuse me? I'm very clean, thank you." I wiped my hands on my pants and lifted my chin. "This took hours of work and an inge-nuity you wouldn't understand."

The door clanked open, and two guards entered, their faces unreadable. I backed up, pinning myself against the wall as I scuffed off a shoe and picked it up. I hated to ruin one of my heels like this, but some things were worth it.

"Don't touch me." I loathed that my voice came out shaky.

"Orders are orders," the first man said, showing no signs of remorse. "You could just walk out under your own power." He shrugged as if he didn't care either way.

He was muscular and scarred, with flat black eyes that hinted he wouldn't hesitate to hurt me if needed. He might even take pleasure in it.

"Well," I snapped, clenching the two hairpins I'd gathered from my hair in one hand like daggers. "I am not afraid to go full psycho."

It wasn't much, but sharp, and I jabbed forward like a fencing champion on a sugar high. One caught my wrist, twisting hard until I screamed, while the other tried to grab my legs. I kicked and flailed, and the other one of my heels flew off like a rogue missile.

"You jerks ruined my outfit!"

My elbow connected with someone's chin. I bit down on the first guard's arm until I tasted blood, so I bore down, ignoring the awful feeling that it was flesh. The man howled as I took a chunk out of his arm. My hair flew wildly as I thrashed, pins scattering, curls everywhere like a whirling dervish. I gripped the base of the heel tightly and slammed it with all my strength, aiming for an eyeball and hoping for that action movie moment where it sank in, making me look like a badass. Sadly, it glanced off his cheekbone, leaving a reasonably wicked slice but failing to do nearly enough damage.

"You bitch! You bit me."

He delivered a strong punch to my ribs, causing me to drop to my knees, my wrists pinned, feet dragging, dirt clinging to me like a second skin as they manhandled me into a hold.

"Enough. No marks." It was the mustachioed guard who had watched my door. "Pick her up."

They hauled me up a narrow flight of stairs into a wide hallway. White columns, wooden floors, tall windows with gauzy curtains—a plantation home. Antebellum and absurd. Frantically, I searched for someone to call out to, someone who might help me, even though I knew that was impossible. I was in Southern Belle horror movie hell.

The opulence, combined with the fact that I was just below in a jail cell and having been punched in the ribs, made me feel ill.

They shoved me hard into a room the size of my old apartment, featuring a four-poster bed and an equally spacious bathroom.

Everything gleamed in white and gold: gilded mirrors, velvet seating, and marble floors. It stood in stark contrast to my previous quarters, so I scrambled forward, trying to find my footing as I moved toward the door.

"Stop," said the Mustache Man. "You won't get anywhere. There is nowhere to go and no one to help you. Clean up. Now."

"Or what?" I sneered even as I tried to assess the options.

It was all bravado, but I summoned every ounce of it I had from the soles of my bare feet, ignoring the ache of my ribs. One guard cracked his knuckles while the other shot me a look that made my skin crawl.

"If that's necessary, you'll find that you'd prefer to tidy up by yourself. There are dresses to choose from. Put one on. If we must return to dress you, I'll let *him* do it." He jerked his head towards the guard who had struck me. "I won't stop him this time. Maybe he can have a little sample," he added suggestively.

Taking a look at the two guards, I could see that they were only restrained by the guard in charge. If he hadn't been here, they would have all been over me. Dread coated my throat. So what was this? Some sort of business like my father's?

"Right," I muttered. "Shower, it is."

They left, slamming the door behind them. I locked it, even though it probably wouldn't hold.

The mirror showed a stranger: dirt-smudged cheeks, bruised wrists, and tangled hair. My eyeliner had turned traitor and fled down my cheeks.

There was an option to ignore orders and not get cleaned up, but that didn't seem very smart. That would only encourage the leechers in the hallway. My job here was to delay. Having already engaged in the little scuffle downstairs, I knew when I was over-powered. It didn't serve me to refuse to clean up. If I did as they asked, I'd be dirt-free and dressed again — and it wasted more time. Please, please, please let my brothers be on their way. I allowed myself one moment in the shower to lean against the tile for precisely two minutes to feel sorry for myself.

I scrubbed myself raw in the shower. Hot water, floral soap, plush towels—like I was supposed to forget I'd been treated like a stray animal. Like this was luxury. Not a cage in disguise. My ribs were bruised, but they weren't broken.

Then I saw the clothes laid out on the bed like an offering. High-end designer, sure. Elie

Saab, Dior, Versace. But none of it was mine. None of it was made by my hands, stitched with love and rebellion.

People never understood that wearing someone else's design felt like wearing someone else's skin.

I chose the least offensive option: a black silk dress with long sleeves and a thigh slit. Classic. Elegant. Tactical. If I had to run, I'd be mobile. The matching stilettos were offensively perfect. Maybe I'd get luckier the next time and land that eyeball shot I'd been hoping for. Squish it right in there and cause some damage. They were nice ones, too. Red bottoms. Louboutins.

I sat at the vanity, brushing out my curls and applying the makeup left for me, as if I were preparing for a gala or a funeral. My hair had always been its own animal—wild, unpredictable, and only vaguely aware that I was the one it was attached to. It was long, naturally curly, and had a flair for the dramatic, as if it knew it was the first thing people noticed when I walked into a room. At its best, it was a sleek, coiled panther draped over my shoulders, all glossy shine and effortless allure. But most days? It was a feral creature with claws, frizzy and defiant, fighting every attempt I made to wrangle it into submission. Brushes? Laughed at. Serums? Momentary peace treaties. Silk pillowcases? A joke. I had stopped trying to tame it. These days, I just worked with the beast—my curls and I, an uneasy alliance at best.

The door creaked open.

I looked into the mirror to see the image reflected back at me. And I knew.

Renzetti.

He resembled a toad, with a broad, heavy-jowled face, a stocky build, and dark hair slicked back. He wore a three-piece suit by a tailor who was either inept or didn't like him very much. There was too much shoulder padding, and the buttons weren't right. He smiled at me, but his face felt all wrong. It was cold in a way that turned my stomach—it felt like a mask worn for too long, almost like a Halloween costume that melted in the sun.

His eyes were wrong. Empty. Cold.

"You must be Theodosia," he said, his smile slow and cruel.

I stood, spine straight. "And you must be that delusional asshole Carlotta mentioned."

His eyes glittered, but I could tell he didn't like it. "You're just as charming as she described. I suppose I'll need to teach you some manners."

"Sorry to disappoint."

Something I learned long ago was not to worry about the preconceived notions people had about me. My goal on Earth wasn't to be what people expected — least of all, this prick.

He took a step closer. I didn't flinch. I wouldn't give him the satisfaction.

"You've caused quite the stir," he murmured. "Fiery. Spirited. Angelo's little doll."

"I don't belong to anybody."

I was startled by his comment. Was that why I was here? Was it because he thought Angelo had some attachment to me? He had crept closer, but there was nowhere for me to go. A chilling, gut-wrenching fear gripped me, yet I forced myself to stand still.

"Oh, but you are." He reached out, brushing a strand of hair off my cheek.

I slapped his hand away, unable to help the instinct to keep his hands off me.

He laughed, low and pleased. "I enjoy a challenge."

I smiled sweetly. "Good. Because you're going to lose."

Renzetti's smile thinned. "We'll see about that. I expect you downstairs and on your best behavior in under five minutes. You'll be escorted down, of course." He added the last part as if he were granting me a favor. Then he turned and walked out, leaving behind the scent of expensive cologne and the stench of decay.

I stared at the closed door. My pulse was racing.

But my mind?

Raced faster.

I wasn't going down like this. I'd memorize every hallway, every face, every weakness. If I had to burn this plantation to the ground in my Louboutins, so be it.

CHAPTER 14
THEODOSIA

THE KNOCK RESONATED like a drumbeat against my ribcage.

Three sharp knocks echoed, and then the door creaked open without waiting for an invitation. Manners? Apparently, they were not on the menu tonight. My favorite silent, mustached guard appeared in the doorway, looking as grim as ever, dressed in all black, as if auditioning for a role in a low-budget vampire flick.

"Let me guess," I said, smoothing the front of my black silk dress. "You're here to walk me down the aisle to meet my kidnapper, Prince Charming?"

Nothing. No grunt, no twitch; he simply gestured.

I gave him my best exasperated sigh and

rose from the velvet stool, taking as much time as possible without appearing obvious. After checking my reflection one last time, I offered him a sweet smile. "Got to look my best," I quipped before smoothing a hand down my dress and moving toward the door. Microseconds could matter, and I'd make sure to extend each one.

The heels clicked ominously against the floor, resembling the countdown of a doomsday clock. The room smelled of lilies and costly decay, and I left a trail of anxiety and Delina in my wake as I walked.

Everything felt overly pristine. Too perfect. Too... curated. High ceilings with elaborate plaster molding loomed above us like the ghosts of bored aristocrats. Oil portraits lined the walls—glowering men and demure women who seemed as if they had all been forced into arranged marriages and afternoon tea. Dark wood paneling gleamed with age and polish, the kind of polish that made you wonder what had been scrubbed away beneath it.

I kept my steps slow and measured, as if I were unsure in my heels, grasping the bannisters as though I could fall at any moment. I could tell he wanted to suggest that I pick up the pace, but I managed to keep going just fast enough that he didn't bother to say anything.

"So," I started, glancing at Mustache Man as we descended a curved staircase that could've easily doubled as a death trap for anyone in six-inch heels, "what do you think of all this? Pretty swanky for a hostage situation. Like Downton Abbey meets American Horror Story."

He didn't even blink.

"You've got the strong, silent type thing going on," I mused. "Very brooding. Do you ever, like, talk about your feelings? Or maybe… grunt a little?"

Nada. This man was a black hole of personality. What a jerk. I mean, if he was just going to stand there while someone punched me, at least he could be funny.

The staircase led into a grand foyer, and that's when I heard it—music. Classical, slow, and lilting. Strings and piano, the sort of stuff that played in the background of old movies just before something terrible occurred.

Beyond the double doors ahead, the sounds of laughter, clinking glasses, and whispered conversations spilled out. I caught the scent of perfume and cologne, champagne, and an underlying aroma that made my skin crawl.

The doors opened, and I was guided into what could only be described as the ballroom from hell.

It was massive—vaulted ceilings and glittering chandeliers that seemed stolen from Versailles, along with a multitude of guests. Many of them were men in tuxedos and women in gowns that likely cost more than an average car. Everyone exuded a gorgeousness reminiscent of the Stepford Wives: artificial, too poised, and too still. The women all had that broken, empty look in their eyes.

A string quartet played in the corner, and servers moved through the crowd with trays of bubbling champagne and hors d'oeuvres that looked like they belonged in a museum.

It was all too perfect. Too smooth. Too shiny.

I was the smudge on the glass.

As soon as I entered, conversations faded. Heads turned. I sensed their gazes—hungry, curious, evaluating. I fought the impulse to pull the slit in my dress closed.

"Try to keep from drooling," I muttered under my breath, my chin held high.

And then I saw Renzetti. He leaned against a marble pillar, as if he belonged on a movie poster for "Dictators of the Deep South." Dressed in a black tuxedo, he held a crystal glass in one hand, while the same hollow toady smile was painted on his face.

He approached me with the grace of someone overly accustomed to getting what he wanted. There was nowhere for me to go. Mustache Man hovered near my elbow. Even if I took off at a sprint, it would do me no good. I had spotted armed guards at every entrance. Delay, delay, delay. My current motto.

"Theodosia," he said warmly, as if we were old friends meeting at a charity gala rather than a psychopath and his unwilling guest.

"Salvatore," I replied, my voice sweetened and tinged with venom. "You host a lovely party. Kidnapping chic is in this season. Thanks for the invite." I flashed a sparkling smile.

He smiled wider. "I knew you'd appreciate the effort." He offered me his arm. I didn't take it.

"Do I get to know what this little soiree is about? Or is that a surprise for later?"

I was beginning to sense what was happening here, and I didn't like it. The eerie music and the women with their downturned smiles and lack of eye contact made me uneasy.

He chuckled and gestured for me to

follow. I complied, albeit reluctantly, catching snippets of conversation as we walked— French, Italian, Russian. As I suspected, these were all cannibal spiders nibbling at the edges of each other's webs.

The crowd parted as we moved through, as if I were the centerpiece of a grotesque art installation. I caught a glimpse of a woman pointing at me as I passed, murmuring something to the man beside her.

We stopped at the edge of the ballroom, where a smaller sitting room was arranged like a VIP lounge. Leather chairs, cigar smoke curling in the air, and a large antique mirror hung on the wall. I saw my reflection — polished, composed, and disgusted.

Renzetti poured me a drink. Bourbon.

"No thanks," I said.

"You might want it soon enough." His thin lips curved into what was supposed to be a smile, but only emphasized the fleshy jowls of his face.

I stiffened. "Why's that?"

He didn't answer. Instead, he turned toward the mirror and pressed something beneath the frame. The mirror clicked and then swung open, revealing a digital, high-resolution screen.

Names. Dozens. With photos. Ages. Descriptions.

I stepped back. My stomach dropped into my shoes. "No. No way."

"You're here as the final addition," Renzetti said, sipping his drink casually, his beady eyes on me watching as I understood the scope of the horror. "A rare piece. The prized lot."

"You're *selling* people."

Everything inside me roiled against the idea. I sensed something like this was happening here, but having it confirmed with such absolute callousness felt entirely different. Trafficking was vile. I'd been so proud of my brothers and their friends for their stance on it.

I understood how my reaction might confuse some people. Perhaps some thought that my father had essentially sold me. Why would I care if I were sold again? Once I learned about the blood oath, I realized one thing: none of the men on the list would hurt me. Sure, they were criminals, and they might not be my choice, but I always knew I would be safe with them. I might have been fighting the chains of this arrangement with Angelo, but fear wasn't part of it. Not this kind of fear.

He tilted his head. "We're offering opportunities. Luxury. Rarity. You know how the world works, Theodosia. Everything has a price."

"Not me," I snapped angrily.

Renzetti remarked lazily, "Don't be dramatic, darling. It's a cocktail party, not a firing squad. Do you want that bourbon now?" he held the glass out for me, his pinky ring winking in the light. "There's nowhere for you to run to."

I ignored him. A drink sounded great right about now, but I wouldn't trust anything from this place. Who knew what they might put in it?

I hoped my brothers killed him.

CHAPTER 15
ANGELO

ANGELO

The trees looked like ghosts in the fog.

Spanish moss draped from the cypress branches like shredded silk, swaying in the humid Louisiana breeze. The plantation loomed in the distance, a shadowy silhouette cloaked in moonlight—grand, stately, and harboring secrets. It was the kind of place that whispered stories even when no one was there to listen.

I stood at the treeline, half-hidden in the underbrush, my Glock warm and familiar in my hand. My heart pounded a hard rhythm against my ribs, steady and unrelenting. I was accustomed to adrenaline. I lived for it and thrived in the chaos. But this? This was different.

Theo was in there. I could feel it in my bones.

"You good, Angelo?" Conall asked, stepping beside me. He resembled a damn war general, all muscle and calm menace, with a scoped rifle slung across his back. His men flanked him, shadows armed with guns and grim determination etched into their faces.

"I'll be good when she's out," I muttered, eyes never leaving the mansion.

Maxim joined us next, having exchanged his suit for sleek black tactical gear. His men moved like ghosts behind him—Volkov-trained killers who didn't need orders to paint the night red.

"The security perimeter is tight," he said with his gravelly Russian accent. "Men are on the balcony, and another four are patrolling the grounds. They aren't amateurs. We'll take the perimeter guards in advance. No guns."

Conall motioned with two fingers, signaling the predetermined patrols, with his right-hand man, Sean, among them. Sean was an absolute savage and was likely eager to get his hands dirty the old-fashioned way. Maxim correctly believed that quietly taking down the perimeter guards was the best approach. It was definitely a stealth job. The bloodier, the better, in Sean's opinion.

"Makes sense," I said, my jaw clenched. "We can't have random shots alerting people inside." Renzetti wouldn't use street rats for this type of operation, so they'd be professionals. But too bad for him; we were a match for whoever he'd brought out here.

Behind me, Ilias, Kostas, and Vaso were quietly and swiftly checking weapons as they spoke to each other in Greek. I didn't understand much of it, but I heard Theo's name mentioned several times. Her brothers were eager for blood. I didn't blame them.

I was right there with them.

Bacco approached from the other side of the trail, wiping sweat from his brow. The southern humidity was a slap in the face after the cool cabin air of the jet, and he was feeling it. My consigliere wasn't built for cardio or this kind of climate, and already he was showing his weaknesses. Still, Bacco would push through when we got inside if he didn't have a heart attack before we got there.

"Front and back entrances confirmed. No guards near the west side veranda. Veronica's intel says the lower-level servants' quarters lead to a back stairwell. If she's still locked up, it'll probably be there."

I nodded once. "We go in quietly, sweep fast, and look for Theo."

Ilias's voice was cold steel. "If she's been harmed—"

"She's fine," I snapped. "She'll *be* fine. Nothing will happen to her." I was going to will it into existence if I had to.

He stared at me for a long moment, and something passed between us—a silent agreement. Theo was family. His blood, my…

Something.

I shoved the thought away.

Not the time for emotions. I could think about it later.

Maxim stepped forward, checking the time on his watch. "We hit in five. My men will breach the north wing. Conall's crew will sweep the first floor and take out the guards. You and your brothers? You go straight for her. Get her out. I have backgrounds on the guests. Some of them won't be walking out alive. If there are innocents there, we'll see about relocating them. Then we burn it down."

I couldn't help but let a grin tug at the corner of my mouth. "That reminds me why I like working with you. You're always going to burn something."

Maxim didn't smile. He simply loaded his weapon. "I thought it was because I was amazing and funny."

"Yeah, none of those." Conall cuffed him on the shoulder. "It's because you're the gun connection."

I snapped my fingers. "That's right," I smirked at Maxim. While that wasn't the only reason, it was a bonus. "We're all about practicality. We don't even like you. Much."

"Right. You guys are all dicks." He rolled his eyes at us.

The night was so dark I could just make out the whiteness of his teeth as he flashed me a grin.

We spread out, slipping through the dark like the kind of nightmares that made grown men cry. I moved with my team—Remo to my right, Bacco behind, Ilias flanking me. Kostas and Vaso brought up the rear.

The grass was slick with dew. I could smell jasmine and gun oil and hear the distant hum of laughter and music drifting from the open windows. It made my blood boil. The fact that they were partying and laughing while having Theo in there against her will was more than infuriating. Veronica had verified what kind of people these were. None of them should even be breathing.

Cocktail party.

For fucking *slavers*.

I would gut them all.

We reached the back veranda in silence, each footstep measured and careful. I couldn't believe we had made it without detection. Our progress was completely unimpeded after the perimeter guards were taken out. There hadn't even been any outside cameras or alarms to disable. Renzetti was either sloppy or overconfident, but if I were one of the attendees, I would be fucking pissed that security was so lax. I was sure these people were paying a fortune to be here, which should include their protection while they were here. However, it was making our job easier, so I shouldn't complain.

Perhaps he thought I wouldn't come for her—the volcano inside me boiled over at the idea that anyone would consider Theo unimportant. Our dynamic was complicated even for us. Maybe we hadn't figured it out yet, but that was our business. Guilt slicked over my insides at the thought that this was my fault. Maybe she wouldn't be in this mess if I hadn't dragged my feet.

The door was unlocked. Too easy. Too confident.

We breached like a well-oiled machine. The guards were weak, surprised, and poorly trained. Only two of them were on the door, and they died like paper mache puppets with their strings cut. Remo and Bacco took point, clearing corners. I swept left with Ilias and Vaso. The house was a museum of decadence —polished wood, antiques, and portraits with eyes that seemed to follow you. The air was thick with perfume and decay. It was one of those houses that felt permeated with it. No matter how much paint you put on a pig, it was still there.

We found the staircase Veronica mentioned. It spiraled upward like something from a horror movie, narrow and claustrophobic. My boots thudded against each step as we climbed. Apparently, everyone was downstairs. Still, you'd think they would have some staff or security up here.

First door on the left. Locked.

I signaled to Vaso. He stepped forward with a silent nod, inserted a small charge, and stepped back.

Pop.

The door swung inward. Empty.

Second room. Same setup. I could feel my pulse throbbing in my neck. Empty.

"She's downstairs," Maxim's voice came through our coms. "We captured one of the perimeter guards."

"Fucking hell," Ilias growled as we

reversed our course pounding back the way we'd come.

"No shit," I growled. "Time to go make a scene."

We didn't creep this time. We stormed and took out the guards as we went. We hit the ballroom like a bomb.

Conall's men flooded in from the front, shouting in their heavy Irish accents, guns raised. Maxim's soldiers took out the balcony snipers in seconds. I'd feel sorry for the party goers if they weren't all dickwads who were going to be shot momentarily. Renzetti's personal guards reacted fast, but not fast enough. I took down two before I reached the bottom of the stairs, gun barking fire with every shot.

Theo turned as chaos erupted around her, and for a heartbeat, our eyes locked. She didn't appear afraid, but then everything tilted as a man with a mustache raised his weapon and a shot rang out. Her body jerked as the bullet tore through her.

"NO!" I roared, adrenaline shoving me forward.

She crumpled to her knees, clutching her chest, blood soaking through the silk of that goddamn dress. I opened fire in the direction of the shooter—some coward trying to blend into the panicked crowd.

Renzetti saw his opening. He slipped away like the snake he was, ducking behind an ornate column and disappearing through a service door while the chaos masked his escape.

"*Piccola*, I've got you," I said, dropping to my knees. My hands were already on her, pressing hard against the wound. Blood coated my fingers. "Nice dress," I added inanely.

She looked up at me, eyes blazing even through the pain. She scoffed. "I hate it. It's off the rack." She gave me a watery smile that was more of a grimace than anything. "Took you long enough." Her eyes drifted closed with a sigh.

And just like that, the world narrowed.

I choked out a half-sobbing laugh. "Sorry, we're late."

Maxim appeared behind me, covering us with his rifle. "We need to move. Now. The crowd's thinning, but we have movement on the east wing."

"Copy that," I growled. I swept Theo into my arms, carefully, blood still seeping from her wound — an alarming amount. She needed a hospital.

She whimpered but didn't fight me. That alone scared the shit out of me. I could hear Ilias behind me, calling out Theo's name, followed by Kostas shouting something I couldn't make out. Conall's men secured the exits while Maxim's soldiers ensured no one followed.

But Renzetti was gone.

Slippery bastard.

As we reached the outside, the night hit us like a wall—humid, hot, thick with gunpowder and smoke. We moved through the wreckage together—through the chaos of bullets and bodies, through Maxim's men pulling out the guests and forcing them to their knees as they compared faces to pictures on their phones. Orders were being barked, but I remained singularly focused. Theo needed a hospital. The others could manage the cleanup.

CHAPTER 16
THEODOSIA

OKAY, no one told me that the afterlife came with a heart monitor's soothing, repetitive lullaby. Or maybe heaven was facing a technical issue.

My eyelids felt like they were made of velvet-covered cement. When I finally cracked one open, everything blended into a pastel smear—ivory walls, pale blue sheets, and a beige curtain with absolutely no sense of aesthetic ambition. Ew.

A sharp ache pulsed in my side, and my brain—a complete traitor—linked it to a memory. There had been sharp, blinding pain.

The auction. Renzetti. The dress I didn't design. The smell of bourbon and blood. The sound of Angelo shouting. And then—

Gunfire.

My chest rose too quickly, and my breath hitched as the machines beeped faster in response. I tried to move as I attempted to sit up, but my body had other plans. My ribs screamed, and my side throbbed. My limbs felt like they belonged to a crash-test dummy. A groan escaped me—elegant, like a dying goat, probably—and that was when I noticed him.

Slumped in a chair beside me, head bowed, one hand hanging between his knees, the other still wrapped around the grip of a gun tucked into the holster under his jacket, was Angelo. A dangerous angel in wrinkled black, his shirt stained with something dark that I didn't want to think about too hard. His hair was unkempt, his jaw shadowed by stubble, and his expression was slack with exhaustion.

And I'd never seen anything more heart-breakingly beautiful. (Aside from a pair of vintage Ferragamo trousers I once saw in Paris, but this was a close second.)

I wondered where my brothers were. My mind replayed the events of the past day. Had it only been a day? Relief had flooded me when I heard the gunfire and commotion from the upper floors. There had been no doubt in my mind that my brothers would come for me. A small part of me prayed that Angelo would be there, too. It made sense that he would be, but I suppressed the giddy girl and needy bitch who reveled in the idea of a white knight riding to her rescue. This wasn't the fucking movies.

"Hey," I croaked or tried to. It came out more like a rasp.

Still, his head jerked up, and his eyes found mine—burning, wild. For a second, I thought I imagined things there, that he had envisioned terrible things while I was gone. His eyes were dark and haunted, but then I reminded myself that he didn't care about me; I was merely an obligation.

"Theodosia," he breathed.

He was out of the chair before I could blink again, one hand cradling my face and the other brushing hair from my forehead as if I might break if he touched me too hard. I was startled, flinching in surprise at the intensity and the feelings that surged within me—old, tired, and beaten down from long ago. I knew better than to harbor them for a man like him. *Stop yourself, Theo,* I told myself sternly.

"You're awake. Jesus, you're awake."

I blinked up at him, trying to focus through the fog. "Hi," I whispered.

"Hi? That's what you're going with right now?" His laugh was low and rough and didn't sound entirely sane. "You got shot."

"Um … yeah. That's what I'm going with. I was also nearly sold off like a cursed vintage handbag," I muttered. "But yes, the bullet thing seems more immediate." The aim was joking, but he didn't seem to appreciate it.

He gave me a look. Half horror, half utter disbelief. "You're impossible."

"Flattering," I said weakly. "You always know what to say to make me feel special."

His hand trembled where it cupped my cheek. "I thought I was too late. When I saw you fall... Theo, I—" His voice broke, and I watched him shut his eyes like he could cage the pain behind his lashes.

I wanted to tell him it was okay, that I was here, and that I didn't blame him, but I couldn't speak through the lump rising in my throat. Instead, in a moment of weakness, I reached for his hand, my fingers ghosting over the back of it, and he latched on like I was his anchor in the storm. Silence settled, thick and heavy.

Then, because I was me and couldn't help myself, I said, "I need a mirror."

It was the last thing I wanted. My hair was probably a mess, and my makeup was definitely running as if a raccoon had eaten my lashes. But I needed him to stop looking at me with this tenderness that was stirring all these *feelings*.

He blinked. "What?"

"I've been unconscious, there are tubes in my arm, I haven't done skincare in—God, how long have I been out? And what did they do with that godawful dress? I want it burned."

He stared at me for a long beat. Then he laughed. Head back, throat exposed, like he hadn't laughed in years and didn't quite remember how.

It made me love him a bit more. Oh God, I groaned. I really was hopeless. The realization that I still had feelings for him made me feel nauseous. He was going to grind me up and leave me in the dust, which was both infuriating and inevitable.

"You'll be happy to know they cut it to ribbons while treating you." He leaned down and kissed my forehead like I was Frankie, though perhaps I could pretend his lips lingered a little longer than necessary. "You're going to be fine," he said as if he were reassuring himself.

"I better be. I still haven't released my fall collection."

He pulled the chair closer, never letting go of my hand. "Your fall collection can wait. Right now, you're getting treated for a gunshot wound. You've been out for two days. We're still in New Orleans."

Two days. The number didn't register. I was still too busy focusing on his face, memorizing every line, every tired crease that told me he hadn't left this room once. I hadn't seen him in a year, and I was drinking him in.

"You had to go into surgery," he continued. "Do you want me to explain what the doctor said?"

"No. Did they fix everything?" The last thing I wanted to hear was the ins and outs of a medical procedure. Those sorts of things gave me the ick. All I wanted to know was if it was fixed. I left everything else to the professionals.

Medical stuff went in one ear and out the other with me. The last thing I wanted to hear was all the complicated terminology. Thinking about all the tubes entering and exiting my body, along with the idea that I was under anesthesia for surgery, made me feel a bit sick. Certainly, having it done wasn't a choice, but just imagining my body limp and pale on the table while they performed surgery made me want to poke my eyes out. I'd never had surgery before, and the thought of being put to sleep like that always secretly freaked me out. I suppose these were the potential hazards that came with being shot, which was part of the mafia life. My hand fluttered up to the dressing on my chest. I was going to have a scar. Just great.

"Yes. They fixed everything," he said solemnly. "You'll need to keep your arm immobile for a while, but the surgeon said everything will be fine." His throat bobbed for a minute.

I slid my eyes away. "Did you get him?" I asked.

A part of me didn't feel safe with the idea of Salvatore Renzetti roaming the world. I hoped he had been killed in the skirmish, but as soon as Angelo stiffened, I knew he hadn't.

A muscle ticked in his jaw. "No. Not yet. He ran when the shooting started. Used you getting hit as cover to escape."

Disgust curled in my belly at the memory of his smarmy smile and vile, possessive gaze. There had been moments when I worried that Renzetti would get his way, and I'd end up sold off. I hadn't even let myself think about what that would have meant. I needed to have a conversation with Angelo about how I ended up there with Salvatore.

"Coward," I whispered.

"Dead man," Angelo corrected.

A silence stretched between us again, heavier now, thicker. Like it knew there were things we weren't saying.

I broke it first. "You came for me."

He looked startled. "Of course I did." He swallowed. "You're *mine*."

The way he said it—fierce and broken and utterly certain—hit me somewhere beneath the bandage near my heart, making it hurt even more because he didn't mean it the way I wanted him to.

"I'm not some pretty doll you can keep in a glass case, Angelo," I said, my voice barely above a whisper.

"I know," he said. "I know. You're fire and thunder and glitter and chaos. No glass case could ever hold *you*."

The last was said ruefully, yet it still broke my heart a little. I wanted him to want to keep me, and that made me stupid. I closed my eyes and let the tears fall.

For everything I'd lost.

For everything I still had.

And for the boy with the devil's smile who had come for me.

"I'm sorry it hurts. Get some rest. I'll be here. Your brothers are here too." He pushed the button for morphine, and I let it carry me away, not bothering to tell him the reason for the waterworks.

CHAPTER 17
ANGELO

THE HOSPITAL WALLS were the color of paper—white, sterile, and so thin that if you pressed too hard, the entire place might collapse under the weight of your sins. It smelled of antiseptic and stale air, and the chairs in the hallway were just as hard. Simply walking inside the place gave me the fucking creeps.

It amazed Remo and me that Frankie wanted to work in places like these, where people were perpetually sick, weak, and frail. She said they were also places of joy, and I looked at them all wrong. My sister wanted me to think of a glass half full. Her perspective was that people came to the hospital for help, got well, had babies, and returned to their families —that they were places where relationships were mended.

I couldn't see it. Walking into this place made me break out in hives. All these people moaning in the emergency room or shuffling around with their IV poles gave me the heebie-jeebies.

But Theo was alive.

That was the only thing that mattered.

Still, the past three days had carved me hollow. I'd been hunting Renzetti like a dog, teeth bared and blood on my hands. I'd been rooting out men that he'd hired for that party of his from every hole-in-the-wall motel that I could find and every back alley bayou. Bacco, Remo, and I had delivered some extremely enjoyable torture sessions in borrowed barns and then fed the remains to the swamps. There were some pluses to being in Louisiana despite the humidity. However satisfying, we hadn't learned any actionable intel other than the fact that all the security had been hired muscle.

I'd left Theo in the care of her brothers—something that had taken more self-restraint than anything I'd ever managed in my life. Every second away from her was like walking with a knife between my ribs. I needed to be moving, to be *doing* something. And if I were going to let off steam, I'd do it the way I knew best: with precision and fire.

Today was discharge day. The day we'd all be returning to New York. Thank fuck. I was cutting it close when I stepped off the elevator. All the Anthakos siblings were already present and accounted for, flanking Theo's wheelchair like some royal entourage.

Clearly, she wasn't too happy to be forced into a wheelchair; she scowled at her brothers as they spoke in low tones, turning at the sound of my boots. She wore oversized glasses and a scarf that she had crafted into a couture-style headband, complete with a trailing bow down her back. The woman had taken a bullet, yet was still somehow on trend. When our eyes met, the tightness in my chest finally cracked.

"You're late," she said, one brow arched above the glasses. "I've been sitting here for hours."

"Don't listen to her. We just got her into the chair. They've taken forever to get her discharged. You'd think we weren't capable of taking care of her or something. The paperwork is a nightmare." Vaso rolled his eyes at his sister, but I knew he didn't mind waiting around if it meant she was taken care of. "We're still waiting on the nurse to bring us our last care package. There are some bandages and stuff I guess that we need."

My eyes swept over her again. She kept herself clear of the wheelchair's arm to avoid jostling herself. Her face appeared almost pale, and I doubted she was very comfortable.

"Listen to you being such a smart ass," I replied, unable to stop the smirk pulling at my mouth. "Starting to feel better. I like it." Directing the question to Ilias, I asked, "Can we hurry the nurse up at all so we can get Theo somewhere more comfortable?" I didn't like that she was sitting out in the open with Renzetti on the loose.

"Spiros is on it. Hopefully, it'll just take a second. Any update on the bastard?" Ilias asked.

My smile dropped like a guillotine. "He's gone to ground. We tracked him to the Gulf, but someone tipped him off. Locals say he had a boat. Could be anywhere in the Caribbean by now."

Theo leaned back in her chair and sighed loudly and theatrically. "Great. The guy who tried to sell me like a human handbag is off sipping mojitos in a hammock while I've been stuck here with ice chips."

"For now," I said. "But I'll find him."

Spiros finally rushed back with the nurse,

carrying what appeared to be a larger bag of items than we could need. It wasn't as though we needed supplies from some backwater hospital. I would have a private doctor visit her twice a day. I'd campaigned to have her airlifted home after the surgery, but I'd been vetoed. My confidence in the care here was almost nonexistent. At least in New York, I would have more control. Here, I felt like I lacked the same contacts. The Anthakos brothers, however, had shut me down, and I didn't have a leg to stand on. Now, my teeth ground together at every second of the delay. There were even more papers to sign, and I barely managed not to snap the poor woman's head off.

"Let's blow this joint." Gripping the handles of the chair, I ignored the scowl of the attendant who had moved in. "I've got it. Step off."

"It's protocol, sir," the man attempted to argue, appearing put out. "Hospital regulations."

But I was more than done, and the Anthakos clan was already moving with me as I started to propel Theo through the hallways, even though the attendant doggedly kept up with me. The dude was lucky I didn't sock him right in the jaw.

"Fuck right off," I ground out, glaring at him.

"Angelo." The quiet reprimand came from Theo. "It's his job."

"No, *piccola*. It's my job. I'll do it. Fuck him."

Every time I looked at her, uncomfortable feelings still lingered, especially now that she was weak and injured. I wasn't used to it. Usually, she was all claws and teeth, fighting me at every turn. I began to feel a little better about closing the door on my complicated feelings for her and the situation we found ourselves in. However, that door had developed a small melted hole, softening around the edges. I wouldn't even touch on the anger that perpetually followed me, but I couldn't blame her for it. It was an old friend from childhood and living with Don Santelli.

"Fine, whatever." Her retort was barely loud enough for me to hear, but I pushed her a bit faster before she insisted that I let her go in favor of one of her brothers.

I helped her out of the chair when we reached the curb and the waiting car. Unfortunately, it wasn't anything special, but I had to prioritize comfort over flash. One thing I loved was cars, but sacrifices had to be made in certain situations.

Theo scowled at me but allowed me to help her, leaning into me so that I felt the tension in her body. The way her hand curled around my arm —both delicate and defiant — made my heart race. She didn't want pity; she desired control, even if she wasn't steady on her feet, and I understood that. After being in the hospital for so long, she seemed smaller, her arm still frozen against her side. The doctors had given her a favorable prognosis for recovery, but it would take time. I'm sure they discussed with her in the last few days that she'd have limited mobility. She'd hate that. I hated it for her.

"We've got the jet on standby," I said as we loaded up the car. "You ready to go home?"

She made a face. "New York isn't exactly home anymore, but I suppose it'll do until I get kidnapped again. I do want to see Frankie," she quipped.

I wouldn't let her comments hurt my feelings, but she was wrong if she thought New York wasn't home. Her days of running away were long gone. It was time to face the music. My feelings about being forced into something were still all over the place, but they were steadier regarding the woman Theodosia had turned out to be.

Kostas muttered something about her

being finished in Europe, and Ilias shot him a glance. I couldn't fault them. If our roles were reversed, I wouldn't let my sister out of my sight either.

Theo turned away from the window as we made our way through the streets toward the airstrip. Her hands were still on her lap, her thigh almost touching mine, and suddenly, I wanted to feel her heat. Slowly, I spread out more so that my leg touched hers. Her eyes shot to me, narrowing, but I ignored her and stared across the limo as if I hadn't done it on purpose, instead turning my focus to Ilias.

"We can discuss strategy when we land," I told her brother, keeping my voice low.

He nodded. "We'd like to get on track right away. We can't let him get away with a move like this."

"Renzetti will surface again. His ego won't allow him to disappear forever. According to Carlo, there are still whispers in the city about the Oliveto territory," I scoffed. "As if we'd allow his ass in New York. We would burn him out before we let him set foot in our city. We should be prepared, though."

Vaso snorted. "He'll definitely make another move, especially after he got humiliated. His little auction fell apart, his men got slaughtered, and now he's a marked man in more ways than one."

I grunted assent. "Maxim's already circulating word through our southern contacts. Conall's got his Irish eyes in the ports. Anyone who tries to help Renzetti'll bleed for it."

There were still several factors I was working through regarding the entire abduction. Things still seemed murky to me about the reasons and methods involved. Renzetti hadn't played a role in our corner of the world until Cosimo was taken out. Granted, we had been the ones to orchestrate that, but still. It wasn't uncommon for a vacuum to form in the underworld and for someone to step into the void, but it was typically someone who was known. Renzetti was an anomaly, and that bothered me.

Theo cleared her throat. "Can we discuss something less murdery while I'm still in these horrendous clothes? They wouldn't even let me shower." She wrinkled her nose.

Leave it to Theo to worry about what she was wearing, although I doubted that was the issue. I expected that much of her attitude was a distraction tactic to keep people from seeing the layers of her real feelings lying underneath. Still, I was willing to play along for now.

I gave her a sidelong glance, watching her carefully. "You're worried about your clothes?"

"Of course I am," she said, indignant. "Fashion is everything. You wouldn't understand."

Her brothers collectively groaned.

"Well, we'll get you all set up soon, and you'll have all the fashion choices you could desire, so don't worry."

"Hmm." The response was noncommittal, and she returned to staring out the window.

I didn't mention that I'd already arranged for Bacco to have her assistant, Vivienne, in Florence, send all her things. Well, I'd arranged for a plane to pick them up. She might be angry, but I knew she would want to work, and she wasn't going back. I had a crew working overtime this week at my house, knocking out a wall and building her a studio where she could work from home for the next few months while she recuperated. I may have also had her apartment packed up — another reason for her to be mad. But ... this ocean between us was over. It was clear she wasn't safe on her own.

We were going to have to get married. Engaged to start.

I kept seeing her collapse onto that damn floor, blood staining her dress. I'd never known fear like that, and I'd known a lot of fear. "We'll get him," I said, more to myself than anyone else.

Theo stirred. "You already said that."

"Doesn't make it less true."

Her fingers fluttered in her lap, and her hand reached for mine, but she changed her mind at the last moment and withdrew it. I placed my hand over hers, squeezed gently, and then released it, allowing her to pull it back to cradle her arm.

"Do you need a pain pill?" I asked, looking at her carefully. The last thing I wanted was for her to be hurting. I may have been out hunting Renzetti's goons the last few days, but I had stayed informed about her medical progress. The doctors had called for her to keep up on her pain management.

"Not yet. Soon. Maybe on the plane." Her head moved in an infinitesimal shake.

I nodded but made a note to remind her. I'd planned to have her lie down anyway. When we arrived, the private jet was fueled and waiting for us. Ilias's crew had done the prep work for us, and a small contingent of

Anthakos and Santelli men remained stationed nearby, keeping watch in case Renzetti attempted anything foolish.

Ilias and I pored over digital maps and communication logs inside the plane. At the same time, Theo rested in one of the plush recliners, declining to lie down until we'd taken off, mainly because she was stubborn more than anything else.

"I'll get sick if I'm lying flat when the plane takes off." Her bottom lip pushed out, making me think about kissing her and sliding my mouth over hers.

Ilias had the nicest plane of all of us, although I'd already complained to him about his flight attendants. I suspected they were all hired by Vaso because they all seemed to think flirting was welcome. I'd already had to tell one of them to keep her hands off me. The girl was like an octopus.

After the plane leveled off, I looked over at Theo. She seemed tired, her mouth pinched in pain. "*Piccola*, let's get you settled in the back, okay? Come on, I'll help you up. Give me your good hand. Slow and steady."

"I can help her," Ilias made a move to get to his feet, his eyes shifting from his sister to me as if he might object.

"I've got it, *fratello*."

She must be in pain because she didn't even bother to argue; she just reached out her good hand for me to help her up. Trying to keep myself steady so I wouldn't pull her forward or jerk her from her chair, I made sure to give her upward momentum so she wouldn't have to do any work. I was worried she would overwork her shoulder muscles that she had to keep still, but I wasn't sure if I was doing it right.

Moving her towards the suite in the back of the plane, I turned down the bed for her and arranged some pillows in the middle.

"What are you doing?" she asked suspiciously as she sat on the edge of the bed. "This is weird." She wrinkled her nose, and her brows furrowed.

I busied myself with my task. "Getting some pillows for your arm, of course." It was a no-brainer. She'd had them at the hospital. I'd just figured she'd need them here, too. The way she was looking at me suggested that I was insane. "What's weird?" I asked, ignoring the fact that I knew exactly what she meant.

She bit her lip uncertainly. "You taking care of me. It's strange."

"Let's not worry about that right now. I'm

going to get you your pain pill and some water."

When I returned, she was still in the same spot, her head bowed, waiting for me. The bed looked too big for her, her feet dangling over the edge.

She cupped the pill in her palm and swallowed the water, gazing up at me through those dark lashes framing her expressive eyes. Dark shadows lingered beneath them, and I realized she hadn't been sleeping well. I thought about asking her if she'd been having any nightmares about the abduction, but I wasn't sure now was a good time to get into it. She looked so tired. Instead, I said, "Let's get you lying down."

I was sweating bullets at the thought of touching her. "Let me know if I hurt you." The wound was near her collarbone on the left side, but the bullet had caused significant damage to the bone, vascular structures, and tissue. The surgeon said that there wouldn't be an issue afterwards, but after his horrifying description of the damage, I wasn't sure I believed him. "I'll help as you move back." Sliding one arm under her thighs and one around her waist, I ignored her squeak as I shifted her over as gently as possible.

"I can do it, Angelo." The protest sounded weak even to me.

"Can't have you hurting yourself, *piccola*. Need to heal up."

My hand slid slowly out from beneath her, watching her every second and feeling the heat of her skin through the thin material of the pajama pants she was wearing. And if she thought I didn't see the blush in her pretty cheeks, she was mistaken. "If you weren't hurt," I let the thought trail off as I leaned a little closer to her mouth. She smelled like flowers and bubblegum — temptation. That's what I associated her with now.

"But I am. Get off." Her breath came a little quicker, the pulse fluttering in her throat. The words were entirely unconvincing.

"In a minute." I made a show of examining her, ignoring the flash of those hazel eyes. Then I added, "I think you owe me a kiss after I took such good care of you."

CHAPTER 18
THEODOSIA

THE HUM of the jet was oddly soothing. If I hadn't been stitched up like a patchwork doll and emotionally ragged, I might have been able to appreciate the luxury of Ilias's private plane. My brother didn't skimp. White leather seats, mahogany paneling, chilled water bottles with French labels, and likely a hidden compartment full of guns.

Angelo took me to the back cabin, which was the kind with an actual bed. I had barely walked in on my own. My body still felt like it had been steamrolled and then sewn together with dental floss. My head was light, my shoulder throbbed like a bitch, and yet somehow, my hair was still trying to maintain its curls. I had cobbled together a scarf and some cute glasses so I didn't look completely catatonic when leaving the hospital, but my choices hadn't been great. Plus, I hadn't been able to wash my hair for days. I wasn't joking when I said they wouldn't let me shower. I was dying to take a bath and get my hair washed. My first order of business was to get Frankie over to help me out.

He helped me lie down, surprisingly gentle for a man who literally crushes bones with his bare hands. I didn't say much. What was there to say? Thanks for the rescue? Thanks for peeling me off the floor? I wasn't exactly feeling warm and fuzzy.

And then he kissed me.

Even as he sealed his mouth over mine, I tried to keep myself from reacting, but as soon as his hand reached up to touch my thigh, I had to bite back a gasp, which was where he took advantage, sliding into my mouth and deepening the kiss. Unsurprisingly, Angelo Santelli knew how to kiss like it was a master class, angling into me so he could taste every corner, pressing into me like he was sampling before diving in for another bite here and there before pulling back to nibble at my lips.

"Mmmm, *piccola*. I've been missing out."

That made me mad. Even as his thumb pressed against my hip bone and his fingers massaged my skin, the retreat only pissed me off more. Of course, he had been missing out. I was fucking awesome. I'd *always* been awesome. Dick.

"I haven't been," I snapped.

I adopted an 'I don't give a shit' attitude. Two could play at this game. No matter how good a kisser he was, Angelo Santelli wouldn't get under my skin. After the scathing setdown he'd given me at fifteen, I'd barely put myself together. Those words had stayed with me for years — they scarred me. After that moment, I avoided him like the plague, torn between embarrassment, anger, and heartbreak. Then, when I saw the blood oath, it struck me that he might not even have a choice but to marry me. That killed me.

I had worked hard on myself with a lot of positive self-talk to reach where I was. There had been dark times for a while —times when I'd thought maybe I shouldn't even be here. Now, I got up fresh every day and reminded myself that I was worthy, strong, a good person, and beautiful. That life was worth living.

The cords on his neck tightened, and his hands clenched.

"And stop calling me that. I don't like it." It was petty, but every time he called me *piccola*, it chipped away at the protection I'd raised around my heart.

His hand spread wider, gripping even more area of my thigh, and I could feel the heat of him through the thin cotton. Why were his hands so big? My traitorous pussy responded immediately to the thought, and it was like he knew because he smiled knowingly at me. Like maybe he knew I was wet.

It pissed me off.

Not because I didn't want it—God, I did. But because I didn't trust it, or him, or myself.

I gave him a look that could have curdled milk. "Don't."

His brows drew together. "Theo—"

"No. Don't Theo me like that." I shifted against the pillow, trying to find a position that didn't make me wince. "You don't get to play hero now."

He ran a hand through his hair, rough and frustrated. "I just spent three days hunting down the man who took you—"

"And what? Now you get a gold star and a kiss for effort?"

His jaw tightened. There it was. That familiar Santelli burn in his eyes, the one that usually preceded a broken nose or a bullet to the chest. "You almost died."

"I noticed," scoffing. I wasn't an idiot.

Sometimes men said the most inane things. Was there some magic world for them where they thought women didn't understand the concept of what was happening? Geez. I knew I got shot.

"I couldn't breathe thinking you might—"

"Don't," I snapped again, cutting him off. My chest tightened, not from the stitches this time. "Don't say shit you don't mean. Don't act like I matter now."

He didn't answer; he just looked at me like he wanted to break something. Preferably me, emotionally speaking.

I hated how good he looked, even when he was wrecked. Wrinkled shirt, stubble shading his jaw, that burn behind his eyes. He smelled like expensive cologne, gunpowder, and regret.

I couldn't take it. So I blurted the one thing I'd been holding back. "It was your mother."

He blinked. "What?"

"Your mother," I repeated, words tumbling out in a messy avalanche. "Carlotta."

He froze. The saying 'deer in the head-lights' — that was Angelo right now. Frozen like one of those statues in graveyards, carved

172

out of marble and then weathered and greyed. His skin had even turned pale.

"I was supposed to meet with an Italian designer I admire, Bassiano Torsiello." Pulling my bottom lip between my teeth, I tried to ignore the anxiety I felt when thinking about it, quickly explaining my business situation. "I'd been excited that someone of Bassiano's caliber would want to meet me, but it wasn't him. Obviously." He nodded, encouraging me to continue. "Carlotta was there, and I was confused."

"Go on," he encouraged. He'd moved away from me now like I'd wanted, his movements stiff and angry. "Then what happened?"

"I caught on pretty quickly that it had all been a setup. There had been no meeting with Bassiano. She had some things to say about our arrangement. She threatened Polina. I wasn't even sure that she knew who Polina was." I skipped over that part and rushed on at the sour look on Angelo's face. "Then she brought up Renzetti. Then she called in the goons and said something about Salvatore owing her."

The silence that followed was glacial. His face didn't change, but the temperature in the room dropped by about thirty degrees.

I pressed my lips together. "I didn't get a chance to tell anyone before. I was, you know, bleeding out." That was probably an exaggeration. "Then you were gone. But I figured I should tell you first. I thought you'd want to hear it privately. I know you're ..." I trailed off. I knew nothing about him, so I didn't bother continuing.

The cold rage rolling off him was suffocating. "She sold you out." He turned away, hands fisting at his sides. "I'll kill her when I find her. She's dead. I swear it."

"Yeah, well. That's a fun family reunion idea." My fingers curled in the blanket, aching to comfort him but knowing it wouldn't be welcome. I was sure the news that his mother was back in the picture and hanging out with the evil villain of the story wasn't what he had wanted to hear. Still, it was information he needed to know.

He turned back around, and for a second, I thought he might punch a hole through the wall. Instead, he sat on the edge of the bed, staring at the floor.

"I didn't know," he said finally, his voice low and rough. "I swear to God, Theo. I had no idea where she's been since she left, and I haven't cared, but it never occurred to me that she would be a danger to you."

"I wasn't sure if maybe you'd be glad I was gone. Out of the picture." The admission was hard to make, but I couldn't hold it back.

He looked up, and there was such violent grief in his eyes that it knocked the wind out of me. "Never."

I nodded slowly, unsure of what to say. I wanted to scream, cry, and tear out the stitches to make someone else feel how much it all hurt. But instead, I reached for the only armor I had left—sarcasm.

"Well, at least if I got shot, Renzetti had good taste in dresses. I was wearing Versace. It wasn't the same as wearing clothes I made, but …" I attempted a shrug as if it was all a joke.

His mouth twitched, almost a smile. "It was Dior."

"Shows what you know."

He reached out, but this time, he didn't touch me. He just hovered as if he didn't trust himself. "You're safe now."

"Am I? Seems like this is one of the worst places I could end up." He didn't answer. The silence stretched. Comfortable, then unbearable. "I don't know what to do here," I admitted. "What to say."

He gave me a small, sad smile. "Join the club. Well, go over what Carlotta said again.

Maybe there is some clue there. Then, I'll go fill your brothers in."

I did as he asked, watching him carefully as I related the encounter. Somewhere over Kentucky, I closed my eyes. Not because I was tired but because I couldn't bear to look at him any longer. Perhaps it was partly the pain pill that made me drowsy, but this way felt easier — his handsome face hidden behind my eyelids.

And in the quiet, I let myself want him— for just one breath. Just one heartbeat.

Then I locked it away again.

Because wanting Angelo Santelli would only ever end in pain.

And I was all out of bandages.

CHAPTER 19
ANGELO

THE JET'S hum was a steady thrum beneath my boots, the vibration resonating through the floor as I stood at the edge of the back cabin. Theodosia lay curled under a blanket, her frame too small and fragile against the sheets. Bruises colored her skin, fading now but not quickly enough for my liking.

She should never have been in that position. Should never have been in Renzetti's hands.

I watched her sleep, her breath soft and even, chest rising and falling in a rhythm I memorized the moment they wheeled her out of surgery. The plane swayed slightly in turbulence, but she didn't stir. She was exhausted, likely drugged on painkillers and fury. Even half-dead, she still managed to hurl insults and try to walk herself out of the hospital. Classic Theo.

And yet, as I looked at her now—quiet, vulnerable—something sharp twisted in my chest. Something I didn't like. Something that felt dangerously close to *fear*.

I didn't do fear. Not since I was little. Small. Now, I <u>caused</u> fear.

But there she was, digging her designer stilettos into the cracks of my armor like she belonged there.

I ran a hand down my face, my jaw tight, and turned away before the guilt swallowed me whole. Back to the main cabin. Back to where I belonged—with men, maps, and mayhem.

The Anthakos brothers were spread out across the seating area, waiting for me impatiently. Ilias leaned over the table with Remo and Bacco, reviewing the satellite images that Veronica had uploaded. Kostas and Vaso were seated nearby, speaking in Greek to one another, which I only partially understood.

I slouched into the chair across from them and tapped the screen with the tip of my finger.

"We believe he's using old contacts from the Gulf Cartel," I said, pointing to a cluster of coastal ports in Belize and Honduras. "Maxim has a contact down there we're waiting to hear from."

Ilias nodded, but his knuckles were white around the glass in his hand. He hadn't said much since that night in New Orleans—not about Theo, just the job—the hunt. We had always been more alike than I cared to admit. Guy was going to blow if he didn't let off some steam. This issue with Theo exploded in our faces, and I knew he had something brewing about Maxim's sister that was gnawing at him. I didn't have the brain space or emotional bandwidth right now to talk to him about that, but I made a mental note to ask him later.

"We need to make a move soon," Kostas said. "The longer we wait, the more he disappears."

"I won't wait," I growled. That feeling just before pulling the trigger, assured and certain, filled me. I would get him. "I'm hunting. Every day. Every hour. We don't stop until he's in the ground."

"And Theo?" Vaso asked, and I didn't miss the accusation laced there or the narrowing of his eyes.

I glanced over my shoulder toward the closed door. My throat worked once before I spoke. There was only one option regarding Theodosia Anthakos that would ensure her safety. I needed to stop dragging my feet. At one time, marriage had felt like a death sentence, but I didn't feel that way anymore. Now, I was looking forward to having her in my space and spending more time with her, peeling back all the layers of what made up Theo. There wouldn't be any claim from me that there wasn't a bitter taste in my throat about how we'd ended up in this situation, but I wouldn't shrink away from the attraction I felt anymore. Or the duty to protect her.

"She'll be coming home with me," I said. "Protected. It's time to make it clear that the blood oath will be honored. We've enjoyed some freedom in our lives, and she's had time on her own. Now that's over." There was unmistakable relief on the brothers' faces. While Ilias hadn't pressed me, the fact that I hadn't pushed forward on the match had been a security issue. I knew he hadn't said anything because he'd been struggling with the blood oath himself, but there wasn't going to be any more running from it. The consequences were too big.

I leaned back, arms folded across my chest, and allowed the silence to linger a moment longer before I spoke again. "There's something else," I said. My tone had turned colder, sharper. "Theo told me who showed up instead of the designer she was expecting: the woman we were trying to identify who set her up." A bitter taste filled my mouth as I tried to get the words out to tell my friends that it was really my mother who sold out their sister.

Ilias stiffened. "Who?" he asked. "We wanted to press her, but she was still really out of it from the surgery and struggling. I figured she would have said something if she knew anything else."

My jaw locked, but I forced it out. "My mother."

A stream of Greek curses erupted from Kostas. Ilias merely stared at me as if he couldn't decide whether I was lying or if he was about to put his fist through the fuselage. A starburst of shame erupted in my solar plexus. Not only did she abandon us, but she also didn't give a flying fuck about her family. Then she had stooped so low as to help kidnap my fiancée and hand her to a sex slaver. Carlotta kept finding a new low, and I shared blood with her. It was disgusting.

"Carlotta Santelli," I confirmed. "Theo didn't initially recognize her. She had gone under the impression she was meeting that designer, only to find Carlotta instead. I'm surprised Theo even knew who she was. She was still little when my mother left." I clenched my teeth. "Anyway, Carlotta had all kinds of crap to say — and she threatened Polina. We still don't know Carlotta's connection to Salvatore, so we'll need to figure that out."

Vaso slammed his glass down. "That fucking bitch."

I wasn't going to defend her. I wasn't even going to try. Whatever pieces of a mother I had in my mind—of what a mother should be—had long been reduced to ashes. If anything had been left, she obliterated them with this stunt.

"We need to get the full story on where she's been," Kostas interjected cautiously. He was trying to prevent the situation from escalating. Good luck. "Carlotta's been... away. We need to understand her connection to Renzetti. You're right about that."

"She knows him," I said flatly. "Knows him well enough to deliver a girl like Theo straight into his arms. That's not just some distant acquaintance. That's a *relationship*."

"It could be business," Ilias suggested, though he didn't sound convinced. "It could be... personal, but she made a critical error by involving Theo." He glanced at his brothers. "And mentioning Polina was a mistake. She is off-limits."

"He's too young to be her lover," Vaso said. "But maybe a protege?"

"I'm not sure he's too young. She wouldn't care about that. Remember, she's a snake. He could be a bastard," I muttered. "Wouldn't be the first secret son of that mafia whore. Nothing she does would surprise me."

No one spoke after that. Maybe I was taking it too far. Normally, I wouldn't disparage a woman for making her way in the world any way she could. However, Carlotta used everything she had to inch forward, showing zero qualms about the tattered remnants left behind.

Ilias finally broke the silence. "If she sold out Theo, she's not safe. Not from us."

"I know," I said. "I'll kill her myself." I twirled the brass knuckles on one finger. Typically, I had rules about women. For Carlotta, I'd make an exception. I might have worn the Santelli name like a badge once, but now it felt more like a stain. I would burn the entire fucking *famiglia* to the ground before I let her close to Theo again.

"So what's the plan?" Kostas asked. His voice was calmer now, but it had that edge.

That 'soldier's readiness.' The brothers were all the same in that way. Rage held behind glass teeth.

"We go to New York," I said. "We set the trap. Let him think he's got breathing room. Meanwhile, we choke off every supply line, every port, every dock. We let Maxim's guy in Central America flush the rats out. Renzetti won't make it to the next full moon."

"And your mother?" Vaso asked.

I stared at him. No emotion. Just finality. "She might be a little harder to find, but when we do, she dies."

The flight unfolded in tense silence, but the wheels were already turning. I could feel the heat rising in my chest again—the fire I only allowed to burn when blood was due. Renzetti had made this personal, and Carlotta had turned it into a betrayal. I was coming for them with everything in my arsenal.

No one—*no one*—betrayed me and walked away breathing. I'd brought death to men for less. I'd buried traitors under concrete, left enemies in roadside ditches, and smiled while their blood stained my boots. But this...

This was different.

Because this time, the woman they hurt was *mine*. I might as well admit it. It had taken me years to come to terms with it, but there was no escaping the truth. She would fight me every step of the way, but it would happen.

Theodosia would be safe. Not because I promised her brothers, not because it was expected.

Because <u>I said so</u>.

CHAPTER 20
THEODOSIA

THE BRONX SMELLED of heat and concrete, exhaust fumes and empty promises, and garlic knots if you walked past the right block. I didn't hate it—this city had a gritty charm and a relentless beat that didn't wait for anyone. It suited Angelo in that brooding, vengeful way of his. It didn't suit me. Not one bit. Or maybe I was lying to myself because it felt an awful lot like home being back here.

Which ticked me off... but it seemed to be my normal state these days.

When we landed, Angelo said he was bringing me back to his brownstone, loading me into a car with his capos. My brothers kissed me and promised to see me soon, but they didn't argue when Angelo steered me away from them. I was surprised they allowed it, and against my better judgment, I didn't protest. I thought Angelo and I shared a moment, and maybe it was time to face the reality of our situation.

Now he was closed off, his face implacable as he helped me into the house I'd known almost my entire life. It was comfortable here, although I typically had limited myself to sneaking around the garage since Frankie had moved out on her own.

I suppose the brownstone he shoved me into—okay, technically escorted me to—was beautiful. A brownstone with high ceilings, polished floors, wrought-iron railings, and a street view that made me yearn for the noise of Vespas and the hum of the chaos I was accustomed to in Florence. Right now, it was quiet. Too quiet in the late stillness of the evening. Darkness had blanketed the house, and Angelo turned on the lights as we went.

"Let's get you settled in," he mumbled as he moved forward.

Exhausted, I followed him through the hallways and up the staircase where I had cried my heart out years ago. There was a guest suite directly across from his room that I had only peeked into once, but it had been empty.

Now, it was full of color and textures, with

a canopy bed that reminded me of my bedroom in Italy. It looked out onto the small gardens. "I thought you might like your own space while you heal." He rubbed a hand down his slacks as I took it all in. Some of my belongings were scattered around the room, including knick-knacks, books, and photos.

"Did you bring my stuff here?" I couldn't tell if I was upset or relieved. I'd already spoken with Vivienne, so I knew he and my brothers had been all up in my business, but I hadn't expected Angelo to have packed up my things.

"Yeah," the words sounded both sheepish and wary at the same time.

"Thanks. Probably for the best." I tried not to look at him as I walked around, thinking about him touching my things. I meant it when I said that it was for the best. When Frankie told me she was going to have her IUD taken out and start trying for a baby, I was thrilled, and I totally meant that I'd come home. Maybe I hadn't envisioned it exactly like this. Still, it was for the best because, in the end, this is exactly where I'd have to be according to the blood oath.

Peering around the corner, I almost moaned at the bathroom that waited for me. It looked glorious.

"I could help you with a bath," he offered. "I know you said you wanted to get clean and wash your hair." He looked at me hopefully.

The offer was too tempting to ignore, and even though it was dangerous in many ways — mostly to my heart— there was no way I could last another frickin' day without washing my hair. I'd been making do at the hospital with sponge baths and wet wipes, and it wasn't enough.

"That'd be great. I can't even stand myself right now." I admitted. No part of me was joking about that, and I wasn't going to be a martyr and turn down his offer. It was too late to call Frankie to help me, and I didn't want to lie down for another night without getting clean.

Thankfully, he didn't provide any additional commentary before he set himself to the task of filling the tub. After examining the closet space where my clothes hung in splendid rows of handmade glory, I watched him from my perch on the chair. Tears even came to my eyes at the thought of things made by my own hands. Angelo had earned himself a lot of grace with this gesture. Unfortunately, I couldn't even undress myself without unstrapping the entire contraption they'd forced me into. My wound was throbbing now, and I didn't want to complain, but I really could use a Tylenol or something.

"Come on then, *piccola*. Your bath is ready. Let's get you in first." He looked sinful beside the tub in his rumpled slacks and that five o'clock shadow. His shirt sleeves rolled up, revealing those corded arms of his that had always driven me crazy.

Methodically, he undressed me, unstrapping the harness that kept my shoulder still and concentrating on the buckles and straps as he went through each motion gingerly. "Tell me if I hurt you."

I nodded, trying to ignore the butterflies that stirred as I breathed in his heat, the scent that was distinctly his—all male—and the awareness that his hands were on me. I winced as the sling came off, and the weight of my arm was suddenly mine to bear again; somehow, it pulled on the muscles in my chest, intensifying the pain.

"Are you okay?"

"Yes. It's fine. Keep going." My eyes found his. There was hesitation on his face, and his mouth was pinched. "I need clean bandages, too," I reminded him. He already had them laid out. "I could call Frankie," I offered. Maybe I should have anyway.

"No, we've got this, *piccola*. We're a team."
He winked at me, which just did me in.

His fingers slid over the buttons on the
shirt I was wearing. I'd borrowed one of
Ilias's dress shirts, tying it at the front, and as
Angelo slipped it off, leaving me in my
lounge pants and bra, each pass of his hands
felt like a brand. I suppose I could help, but I
was supporting my other arm, trying to
relieve the strain and ignore the throbbing
that seemed to radiate from the wound like
the heat of a thousand suns.

"Whose shirt is this?" his tone had darkened, but his head was bowed as he lowered
my pajama pants until they pooled around
my ankles.

"My brother's. Thank you for bringing my
things here. That was kind." His fingers
moved to my panties, and he hesitated. "I
can't take a bath with them on." I'd shrug, but
it would hurt too much. I wasn't ashamed of
my body—the thickness of my thighs or the
softness of my belly.

"You're beautiful, you know?" He eased
them off and let me step out, starting on the
bralette I was wearing. A nurse had kindly
helped me with it, as my brothers weren't an
option. "I should have been faster," he said,
swallowing as he looked at the bandages.

"You came. That matters. I'm safe." I wouldn't touch the comments about my physique. Angelo blew hot and cold, and I still felt it was important to remember that he wasn't here by choice. This was all a forced arrangement.

I slid into the warm water with a hiss of pain and pleasure, the ache in my shoulder a dull roar, yet the comfort of being submerged (at least my lower half) almost brought me to tears. I wished I could fill it up, but the doctor had been firm about keeping the wound as dry as possible. My breasts were bare except for my long hair that draped over them, but Angelo's heated gaze told me he didn't mind the free show. My traitorous nipples were hard under his stare. Maybe I should care that he could see, but I didn't. I leaned my head back against the curved porcelain, closing my eyes briefly and letting the scent of lavender and chamomile envelop me.

"Too hot?" he asked, his voice low.

"No. It's perfect," I breathed, then cracked one eye open to find him still watching me. His sleeves were rolled higher now, his forearms dusted with water droplets, veins pronounced, and skin glowing under the soft lights of the bathroom.

Angelo knelt beside the tub like some

Roman statue come to life, a contradiction of violence and gentleness, a man whose hands were capable of ending lives and yet, somehow, were tender on my skin.

He was quiet, waiting.

I wanted to say something snarky, to cut the tension that had wrapped around us like thin but unbreakable silk thread. But the words got stuck somewhere between my lips and heart.

Instead, I dipped my good hand into the water and began washing what I could, stubbornly maintaining the illusion of independence. My hair was a whole other story—a tangled mess of curls and frustration. I poked at it with a sigh.

"You're going to let me help you with that, right?" he asked.

I hesitated. There were so many levels to that request. But that was what had gotten me in the tub, and I wouldn't bow out now. Letting Angelo Santelli touch my hair was far more intimate than the bath. I opened my mouth to object, but he was already kneeling behind me, taking the pitcher in his hand and pouring warm water over my hair with agonizing care.

"I'll be gentle," he said, sensing my hesitation.

"You're not exactly known for that," I muttered, but there was no heat behind the words.

His chuckle was low and deep, trailing across my neck like a gentle caress. "Perhaps I'll surprise you. Maybe I've grown up a little."

His fingers moved through my curls, detangling with gentle patience. The pads of his thumbs grazed my scalp. I felt myself begin to unravel under his hands, strand by strand.

"You don't have to do this," I whispered, unsure if I wanted him to stop.

"I want to." His voice was gruff. "After everything… I need to."

And that did it. The words twisted in my chest, splintering something that had been rigid since the plantation. Since the bullet. Since I'd felt like maybe I wouldn't make it out at all.

I turned just enough to see him. His face was shadowed, but his eyes were sharp. Full of unspoken things.

"I hate you," I said, my voice barely rising above the splash of water. The words weren't entirely a lie, but there is no more accurate saying than, 'There's a thin line between love and hate.' That encapsulated my feelings towards Angelo over the last decade, constantly vacillating between the two.

His jaw flexed. "I know. I'll fix it."

"I'm not sure you can." It was as honest as I could be. Deep in my heart, bitterness had clouded over that childish love that I'd had for him, and it had turned into acid. It had colored everything I did through the years.

He paused for a moment. "I knew about the blood oath. It made me want to break something —the very idea of it. My father forced me to sign. He beat me right at the table and made me press my finger to that paper." There was a hearty sigh. "I've just always had a lot of feelings about it."

God, what were we doing?

I dipped my chin, eyes burning.

The water had stilled. Even the city noise outside seemed to have hushed in respect for whatever was unraveling between us. Angelo's hand moved from my hair to my cheek, wet and trembling, and I leaned into it despite myself.

"You scare the hell out of me," I admitted. "Not because you're violent. Not even because you're the most dangerous man I've ever known. But because... because of this thing we have to do. Neither of us has a choice anymore."

"No," he said, voice raw. "We don't, but I'm not sure I'm mad about it anymore, *piccola*." His thumb brushed across my cheekbone. "Are you?"

I closed my eyes. "I don't know." My feelings felt too big and jumbled for me to be more specific.

He let out a breath that sounded like it'd been trapped in his chest for years. "That's honest, at least."

I opened my eyes to find him closer, kneeling at the edge, still with that wretched restraint in his body, like he didn't trust himself not to burn us both alive if he moved.

And maybe that was what I wanted. Maybe I wanted to feel something other than pain and fear and the suffocating weight of obligations I never asked for.

"Angelo," I said, and it came out like a plea.

He leaned in, lips a breath from mine, his eyes locked on me. "Say it again."

"*Angelo*."

The kiss that followed was not gentle. It was reverent and ferocious, a claiming and a surrender, our mouths crashing together like we'd both been drowning and just found air. His hands cupped my jaw, careful not to touch my shoulder, but everything else was wild. His breath ragged against mine, the water lapping at the tub's sides with every movement. My fingers anchored the back of his neck to me as if I couldn't get enough.

I gasped when he pulled away.

"This isn't done yet," he said, voice thick.

I blinked. "What?"

He stood, clearing his throat. "When you're better. When you're whole, I want you to choose it. Me. Not because you were forced into it, but because you want it."

Damn him. And damn me... because at that moment, I wasn't sure I had ever wanted anything more, even if it terrified me.

Even if it meant letting him in.

Later, when I was ensconced in the sheets and clean, with my hair dried, I let my eyes drift shut, thinking hard about the circumstances that had brought me here. Angelo didn't realize it, but underneath everything, I did want to choose him—every time. I just needed him to choose me first.

CHAPTER 21
ANGELO

NEW YORK WAS different when you were at war. It wasn't the usual pulse of grease and exhaust and Wall Street sweat— this was something darker. Like gunpowder soaked into concrete. Like the stink of fear bleeding from rats who thought they could nip at my empire and scurry away without losing teeth.

I stood in the shadows of *Fortune* after checking in with our manager, Oscar, who filled me in on what I had missed while I'd been away chasing Renzetti all over the map. Thankfully, he was more than capable of running the place without me. He managed the soft launch and opening night without a hitch. It was meant to be exclusive anyway—

more of a gentleman's club, and I was proud of it.

Now, the VIP level had been cleared—no bottle girls, no hangers-on, just the men I trusted with my kingdom. We had a lot to review this morning, and it seemed essential to formulate a game plan. The idea that Renzetti and my mother were collaborating felt like a worm in my brain, gnawing at me from the inside out. There must be some fundamental reason she had resurfaced and gotten involved with this guy. I just needed to figure out why.

Maxim leaned against the bar, his black suit immaculate and his eyes as cold as the Siberian tundra. Ilias paced like a caged wolf, filled with restless energy and volcanic fury. Conall sat at the far end of the table with a tumbler of whiskey in his hand, his knuckles white around the glass. Scattered around the booths were the rest of our men. Although he was engaged in a card game with Lev and Remo, Bacco insisted on joining us. It had become a trend for the Commission to come together, with our men forming friendships. I appreciated this new facet because it fostered trust, leading to better coordination in our businesses.

Me? I was trying not to break my phone in half.

Theo had texted me earlier. One word:

> Theo: bored

Bored. After everything. After almost bleeding out in my arms. After being in the hospital for a week. Being kidnapped. After being almost trafficked.

> Me: Text Frankie

> Theo: Already did. Bring me something fun.

I didn't know what that meant. Fun?

> Me: Fun ... like?

> Theo: Surprise me.

I could picture her now, curled up on the couch in one of those kimonos that hung off her shoulder, surrounded by half-finished sketches and bolts of silk I had brought in. Her curls piled up in that effortless way that drove me insane: surly, stubborn, untouchable. When I told her I needed to go out this morning, she narrowed her eyes at me but didn't complain. She mentioned that she might redecorate the garage, which sent shivers down my spine. Theo had always been hell on my cars. It had been a little game we'd played. I loved them, and she tortured them.

Her sneaking into my garage had been my penance for her catching me all those years ago. We had never spoken about it, but I knew that's what it was. It hadn't even been so much about the woman … it was about the words after. I deserved everything she did — each tire she slashed, each car she keyed. She'd become less violent over the years, only letting the air out of the tires instead of slashing them. Her small rebellions had slowed down to just once yearly, and I'd almost been sad.

I had left her at the brownstone in the Bronx that morning with two of my best men stationed outside the door. Norris was also there; he was combat-trained and could cook. He had been with me for ages, long enough to fully understand my tragic history with Theo.

I might also have had another squad of men parked in a brownstone I owned across the street, keeping watch just in case. Additionally, another team monitored the security feed from a block away. This time, there would be no kidnapping.

Renzetti had slipped through my fingers like oil. Humiliated in Louisiana, his sick little auction burned to the ground, and now he was striking back. Two warehouses were torched in Brooklyn. One of our cash fronts in Hell's Kitchen was turned upside down. Earlier this morning, one of my men had been shot on the stoop of his own home. Renzetti wasn't going to lie down and take it.

"I want blood," I growled, the words bouncing off the dark-paneled walls. "We need to get this fucker."

"Join the club," Ilias muttered, dragging his fingers through his hair. "If I don't put a bullet between that little toad's eyes myself, I'm going to lose my mind."

Ignoring the fact that Ilias wanted to take my kill, I focused on what we knew. "We think he's using old contacts from the Gulf Cartel," I told them, pulling up the digital map on the screen we'd installed behind the bar. I pointed to a cluster of ports in Belize and Honduras. "Maxim has a guy down there we're waiting to hear from, but he's making plays here as well."

"*Da*, he's getting closer to the answers we need, but this is tricky business with the cartels." As always, Maxim sounded bored.

"We need to make a move soon," Kostas

had appeared in the doorway like a shadow. "The longer we wait, the more this makes us look like fools."

"I'm not waiting," I said. "I'm hunting. Every day. Every hour. We don't stop until he's in the ground. I've been taking out any of his men that I find." We'd caught one down near Oliveto territory and torn him apart, leaving his body steaming there for the vultures.

"And Theo?" Vaso asked. He was seated beside Ilias, arms crossed, gaze sharp. "How's she doing?"

"She's good," I said, my voice firm. "Protected. She slept well." I offered the last piece reluctantly. She had indeed slept well. I'd checked on her every half hour and eventually caved, remaining in the chair by her bed and watching the gentle rise and fall of her chest.

It took everything in me the night before not to touch her. She had been Venus de Milo come to life, stripped bare. I would have taken her right there if she hadn't been injured and wary. Theo didn't trust me, not like I wanted her to. She said she hated me last night, and I couldn't blame her for that. She'd been so beautiful with those tiny dusky nipples of hers and all that bronze skin that glowed in the light of the bath. Just getting to touch her at all had been a gift. She'd had no idea that I'd knelt behind her and struggled to breathe through the hard-on I'd had the whole time, trying to center myself and be mindful that she was injured.

I turned my back on them for a moment to breathe. What I didn't say—what I couldn't say—was that every day I left her behind felt like leaving a knife in my chest.

Theo had changed everything. Or maybe she had just shown me what I hadn't wanted to see. That I wasn't a man immune to attachment, that I couldn't keep pretending she was merely a strategic match, a duty fulfilled. She had bled in my arms, and she'd curled into a space in my heart that somehow I didn't realize was empty.

And then I'd locked her in my house like a fucking prisoner.

Because I had to, Renzetti would come for her again. That bastard didn't like losing; that much was obvious. This was personal. The way he'd gone about it—who he'd picked—was specific. If it wasn't about me, it was about Theo. Then there was the Carlotta factor. My mother was helping him—or, at the very least, she had opened the door.

"So … Carlotta…" Ilias said slowly, as if

he were reading my thoughts. "Any leads? I'm worried for Polina, too. You said that she was mentioned? It isn't good for her to be on anyone's radar." He frowned.

The other Anthakos sister, who was kept away from criminal enterprises, should be checked on. I clenched my jaw. "Theo said Carlotta knew of her, so I would ensure she is secure." Ilias nodded, but his scowl deepened. "I've torn through every known safe house she ever used. Every contact. Every whisper of where she might've gone. It's like she disappeared off the goddamn map."

"Or someone's protecting her," Maxim said coolly, swirling the drink in his hand. "She was always good at manipulation. That woman is a master at that."

"She handed my fiancée over to that psycho," I said, voice a snarl. "There's not a universe where she walks away from this."

"Upgraded to fiancée already?" Ilias was cool in his reply. "Did she finally accept the proposal? I better see a ring on that hand."

"You'll see one." Theo still needed to agree, but I was focusing on my approach.

"I agree that there isn't a world where Carlotta walks away. She's in too deep," Remo groused from his card game with Bacco. He had taken our mother's involvement even harder than I had if that was possible.

Conall rolled his glass between his hands. "You think she knew what he planned?"

That was the big question I'd always had about my mother, and maybe an answer I hadn't wanted to face for a long time: how far the rot went. "I don't know. But I don't fucking care. She knew enough to set Theo up," I paused. "I think she knew. There's something else," I added, flicking to another slide on the monitor. "I found an old Santelli financial account—one only Carlotta had access to—was drained. A couple million."

Ilias swore under his breath. "You think she was helping fund Renzetti."

"Maybe," I muttered. "Maybe she has always been involved in the sex trade. Trafficking." I'd always wondered if she was more of the mastermind of my father's trade routes — the impetus for pushing him into the alliance and the blood oath.

Maxim cocked his head at me in that way he did when he was contemplating something. "It's possible for sure, but she's never shown her hand before or since. Then we cut off everything else," Maxim said. "Burn every contact. Isolate her and Renzetti. Starve them."

I nodded. "I've already started. I've pulled back on every Santelli-funded deal, even remotely linked. The ripple will reach her. She'll come out of hiding when the money runs dry. My men are roaming the streets here in New York, looking for any of Renzetti's men and grabbing them on the spot."

A smile stretched across Maxim's face, wolfish and sharp. "I caught two of them last night. Lev and I enjoyed that." He glanced at his vor, whose answering grin confirmed that Renzetti's men had not reciprocated the feeling.

"We've been on the lookout but haven't seen any," Conall added. "Not that we haven't been looking. O'Kelly turf has been quiet, except for a call from Nico."

Ilias went still. Nico should have warned us, at the very least, about this mysterious cousin of Cosimo's. "Oh? What did that fucker have to say? Did he have a good explanation for why this psychopath was coming out of the woodwork?"

"Not really. He was quick to mention he wasn't involved in whatever Renzetti was up to, which is smart. Nico said he had the men who were loyal looking for any intel they could find, but obviously, I don't think we should bother too much with Nico. I'm not

saying we should write him off, but ..."
Conall's massive shoulders rolled as if he were trying to work out a kink. He felt uncomfortable with the situation involving Cosimo Oliveto and, by extension, Nico Balestra, but he was trying to navigate it for Theo's sake.

Silence settled like ash. At times, that dream floated forward — the one where I took my family and found a place where blood didn't fall from the sky and the pavement wasn't perpetually boiling beneath me.

In my head, it was quiet. It was her voice. Theo. Laughing. Swearing. Telling me I was being dramatic. That I looked like a mob boss straight out of a movie. That I was capable of figuring it all out. She was right, of course. But the difference between me and the caricatures was simple—I didn't bluff.

My phone buzzed again—another message from Theo.

> Theo: You better be bringing home pizza. Or I'm setting fire to your ties.

I smirked despite myself.

"My sister still causing trouble?" Ilias asked, watching the way my mouth twitched.

"She's—" I paused, then exhaled. "She's driving me insane."

Conall laughed knowingly. "You're a goner."

"She sees me." My voice was quieter now. "But I have a lot of work to do to get her to trust me."

I hated leaving her behind. I hated the way her eyes followed me to the door that morning. She hadn't said, *'Don't go,'* but she hadn't needed to. It was in how her breath caught as I helped her dress and checked her bandages. Her eyes were wary, even as I wanted to press my advantage.

And maybe I shouldn't have kissed her. Or I should have kissed her more.

Maybe I shouldn't have tucked the sheets around her, knowing damn well that the only place I wanted her was under me, in my bed, screaming my name.

But she'd been pale. Still healing. And when she'd curled into the pillow and whispered my name in her sleep, I'd felt something splinter in my chest. I didn't want to deny what was in front of me anymore. There was that tug and pull to her that was undeniable.

I wanted to keep her.

Protect her.

"She doesn't deserve this," I murmured. It was a difficult realization that the lives we crafted weren't conducive to safety, no matter how hard we tried. It felt like grasping at a pile of pick-up sticks. I didn't think the others knew how uneasy it all made me, how uneasy it had always made me. How conflicted I felt.

"No, she doesn't," Ilias affirmed. "But we take care of our families."

"Even when they despise us for it," Conall said, raising his glass.

"Amen to that," Maxim remarked with a faint smile.

We all appeared to bear that burden, particularly lately, with the shadows looming over our empire.

The meeting extended well into the afternoon. Plans were crafted. Insights were exchanged. Names were mentioned.

And all the while, my mind drifted back to the brownstone in the Bronx. To a woman who stitched silk like magic and threw knives with her words. To the way, she'd looked at me in that bath, soft and suspicious, aching and proud.

Theo Anthakos was going to be my wife.

And God help anyone who stood in the way of that.

Especially Renzetti.
Especially my mother.

CHAPTER 22
THEODOSIA

I PADDED barefoot down the stairs in Angelo's shirt—one of his good ones, might I add. Silk blend, crisp collar, and still faintly smelling of sandalwood, gunpowder, and the kind of expensive rage that said, *"Don't mess with me unless you want a bullet through your kneecap."* Honestly, that was the kind of vibe I was going for these days. I found a pair of my favorite silk lounge pants, which I adored, stitched with tassels on the bottom that swished when I walked and tickled my toes.

The hospital had allowed me to remove the sling for a few hours at a time, so I was taking a short break. I'd slept well, and my physical therapist was scheduled for a home visit. I wasn't looking forward to therapy since it would likely be difficult, but I would work hard to ensure I regained full mobility as quickly as possible. The one thing about design work — you needed your hands. Thankfully, I was young and a good healer. There was a lot to be grateful for.

I tried to center myself after last night. Angelo had been gentle and responsive — it was confusing. The Angelo I remembered and found off-putting was anything but those things. Just the memory of his calloused fingers on my scalp, while he worked the shampoo and conditioner through my hair, made me shiver. It had been an experience I'd like to revisit when I wasn't exhausted and wounded. Even last night, every part of me was hotwired to those fingertips that hesitated along the shells of my ears and the nape of my neck as if they might wander, although they never did, much to my disappointment.

The soles of my feet stuck slightly to the hardwood floors, the only sound in the house aside from the distant hum of traffic outside the glass windows that I had no doubt were bulletproof. Since arriving last night, I still felt as if I were doped up on a blend of pain meds and sarcasm when Angelo half-carried me through the front door as if I weighed nothing.

Now, it was morning. And I was hungry. And maybe a little nosey.

I rounded the corner into the kitchen and nearly jumped out of Angelo's shirt when I saw a man at the stove. Slight, dignified, probably in his sixties, with silver hair and a calm expression that screamed, *"I've seen some shit."* He stirred a saucepan with all the grace of a Michelin chef, which was odd because I was fairly certain he didn't know I existed.

"Oh!" I halted, clutching the hem of the shirt dramatically. "Either I'm still dreaming, or Alfred from Batman has a twin."

The man turned slowly toward me, one eyebrow arched, and gave a slight bow of his head. "You must be Miss Anthakos."

"You must be...?" I trailed off, waiting for him to fill the void.

He cracked a smile. Barely. "Norris. I run the household and the kitchen."

"Theo." I extended my hand. "Resident chaos goblin, lover of tiramisu, and current squatter in your boss's shirts."

He shook my hand with a faint twinkle in his eyes. "I figured as much. There's coffee brewing. And a lemon ricotta pancake if you're quick."

I decided that I loved him. "Marry me?" I offered with a wink.

"I'm flattered, but I'm taken."

I grinned and sauntered toward the counter, already liking this man immensely. "You always this composed?" I asked, pouring myself a cup of coffee from the elegant silver pot.

"Only when I haven't had to clean blood off the floor in the last twenty-four hours," he said nonchalantly.

"Yikes. Too soon."

"Mm." He handed me a plate stacked with the fluffiest pancakes I'd ever seen. "Find yourself a seat and I'll get you some lemon syrup to go with those."

I took a bite and moaned. "Okay, seriously. Are you some kind of mafia wizard?"

He merely turned back to his stove. "I do my best."

Seemed to sum him up. A man of few words, a dry sense of humor, and the ability to make pancakes that could cause spiritual awakenings. And as I sat there, barefoot in a borrowed shirt, eating food made by a stranger in a house that wasn't yet mine, something strange happened.

I felt like I was home, and that scared me more than anything.

I texted Frankie an hour later.

Bestie Chat

Me: Come over. Bring your judgey eyebrows.

Frankie: On my way. Is there food, or should I stop?

Me: I met Norris.

Frankie: He's great, isn't he?

Me: Already proposed. He rejected me.

CHAPTER 23
THEODOSIA

FRANKIE SHOWED up with a bottle of our favorite cheap Chianti, which we used to buy when we lived in our shitty apartment and an armful of hydrangeas, which she plopped into a pasta pot because, quote, *"Vases are for boring people."*

Squeezing her tightly with my good arm, I savored the hug. "They are bestie, they are. It's like you know me."

"It's so good to see your face. Let me take a proper look at you. Angelo sent updates, but..." She peered at me before guiding me into the family room. I didn't argue as she peeled my shirt off my shoulder to peek at the bandages. Frankie was a registered nurse at a local hospital, so I wasn't surprised that her first order of business was to see if I was healing all right.

It felt like forever since I'd seen Frankie. It had been a year, but it still seemed like longer. She looked happy, her hair down around her shoulders and her eyes less shadowed than they had been when I had left.

After she had rebuttoned me and talked me back into the sling, I asked, "How's married life?"

A grin spread across her face. "So good. Better than I could have imagined, really. If you had told me it would be like this, I would have laughed in your face. But he sees me and doesn't judge. He even lets me put plants in the bedroom."

"I'm happy for you. Truly. Plants in the bedroom are a big deal for him." I laughed, but for Conall and his OCD tendencies, that was a significant step. When Frankie moved in, she did a little redecorating in the living area but left the other sections of the house untouched. That was quite a big deal if he felt comfortable enough to let her extend into the penthouse.

"I know, right? I'm happy." She gave me a mischievous grin. "Happy enough that I had an appointment and got my IUD removed."

We had the conversation via text, but I

was still excited that she felt safe enough to take that step. Her mother had done a number on her, bringing up another point. I wondered if anyone had informed her that Carlotta was involved in this fiasco.

"Conall is great with Maxim and Cora's baby. Just wait until you see Vasily. He's so adorable. Angelo is in love with him, too." She gave me a sly look.

I wagged my finger at her. "Don't get any ideas. I'm not there yet." However, the thought of a baby Angelo with those eyes and cheekbones was tempting. Deep inside, there was a strong desire for children — a lot of them. However, I wasn't sure about this life and the violence that followed. "So, when will you tell Conall? Or are you just waiting on those two little pink lines? He's going to be thrilled, I'm sure."

"I'm going to tell him tonight. I don't want to spring it on him, you know. That wouldn't be fair." She bit her lip in hesitation. "He's been really good about not pushing, but it wouldn't be right for me not to discuss it with him without first telling him that I wasn't on birth control, especially after I made such a big deal about it."

"Of course, bestie. Consent is a two-way

street." I nodded. Frankie looked at me with gratitude, thankful that I understood.

"So …" she picked at a thread on the sofa's edge. "This whole Renzetti thing? Do you want to talk about it? You got nabbed in Italy?"

There was hesitation in her voice, and she had her head down so I couldn't see her face. Frankie had been through a lot, an assault and her own kidnapping, so I knew she'd understand. "Yeah," I hedged. "What did Conall tell you?"

She tugged fiercely at the thread, pulling it as if it were the poor couch's fault. "I could tell it bothered them a lot. Initially, Conall and Angelo didn't want to tell me, but I kept asking until they caved. I know it was Carlotta who took you. They said you were taken from a meeting, then flown to New Orleans and given to Renzetti. Conall flew there with Maxim. I guess Renzetti is here trying to get territory that used to belong to Oliveto." She looked over at me hesitantly. "If you want to talk about anything, you can," she offered.

The whole Oliveto situation was an unfolding mess that was a ripple effect from an incident between Fausto Oliveto and Frankie years ago when he tried to rape her, and she'd killed him. Frankie and I burned the body, but his brother, Cosimo, had never stopped trying to find out who killed him. It became his obsession, ultimately leading to the loss of his territory. Yet, vacuums like that in the underworld just sucked in more evil. They never remained empty. I wasn't sorry about the Olivetos — they got what they deserved. So would Renzetti.

"I'm honestly fine. You've summed up the experience. Nothing happened. I got shoved into a nice dirt cell for a while, but that wasn't bad. There were some threats. I fought back a little." I frowned. "I tried to stab someone in the eye with my heel. You know," I quirked an eyebrow at her. "It doesn't work like it does in the movies. I really tried." That still pissed me off.

"That's what you're upset about?" she laughed. "Really?"

"Well, yeah. It should work. It's a stabby thing. It should stab."

"I suppose you're right." Her fingers returned to the thread. "So, Carlotta? Did she say anything about us? I hate to ask. I'm not sure why I am."

Gripping her hand, I brushed my face against her shoulder. "Frankie, it's okay to ask. It's okay to care and be curious, to hope

221

that she has somehow changed. It's okay to be disappointed that she hasn't." Recalling the conversation was a bit of a chore. Angelo wanted details, too, but not for the same reasons as Frankie. I think he had more insight into Carlotta than she did because he was older, and he was searching for clues instead of a reason why she was built the way she was. Angelo already knew. "She seemed to be working with Renzetti, but Angelo wasn't sure why. She knows I am arranged to marry him, so I assume she knows about you and Conall, but that's all. She was very focused on getting me to that meeting."

"What do you think her angle is?"

"The boys aren't saying much, but I wonder …"

Her eyes searched mine before she nodded. "Me too. I think she's always been involved. Maybe she's found new people to help her, or she's the mastermind. Which is gross." She shuddered, then did a whole-body shake. "Hey, enough of that. My brother hasn't let me in here for months." I already knew that was likely false. Angelo allowed Frankie to do anything, and this was essentially her childhood home. "Let's find snacks and see what he's changed around here. I want to explore and see if my room is the same. Let's not talk about Carlotta anymore. She's depressing."

Letting her help me up, we did as she wanted, and the rest of the day became a blur of exploring the brownstone, giggling at how impeccably clean Angelo maintained things (thanks to Norris), and eventually stumbling upon the studio.

Tucked in the back of the first floor, past the hallway that led to his precious garage that was very clearly "Angelo's Don't Even Think About It," was the space he'd created for me. An actual studio. With real light and mood boards, bolts of my favorite silks stacked in neat rows, and my sewing machines gleaming in the sun. It looked like something from a Vogue feature on "Chaotic Artist Quarters: Mafia Heiress Edition."

He had sent for all my belongings: every sewing machine, every bolt of fabric, and every pair of tiny antique scissors I had collected from flea markets across Europe. The studio was perfect—white-walled, sunlit, and organized.

I hadn't cried when I got shot. I hadn't cried when I woke up in a hospital, but this little room full of silent, thoughtful care was too much.

"Wow." I was speechless as I wandered

around, touching each familiar piece and examining the new additions. Even my notebooks, computers, and business accounts were laid out on a table that looked so identical to my desk in Florence that someone must have taken a picture. "It's like they just transposed the workspace."

"I take it he didn't mention this?"

I shook my head. "No. Not a word."

She smiled. "Typical Angelo Santelli. Expresses love through violence and real estate."

I tried to laugh, but my throat felt tight. "He brought my stuff from my apartment, too." I didn't mention the 'L' word she'd dropped. Love didn't enter into the equation of our arrangement. "It was thoughtful of him, " I said as I caressed a spool of gold thread as if it were made of magic.

Frankie hummed as she moved around a dummy with a partially finished project, before looking through a few completed pieces. "My brother is sometimes more empathetic than I expect. He's always been angry, but beneath all that is someone searching for connection. I hope he finds that with you, Theo. I hope you find that with him."

My throat felt tight. "Me too, bestie. Me too, for both of us."

CHAPTER 24
THEODOSIA

LATER THAT AFTERNOON, I texted Angelo.

> Me: Bring pizza. And
> something fun. I'm bored.

He didn't answer immediately, but I figured he was still busy with his meeting. Not to mention, I didn't want to come off as clingy.

Frankie had already gone home, and Norris had retired after preparing some absurdly huge sandwiches for us. I wandered through the brownstone again, barefoot and buzzing with nerves, like I was waiting for something to happen.

Something did. Memories.

The gunshot. The pain. The weightlessness of falling.

It came back fast, hitting me like a sucker punch to the ribs. I sat down in the studio where my favorite lavender silk draped over a chair like a shroud and pressed my face into my hands, breathing deeply.

It wasn't until a knock came on the doorframe and Angelo stood there with a pizza box and a bottle of limoncello in one hand, like some deadly delivery boy from my fever dreams, that I pulled out of it. As always, he took my breath away—those thick thighs and beefy shoulders made me feel he was sturdy and reliable. Yet, it was always his hands that captivated me—the veins stood out in sharp relief, showing how *alive* he was. And those eyes burned with all the emotion he felt about everything.

"*Piccola.*" He entered the room, eyes searching my face and taking everything in. I was sure he saw the signs of distress and tears.

"You brought limoncello?"

"You mentioned something fun, but I wanted to get back as soon as possible, so this will have to do. Maybe we can make our own fun."

He stepped closer, eyes scanning me, and I

knew he saw it all—the stiffness, the paleness, the leftover fear still clinging to me like shadow.

"You okay?" he asked, voice low.

I swallowed hard. "Not even a little."

And when he came inside and sat beside me, brushing his hand against mine, I didn't pull away. After setting the pizza box and the limoncello on one of the tables, he pulled me against him, running his fingers up into my scalp. "Lay your head on my shoulder, *piccola*. I'll make it better."

Closing my eyes, I breathed him in, letting my tears soak his shirt and allowing myself to feel the strength behind the cotton. The heat of the muscles underneath it made my fingers itch to pick up some fabric, thinking about the buttons I could use to craft the perfect shirt for him, wrapping him up the way he deserved, stitching each detail myself. Tilting my face up towards his, I found him already looking down at me, his eyes soft and open.

Maybe it was time for another risk. "Kiss me. Help me forget."

Our mouths were so close already, we were almost there. It was no effort for him to take that next step. I could smell the heat of his breath as it mingled with mine. I breathed in that cinnamon taste before he settled his mouth, his kiss demanding and hard. Angelo kissed with ferocity, that gentleness leaving him as he took and took, sliding his tongue against mine, cradling the back of my head as he dove in over and over. My core throbbed, and my whole body wanted to twine itself around him.

"That's my good girl," he murmured against my lips as he slid to his knees, laying a hand on each thigh. "I'll help you."

Oh my God. Was he going to do what I thought he was? I watched under hooded lids with bated breath, liquid pooling between my thighs as he slid off my loungers and my panties. My focus was one hundred percent on the man between my thighs as he pushed my knees even further, massaging and kneading, peppering little kisses as he did.

Almost in a whisper, he said, "You're already dripping for me, aren't you?" He circled my pussy lips with his fingers as I whimpered. "So needy." His eyes fluttered for a moment. "You'll be the death of me. Fuck. Time to taste, baby."

Groaning, he licked me, taking his time. He rubbed against my folds with his tongue, sliding it into my channel before he began his assault on my clit sucking it into his mouth as he pushed his whole face up against my pussy while he held my thighs wide. Holy hell. Unable to stop myself, I ground against him the pleasure taking hold of me as he kept up a steady rhythm as he sucked and pulled on my clit. Throwing my head back against the chaise, I allowed my eyes to close as the sensations swept over me.

"Oh God. I'm so close." Everything hummed inside me as he spread me even wider, pushed even harder into me until I was screaming his name, white stars flashing behind my eyes.

He stroked me gently before redressing me, kissing me again so lovingly it almost brought tears to my eyes. Sitting on his heels, he watched me with satisfaction. "Hmm, that was my favorite meal of the day." He caught me staring at his obvious hard-on and smirked. "Can't help how you turn me on, but don't worry about that right now."

"I could help you out," I offered. I wasn't sure I wanted to take that step. I loved what had just happened, but if we took another step, then it would get even more complicated.

His eyes banked, and immediately the intimacy that we had been sharing passed. "That was just for you. Let's get you fed, *piccola*." He reached for the pizza.

I nodded, trying to banish the shadows from my thoughts. I was starving. It was hard to feel bad when he was with me. Angelo had always made me feel safe. Shoving a slice of pizza into my mouth, I took a giant bite and was rewarded with an approving grin from him.

Later, when he put me to bed in the guest room, I allowed myself time to wallow in my thoughts. If I gave in and agreed to the inevitable, maybe I wouldn't be sleeping alone anymore.

CHAPTER 25
ANGELO

KOSTAS AND VERONICA had been searching for a week now, and they concluded that the Salvatore Renzetti we'd stumbled across was a fraud. He was someone who had taken up the name of Cosimo Olivetto's third cousin and had a passable Italian heritage, so he hadn't been questioned too much about who he was. Plenty of cash had been flashed about, and people liked that. Still, when Veronica compared facial features from early school photos of Salvatore Renzetti, they didn't match the ones captured from security footage we'd been able to grab from cameras in the New Orleans area.

Which begged the question … who was he really? Because we had no idea.

What we did agree on was that Carlotta Santelli was at the center of it all. As Veronica and Kostas dug deep, they'd hit on more and more aliases that she used — more people she'd manipulated as she spread her evil around the globe. Each time I learned another piece, it made me sick to my soul.

For now, I needed to focus on ensuring that the Five Families knew Renzetti wasn't who he claimed to be, which meant meeting them one-on-one, including that fuckface Scarpato.

Earlier, I planned a meeting with the don of the Cardoni *famiglia*, a family whose allegiance we needed locked down. The Commission couldn't afford splinters right now, especially with Renzetti crawling out of whatever hole he had been hiding in to light fires on the edges of our territories.

These endless meetings kept me from Theo, and I hated that. It had been days since the moment when she'd let me get close in her studio, and I found myself searching for other opportunities to spend time with her, but she'd been slippery, taking her meals before me and going to sleep early, claiming she needed the rest. I'd seen the moment she shut down in the studio when she thought I wanted to go a step further. Maybe she thought I didn't realize that she was still vacillating about her commitment to a marriage to me, but I saw it. I wouldn't force her into anything. Everything I gave her would come without strings attached.

I had to remind myself that these meetings were just additional steps towards figuring out ways to keep her safe. All of these things I was doing were for her protection.

The lights in *Fortune* were dimmed, and staff activity was minimal, but Bacco and I agreed it was the best place for a meeting we could control. Since the rebuilding, we had beefed up security, built bulletproof panels into some of the walls, and even added secret back passages and a safe room. The catastrophe at *Mirage* last year, where Frankie had been kidnapped, taught us all a valuable lesson. We needed to up our game and prepare for the worst eventualities, including other crews coming in and shooting up the place.

I sat in the back of the club, one arm draped across the leather, the other scrolling through encrypted messages—each one more frustrating than the last. Renzetti was still alive, still hiding, and still carving pieces out of our operations like a butcher with a dull blade—messy, deliberate, and personal.

Valentino Cardoni arrived with two guards, exuding enough confidence that I could tell he wasn't concerned about being in a location over which he had no control. When we spoke, I wondered if he might want to dictate the terms to a more favorable venue; usually, this wasn't something I would have suggested. Far be it from me to hint that I wasn't willing to meet on his turf. However, with everything going on with Renzetti, I couldn't take any chances. There was Theo to think about.

Valentino had taken over from his father just a few years earlier — he was second-generation mafia like I was. Still, he had been a second son not destined to be a don until his brother had died in a skiing accident in Tahoe. He was also the father of a little girl, if I wasn't mistaken, based on the dossier I had on him. However, there wasn't much information available on her or her mother, as he wasn't married.

"Angelo," he said, shaking my hand. His smile didn't reach his eyes. "You've been hard to reach."

"Been hunting ghosts," I said flatly. "But

we're here now. Let's talk." I kept my voice even, but I knew I was struggling to maintain my patience.

He didn't seem fazed as he motioned for his men to stand by the door and moved further into the lounge. "Nice place you've got here. I came once before, but this is even better."

Motioning towards a booth in the back where Bacco sat, I said, "We made some improvements—learned some things last time that I wanted to implement here. Always making notes with each build. I'm sure you understand, but I appreciate the compliment." Waiting for Oscar to pour our drinks, I leaned against the cushions and observed the other man.

The Cardoni *famiglia* was cautious and intelligent. Valentino's father, as well as his brother during his brief tenure, adhered to a modest plan that kept their mafia close to power without overreaching. I respected that. They weren't spoken of with fear, but they didn't shy away from eliminating people either. The Cardonis stuck to their business and left ours alone.

Rubbing the edge of the crystal glass with the side of his thumb, he watched me. "You want to talk about Renzetti? That what this is about? Or you just wanted to have drinks?"

Nodding, I pushed my drink over and leaned forward. Bacco and I had discussed how forthcoming to be. My consigliere didn't agree with me about divulging information, but there was a line, and I was going to walk it as close as I could. It didn't make sense not to try to bring in everyone we could. "You're up to date on what happened with Oliveto?"

"Yes. I think I have the story straight. Cosimo was constantly searching for his brother's killer. He just couldn't let it go, but he also couldn't accept that Fausto was a pig." He gave me a considering look. "Too bad they both ended up dead."

Bacco gave a harsh guffaw. "Sounds like you're sorry."

The sarcasm wasn't lost, nor unappreciated. It was how I'd hoped that Valentino would lean.

"As for Renzetti, word on the street is that he's some kind of lost cousin, but sounds fishy to me."

Well, well, well. He was smart. Adjusting slightly in the booth, I relaxed a little. "You're right to be suspicious." Sliding my eyes to Bacco, I ignored the way his shoulders tensed. He definitely didn't want me to share this next piece of information, but nothing ventured, nothing gained. "We've discovered that the man masquerading as Salvatore Renzetti isn't who he claims to be. At one time, there was a Salvatore Renzetti who was very loosely connected to Cosimo Oliveto, but it isn't the man who is parading around today. We aren't sure who he is."

Valentino draped an arm along the back of the banquette, his eyes narrowing. "And ... I sense something else there."

"And ... Carlotta Santelli," I couldn't bring myself to call her my mother, "has been working with Renzetti in the flesh trade. We are committed to stopping both of them at whatever cost."

Finally, his eyes showed surprise, as if I had given him information he hadn't had. "So you'll kill her then if you can?"

"Definitely. She was instrumental in the kidnapping of my fiancée. She's also definitely involved somehow. We've struggled to figure it out, or find where she's at — or Renzetti. There has been motion along the periphery of our territories, but not the man himself." Bacco made a slight choking sound. That was definitely too much information, but I could sense the genuine interest in Cardoni.

He looked at me with consideration, and

then after a moment, he seemed to come to a decision. "Well, we're a small *famiglia*, as you know. There are some ways we could help." He ran his hands over the rim of his glass while I waited for him to make the fucking point. "Carlotta knew my father."

I didn't say I was surprised, but still, my eyes slid over to Bacco. I wanted to swear out loud or kick something.

Valentino continued, "She stayed sometimes at our summer home. There has been activity there recently, but I haven't been too worried since we have staff there sometimes. It might be worth a look." He watched me consideringly.

"We have been wondering if there are places she might stay," I said thoughtfully as if this was earthshaking news. Inside, I was jumping up and down.

"There are a few other locations that I can check, which might be more likely. She stayed with us when I was growing up." His mouth tightened as if the memory of Carlotta stained his adolescence.

"Thank you. That would be very helpful," Bacco interjected. "We had no idea that Carlotta had been around Don Cardoni after she'd left the Santellis."

Valentino reddened, "It was even before that, and after."

"I see. Did you know that Vallone is my sister's father?" I threw the last out lazily on instinct. I didn't think that Valentino liked Carlotta much either. "Carlotta liked to whore herself out."

Valentino's eyes slid to the side away from me as rage pooled deep inside my belly at the thought of the woman jumping from don to don looking for power grabs.

A flush rose on Valentino's cheeks before he added, "My father kept diaries."

Very interesting."Did he talk about Carlotta?"

"He did." Valentino looked over towards the door for a moment, and I wondered if he'd end the meeting right then. He didn't really owe me anything, least of all a detailed description of what was in his father's private diaries. Then, he said, "She wanted a seat at the table with the Five Families, and he had been inclined to help her get it. My father frequently wrote about how Carlotta wanted to control the mafia herself. How she wouldn't be satisfied until she could do that, but she didn't think she would be able to get the men of the Santelli mafia to fight for her. He'd speculated that she'd be back when you were older and that she would try again." He paused. "My father wasn't stupid about her. I think he used her, too. Carlotta would stay with us or at our properties, but she was never allowed near our meetings or men. My father was well aware of her dealings with the other dons and the power struggles. At the same time," Valentino smiled softly, "My father was lonely, and Carlotta amused him with her machinations."

Taking a swallow of my drink, I considered what he'd told me. It provided information I hadn't had and was immensely valuable. Hidey holes that we didn't know about could lead to another location where she might be staying. Not to mention, we could also check properties associated with other mafia dons or past dons she could be linked to."I appreciate the insight you've shared. It'll be helpful to us."

There was an imperceptible incline to his head, but he held up a hand. "Just so we're clear. I'm not on anyone's side but my family's. Renzetti has blood in his eyes, and Carlotta? That woman has always been crazy."

Bacco's eyes sharpened at the slight hint of dissent, but I understood Valentino's perspective. His mafia was small, and the last thing he wanted was to become involved in a war that could spread beyond what they were prepared for. Even though we were still trying to navigate the undercurrents of what we were facing, Cardoni was smart enough to realize that he needed to proceed cautiously. No one could fault someone for not wanting to get too deeply involved.

"Of course, we understand where you're coming from. You need to think of your *famiglia* first. Any help or information you provide is appreciated, but most of all, any help you <u>don't</u> provide them is also important." I made sure my point was clear.

Val sneered. "You can be sure that won't be happening." There was a considering pause. "That woman will get no help and no quarter from me."

"Good to hear. She deserves none."

Val leaned forward. "You'd better get ahead of this. Fast. This whole situation stinks to high heaven. Her coming back."

I let my smile stretch slowly across my face. Cold. Empty. "We are moving heaven and hell to make sure she finds a cold grave. Everything the Commission has, we will throw at her." Rising to my feet, I reached over with a hand to shake his. "I appreciate you coming all this way to meet."

"Not a problem. I was happy to discuss this with you. I'll check out those locations and send you an update."

Watching him go, thoughts of other spots to check occurred to me. I sent an update to our group chat about the meeting and then followed up with another text to Veronica so she could follow through on those leads. Hopefully, something would pan out soon; chasing Renzetti and Carlotta was getting old when all I wanted to do was focus on Theodosia and how crazy she'd been making me.

Almost two weeks had passed since the plantation. Since Theo had nearly died in my arms. And still, every time I looked at her, I saw the blood soaking into her clothes. Heard her broken whisper. Felt the helpless rage clawing up my throat.

She was healing. The doctors said the surgery had gone well. Her physical therapy was progressing. Norris said she'd even started eating more, but I could see the restlessness in her eyes. She was bored. She was angry. She was trying not to let it show.

And I couldn't blame her. She had lost the life that she had been carving out for herself, and now she was thrust into something she had fought against.

Still, we had broached something new that

night in her studio — uncovered a new corner to explore. I wanted her to choose me. So I'd continue to bide my time and try to breach those defenses. Her asking me to help her forget had been the catalyst to move our relationship to a different phase, so I'd made sure to take advantage — to touch her at every innocuous opportunity: a hand at the small of her back, a caress along the back of her hand, a light kiss on the back of her neck. Everything about her called to me like a siren—the fall of her hair, the glow of her skin, the taste of her.

Every night I stroked myself to the thought of her, the smell of her, the image of her tits until I came hard with the promise that one day soon I'd be balls deep in Theodosia Anthakos.

———

Norris met me at the front door of the brownstone when I got back just after midnight.

"Angelo," he greeted with a polite nod, his voice the same calm gravel I'd come to rely on.

"How is she?" I asked immediately.

"Restless," he replied, confirming what I

already knew. "She was in the studio for most of the evening. Fell asleep in there with all of her fabrics."

I sighed. "Thanks, Norris. I'll just check in on her quickly."

"I'll reheat dinner for you," he lifted an eyebrow.

I gave him a faint smirk. The man knew me too damn well.

When I peeked into the studio, Theo was still asleep. The room glowed softly from the dimmed sconces, gold light pooling against walls lined with fabric. I'd pulled every favor I had to get her things from Florence. Since then, I'd had more fabrics flown in, from hand-painted bolts of silk to hand-dyed cottons from Delhi, and textures I didn't even understand but knew she loved.

She was curled on the chaise, her dark hair spilling over the cushions, lips parted, her injured shoulder tucked protectively under her body. I wanted to wake her up in the most delicious ways, and I was tempted for a moment. However, she was still fragile from the ordeal my mother had put her through and I wasn't that much of an asshole.

God, she looked breakable, but I knew better.

She was fire. Dangerous. Too smart for

her own good. Which made everything harder. Because all I wanted was to keep her close and carve out the throat of anyone who so much as thought about hurting her again.

Moving back down the hallway to the kitchen, where Norris was humming around the darkened kitchen, I slid onto a stool and watched him as he bustled around before setting a heaping serving of lasagna and garlic bread in front of me.

Shoveling in a bite of food, I sighed with satisfaction as ricotta and tomato meshed in perfect harmony. "How are you, Norris? Anything new with your collection that I don't know about?"

He grinned back at me. "I'm good, sir. I found a new piece. Very special. Not a crack. I've got the perfect spot for it."

Grinning, I broke off a piece of bread while listening to him rave about his new flamingo cookie jar. Norris was obsessed with cookie jars, all of which were different, according to him. He was a passionate collector, always on the hunt for his next purchase on auction sites, in antique stores, or through garage sale listings. "You'll have to show it to me."

"I'd love to, sir. I confess that I've been

waiting to show the new missus. Maybe she'll think it's strange." He looked unsure.

"Of course she won't. We're all a little wacky on the inside, Norris. It's what makes us interesting. Theo understands and appreciates that. It's one of the things that I like about her."

CHAPTER 26
THEODOSIA

I WOKE up with a pencil stuck to my cheek and a bolt of pink organza trying to suffocate me.

Classic Theo.

It took a moment to orient myself—high ceilings, raw silk draped over the chaise lounge, a mood board speckled with dozens of clippings, and sketches scattered like confetti. Right. Angelo's brownstone. My studio. *My* damn studio.

Earlier, I had wrapped myself in lavender silk and lay on the chaise, staring at the ceiling and willing myself to dream up a design. I video-called Vivienne to discuss closing everything down in Florence, but it seemed that Angelo and my brothers had already taken care of that. They even paid her salary for the year, along with a generous bonus. Vivienne would take advantage of the time off and travel a bit, and then she thought she would try again with design school. She had tied up all of our outstanding orders, so I didn't need to worry about those, but my brain was trapped in gossamer thoughts that seemed to fight against shadows.

I was still trying to puzzle out what had gone wrong in Italy even before I'd been kidnapped and taken to some Gothic horror movie scene. If I had any hope of resurrecting something here and continuing with my fashion work, that mystery needed to be solved. Someone had been conspiring against my label for reasons I couldn't figure out. Maybe it was time to ask for help on that problem before it really twisted me up.

Eventually, I'd passed out on the floor like an overworked fashion student after her final critique. I'd only come in to "organize" and think about things. Apparently, that meant dozing off while looking through my sketch-book for inspiration for a new idea to hit me.

I groaned, sitting up slowly. My shoulder throbbed with a dull ache in protest, and I winced. Guess that's what happened when you lie curled in a fetal position on your injured side for two hours. It was much better than it had been, but sleeping like that wasn't ideal. A doctor had already visited the brownstone to check on me, and Angelo had arranged for a physical therapist for daily grueling sessions. Still, I was thankful he'd made arrangements for me.

The house was quiet. Late quiet.

Outside the window, the city was as dark as it could get, the streetlamps buzzing like secrets. I rubbed my face, smoothed my hair back into something semi-human, and padded barefoot into the hallway. The kimono I wore was barely acceptable for housewear. The brownstone creaked underfoot, the kind of rich, old noise that only came from actual wood and generational money.

That's when I heard them—muffled voices from the kitchen below.

I hesitated, one hand on the banister.

It was Angelo. His voice was lower than usual, tired and gruff in that way he got when he thought no one was listening. And Norris, ever the butler-with-a-soul, was talking back.

I crept to the edge of the stairwell, half-hidden by the shadow of the hall, and stilled.

Dinner plates clinked. The scent of roasted garlic and tomato lingered in the air, and I was tempted to move forward just for food. Even though it was very late and Norris had fed me, I could definitely eat. I could make out the warm amber glow of the kitchen lights pooling across the dark hardwood floors. One of the things I appreciated about the brownstone was the richly colored coffee floors, which were covered haphazardly here and there with rugs. The brownstone did have a nicely lived-in feel — a family had lived here, and it showed.

"—and she hasn't touched most of the stuff in the studio," Angelo said, frustration sharp around the edges. "I'm not sure she likes it."

My breath caught.

"I think she's trying," Norris offered gently. "Sometimes trying looks like nothing at all, at first."

There was a pause. A fork scraped against a plate. Norris began to rave about something he was collecting. It took me a few minutes to figure out, but I thought they were talking about cookie jars? Maybe? I blinked, trying to picture it. The don of the Santelli mafia having a wholesome dinner conversation about decorative ceramics.

"You'll have to show it to me," he said to Norris, his tone lightening.

"I'd love to, sir," Norris replied, hopeful. "I confess that I've been waiting to show the

new missus. Maybe she'll think it's strange."
His voice dipped, uncertain.

My heart squeezed.

Angelo didn't hesitate. "Of course she won't. We're all a little wacky on the inside, Norris. It's what makes us interesting. Theo understands and appreciates that. It's one of the things that I like about her."

I backed up a step, like his words had physically touched me. A stupid, stinging warmth spread up my throat. I hadn't expected that. Not from *him*. Not after nearly a week of tiptoeing around each other, trading glances like live wires, and pretending we weren't both on edge whenever we shared the same space.

I had told myself he was too busy, too cold, too complicated. I had convinced myself that he hated me, but this almost sounded like he … liked me.

And yet there he was, defending my weirdness like it was something to protect.

I scrambled away from the landing, heart hammering, and darted back into the hall just as his silhouette stepped out from the kitchen. My back hit the wall near the upstairs railing, and my breath caught in my chest.

Angelo stilled, one hand braced on the

stairwell's carved banister."You were listening," he said softly, voice low and unreadable.

I swallowed, eyes wide. "Technically, I was sleepwalking. Entirely unconscious. This is all a dream."

One dark brow lifted. "You dream about me complimenting your quirks to Norris?"

"I dream about worse things," I muttered, pushing off the wall and walking toward him. "Like falling asleep in a pile of tulle and waking up with 'Vogue' stuck to my face. Oh, wait—that actually happened."

His eyes followed my movements, lingering on the outline of my bare legs. There were sleep shorts underneath the kimono, but it was hard to tell. He didn't say anything at first.

Then: "You okay?"

I nodded, then shrugged, regretting it immediately as pain flared in my shoulder.

His expression darkened. "You should've called for me."

"And ruin the moment? You, being nice? That's rarer than Norris's banana-shaped cookie jar."

He exhaled a sharp laugh and looked away, his jaw tense. But he didn't retreat. He stayed rooted on that step, as if something in him didn't want to let me pass just yet. "I don't think it's banana-shaped, but he'd probably love that." His voice dropped as he stepped closer. "I meant what I said, Theo," he murmured. "About you being interesting. About liking that."

I sucked in a breath. This was dangerous ground. The kind with no footing and too many sharp drops. "I don't need compliments, Angelo."

He moved closer, just enough to eliminate the distance between us. "That wasn't a compliment. That was a fact."

Something flared between us then, silent and hot and old as sin. I could see it in the hard line of his jaw, the way his eyes flicked to my mouth and then back again like he was fighting himself. Like he wasn't sure if kissing me would fix things or make them worse. I should've said something. I should've told him I wasn't ready, or that I didn't know what this was, or that my heart was still too bruised to be touched like that. Instead, I whispered, "Show me."

He blinked. "What?"

"The cookie jar," I said, chickening out, breezing past him and down the stairs before I lost my nerve. "I want to see this cookie jar in all its flamingo glory."

Behind me, I heard his chuckle—quiet, surprised, warm.

The brownstone's kitchen resembled something out of a mafia housewife's dream —warm lighting, old-world tiles, and cast-iron pans hanging in a neat row. It always made me wish I could cook, which, to be clear, I couldn't. While I could whip up a mean tutu, lion costume, or jumpsuit, baking bread or making pasta sent shivers down my spine. No part of me was interested in learning either.

The scent of garlic, basil, and whatever else Norris had been cooking clung to the air like perfume. It smelled pure Italian and 100% delicious. I was already drooling.

And in the center of this dream was Angelo, sleeves rolled up, looking like sin and Sunday dinner.

Norris perked up from the sink like a startled meerkat. "Miss Theodosia! You're awake."

I smiled at him, sliding onto one of the barstools at the island. "Barely. But I heard there was a flamingo cookie jar, and I couldn't resist."

Norris beamed. I mean, *beamed*. He looked like he'd just gotten front row tickets to the

Antiques Roadshow. "Oh, you're going to love her. Her name's Loretta."

Angelo moved to the counter behind me, his presence a low hum I could feel even without turning. He was always like that— more gravity than man.

"Did you give her that name, or did she come with it?" I asked, watching Norris pull a bubble-wrapped monstrosity from the cabinet.

"She *told* me her name," he said, deadly serious. "Look at her eyelashes. That's a Loretta if I've ever seen one."

He unwrapped the jar and placed it like a rare jewel on the counter. It was... glorious. Bright pink, with one leg in the air, sparkly gold eyeshadow, a little hat with a bow, absolutely unhinged. I wasn't sure how many actual cookies it could hold, but it was amazing.

"I <u>love</u> her," I whispered.

Angelo leaned in close to my ear, pressing against me so I felt him unmistakably hard right up against me. His cock fit right between my ass cheeks making me want to rock back into him. "Told you she'd like it."

His breath tickled my neck, and I pretended my entire body didn't light up like a cheap neon sign. I focused on Loretta.

Loretta was safe. Loretta didn't make me feel like my stomach was turning inside out.

"She looks like she moonlights in Vegas," I said, grinning. "Like she's been married six times and only regrets the fourth one."

"Fourth was Gary," Norris said solemnly. "We don't talk about Gary."

Angelo actually laughed. A low, rough sound that rumbled through his chest. My eyes darted to him before I could stop myself.

God, he was stupidly handsome. Dark shadows were beneath his eyes, and the crease between his brows looked deeper than a few days ago. His body was here, but his mind was still out there, hunting ghosts.

"Have you eaten?" he asked me suddenly, and I blinked.

"Do three Tic Tacs count?"

Norris gasped in horror. "Blasphemy. Sir, I made her a sandwich. She ate lunch." He glared at me.

"It's after midnight, Norris. That was yesterday." I winked at him unapologetically.

"I'll heat something up," Angelo said, turning to the fridge.

I watched him for a second, something squeezing in my chest. Was this who he really was? The kind of man who did things like this? Meals? Small talk? Cookie jars?

"Hey," I said softly. He looked up. "I know things are… messy right now. Thank you. For this. The studio. The food. Loretta."

Angelo's gaze held mine for a second too long. Then he looked away. "You're welcome."

Norris nodded as if he were about to cry, but he rallied. "I'll let you young people get on with your evening. Let me just get Loretta settled with the others." He scooped up his prize and gave us each a pointed look before ambling off into the darkness toward his quarters, where he apparently had a treasure trove of cookie jars.

A beat of silence stretched between us. He slid a plate into the oven, and I picked at the corner of a napkin, nerves making my fingers twitch.

"Do you want to talk about it?" I asked finally.

He stilled. "About what?"

I gave him a look. "Don't play dumb. You're spinning. I can see it." Clearing my throat, I tried again. "Look, if we're going to do this, then I want us to communicate, you know?"

He leaned back against the counter, arms crossed—that classic mafia don stance—all quiet power and dangerous restraint.

"I'm trying to protect what's mine," he said simply. "That takes work. Especially now."

His voice was clipped, like he didn't want to let too much slip.

"Carlotta," I said. The name was bitter in my mouth, but Frankie and I had been trying to process together the involvement of the woman who had given birth to the Santelli clan and the way she had used her children to manipulate the criminal underworld. "Frankie and I have talked about her role in all of this."

His jaw tightened, his hands clenched against the granite edge of the counter. "I talked to Valentino Cardoni today. She was seeing old Don Cardoni, too, back in the day."

There was no mistaking the anger on his face. "We think she's always been the one pulling the strings," I offered instead. "That Renzetti is just another mark."

A sharp nod. "Yeah, that's what I think. What we all think."

I watched him carefully. "You think they're connected?"

"Renzetti is the one who is trying to bleed my territory, but I think Carlotta is behind it all."

I sat with that—the idea of someone

picking apart Angelo's empire piece by piece, watching him bleed out. No wonder he was exhausted. No wonder he was holding the whole world at arm's length—even me. I agreed with him, though this was all connected. "I hate feeling useless," I said quietly.

His eyes softened. "You're not."

"You're out hunting a ghost who put a bullet in my shoulder, and I'm stuck here. That feels a lot like useless." Now, I realized I was complaining, which was even worse.

He pushed off the counter, crossed to me, and braced his hands on either side of the island where I sat. His face was inches from mine.

"Don't ever say that again."

"Angelo—"

"You are healing. That takes strength, too. You were shot because of *me*. Targeted. You almost died, and you're still here. We're still here. Becoming *something*. That is not nothing."

There was an offer in that I realized, looking up at him. My breath caught in my throat. "You can't fix this with a flamingo and a piece of lasagna."

"I'm not trying to fix it," he growled. "I'm trying to be here. With you."

That did me in. Because that was the thing, I didn't want him to fix anything. I didn't want vengeance, apologies, or heroics. Maybe there was life after being a teenager. Perhaps I'd held on long enough.

I just wanted *him*.

A long, charged moment passed. His gaze dropped to my mouth, and I saw the flicker behind his eyes. He was holding himself back. Barely.

"Angelo…"

"Yeah?"

"I'm scared." That was the thing I was scared of: what these feelings were. I had locked myself so tight for so long that I was afraid I would fly into a million pieces and would never be able to put myself back together.

He pressed his forehead to mine. "Me too."

Another beat. Then I whispered, "So what do we do?"

His lips brushed the corner of my mouth —feather-light. "You eat. We sit. We talk. And I don't go anywhere tonight."

"Okay," I breathed.

He pulled back just as the oven dinged, and I let out a shaky laugh. And I didn't feel so alone for the first time in weeks.

"What were you working on today?" He asked.

"Nothing much. I've got creator's block." Shoving the too-hot food in my mouth, I chewed around the scalding hot mess, not caring that it slid down too fast. "I talked to Vivienne. Thanks for handling all that, by the way. I appreciate that. Just before all this happened, I'd been experiencing some issues with the business, so we were reviewing some leads we had. I went back over my contacts again. Just typical stuff." Picking through the layers, I speared some sausage and mopped up some sauce with a piece of bread.

Angelo took a seat next to me, his eyes intent on mine. "Slow down a second. What kind of problems?"

Outlining the basics, I reviewed what had happened with *Mythos*, how our client base had ghosted, and how orders had dried up. "It was unusual. We were doing really well. Like, super well. I was proud." Choking up a little, I took a sip of water, ignoring the man beside me, who I knew was turning everything over. I hoped he wasn't too ashamed that his future wife was an utter failure in business.

"Someone sabotaged you. We need to look into that, because I'd bet money it was Carlotta." The tone was flat, and when I looked over, there was pure rage in his eyes, knuckles fisted as if he would pound something to dust if he could.

I raised an eyebrow at him. "Really? You think so?" The thought hadn't even crossed my mind.

"I do think so. I think it was intentional so that when the invitation came, it would be more appealing and you wouldn't think twice about heading out the door for a meeting. She probably set everything in motion with a few calls." He cocked his head at me. "You didn't ask your brothers for help?"

"No, I wanted to work it out myself." Now it seemed stupid. If I had asked them, Kostas might have figured this out sooner. The whole situation might have been avoided. My shoulders slumped in defeat.

"*Piccola*," Angelo squeezed my hand. "Let's put that aside for now. Finish your food. In the morning, we'll focus on figuring out who is behind sinking your business. Everything will be right as rain. I promise."

The words spread through me and shot straight like an arrow to my panties. First, an unsolicited compliment, then food, and now acceptance and help. He was speaking my love language.

CHAPTER 27
ANGELO

SHE HAD BEEN STANDING THERE in the kitchen doorway like some sleepy angel.

Tousled curls springing away from her face, shadows pooling under her wide eyes, and that thin robe belted haphazardly around her waist like she didn't even know she'd seduced every damn molecule of air in the room just by breathing.

I knew she'd overheard me. Heard the damn truth spill out when I wasn't thinking, when I let my guard down for once with Norris. Of course, she had. She always heard the things I didn't say. Theodosia had a way with getting words out of me — even words I didn't mean.

That was the problem with Theodosia Anthakos—she saw too much. Knew how to get under a man's skin, and I was letting her. Each day, I found that I liked having her in my space, and my fear of the arrangement that had been made was just that … fear. I had misplaced my anger all these years. Maybe I cheated us out of time we could have enjoyed. The thought didn't sit well.

Now, we were in the kitchen while she forked the last bit of lasagna, pushing the plate away with a satisfied smile."I wasn't planning on eavesdropping," she said, voice low and a little raspy. "But then you started talking about me and… cookie jars."

I smirked, head tipping as I watched her try to play it cool. "You jealous of Norris's cookie jars, *piccola*?"

"I'm jealous of anyone who gets your compliments. You hand them out like rationed whiskey."

Jesus Christ.

That should've made me laugh. Instead, it made my stomach clench and my hands twitch with the need to touch her. I reached out and tucked a strand of hair behind her ear, slow, deliberate.

"I meant what I said," I murmured. "You're different. You see people. Even me. And you don't run from what's broken."

Her breath hitched, but she held her

ground. "Maybe I just collect broken things. Dresses, vintage fabrics, mafia bosses with mommy issues…"

That earned a brief, rough laugh. I leaned in, brushing my nose against hers. "Careful, Theo. That mouth of yours could get you in trouble."

"Promises, promises," she whispered, and suddenly the air felt electric, as if it might snap if we breathed too loudly.

That was the second time she'd tempted me, and my leash was pulled tighter than a hangman's noose. "Theo," I said softly, more breath than voice.

She didn't move when I came even closer and spun her around so those long legs automatically opened to accommodate me as I slid between them. She tilted her chin and looked at me with those hazel eyes like she wanted to fight and kiss me in the same breath. The fabric of her robe parted slightly, and I forced my gaze to stay on her face.

She lifted a hand, fingers brushing over the stubble on my jaw, her short nails rasping over the whiskers there. "Kiss me then."

Diving forward and wending my fingers through her hair, I pulled her head back to expose her throat. Her pulse fluttered wildly as my hand pressed against her skin. "Do you feel what you do to me, Theo?" Pressing myself against the seam of those ridiculous little barely there boyshorts, I let her feel how hard I was. "I'm so hard for you. Always." A little whimper escaped her and I increased the twist on her hair as she rocked onto my cock.

Leaning down, I took her mouth, nipping at the corners of those lips that drove me wild, licking into her as she moaned those whimpers of hers that I'd be happy to hear every hour of every day. I could practically feel the heat of her against me as she ground against me. I wanted to touch, lick, and taste so much of her. Ignoring her startled squeak, I swung her up into my arms.

———

Lying her against the pillows, I tried to remind myself to treat her with care, to mind her wound. The belt of her robe had already slipped, showcasing tantalizing expanses of skin that begged for my touch.

"You choose this?" I needed her to, desperately, but I wasn't sure if I had read her correctly or if I had scooped her up and was doing what I did naturally — being an asshole.

"Yes." The word was barely a sigh — a moan.

"*Piccola*, you'll tell me if you need to stop. If I'm hurting you?" I sat back on my heels, pulled off my shirt and tie, and threw them to the floor, watching her eyes darken in appreciation.

"I'm not going to break. I want this. You're so beautiful."

Huffing a little laugh at her, I traced a finger along an ankle. "I'm not supposed to be beautiful, Theo. Men are handsome."

My little hurricane firmed her chin. "Don't be silly, Angelo. Men can be beautiful. You're beautiful like the statues in Rome. You could be carved from marble. Maybe I'll make you a toga. We could … oh!"

Her words were lost as my mouth latched onto one of her thighs, parting them and sinking my teeth into the flesh just hard enough to leave an indentation. I sucked hard enough to bring the blood to the surface. I wanted to mark her everywhere. Leave love bites — evidence that she was mine. Her scent was now so close that it overwhelmed me, driving me to a frenzy as she mewled, her fingers clenched against the sheets. Letting my hands roam freely, I moved up those beautiful legs, memorizing the feel of her satiny flesh, the divots in the backs of her knees, and the bones of her ankles. I was deliberate in making myself wait until I allowed myself to pull down the little shorts she wore.

"No panties?" Easing them over I settled by her pussy allowing myself to rock against the mattress a little. Fuck. I could blow in my pants right now, smelling her. I'd been fucking my hand for over a year now since I had known for sure that Theodosia Anthakos was mine for certain. Since this whole blood oath had been set into motion. Now that she was literally beneath me? My cock was struggling to get the message that it needed to calm the fuck down. It was raging behind the zipper, the teeth only making the pleasure sweeter. Gritting my teeth, I narrowed my focus on Theo. "You're so wet for me, *piccola*. Look how pretty you are." Blowing lightly on her pussy I watched her whole body shiver.

"You're a tease. Touch me already. Please." There was a want in her voice that I wanted to rise to a fever pitch.

"Hmmm," I said thoughtfully, giving her opposite thigh a matching love bite, then arranging that leg over my shoulder. "I could come in my pants right now looking at you like this, do you know that? You're so beautiful. I'm going to make you feel so good."

"Angelo …"

Spreading her legs even further, I slid two fingers into her tight channel, groaning out loud at how wet and slick she was. I could just imagine how my cock would fit in that wet heat sliding in and out. How tightly she was going to clutch me. She was like a flower right now, all moistened petals opening to the sun. "I've got you, Theo." Latching my mouth onto her clit I sucked the little bud into my mouth, rimming it with my tongue. I wanted to make her fly. Keeping up the rhythm I drove her with my fingers up against her slick folds as I worked her clit mercilessly until she ground against my face just how I wanted. I couldn't wait until I could get her above me riding my face until she came..

"Don't stop." Her fingers tangled in my hair pulling my face to her pussy. I'd tell her that nothing would make me stop, but I didn't dare interrupt the flow that I'd started. Instead, I kept the pace until my *piccola* arched her back off the mattress and came apart. Her thighs trembled hard as I lapped against her pussy. "Oh, my God."

She was flushed, a rosy glow rising over her as I shucked off my slacks and boxer briefs. I hadn't even given proper attention to those tits of hers, but I would be rectifying that right away. Palming my cock I squeezed it trying to remind myself to calm the fuck down and not be too eager. Every part of me wanted to make this good for her. She wasn't some corner girl. Theodosia Anthakos was going to be my wife.

CHAPTER 28
THEODOSIA

THERE WAS nothing shy about Angelo Santelli, which did not surprise me. He was cocky and confident in everything he did, so it followed that he would be that way in bed and boy did it work for me.

When I said that he looked like the statues in Rome, I was not lying. His body was drool-worthy, and for a moment, I doubted myself, those words creeping into my psyche that I was too soft or not pretty enough to be with someone like him, but I shut that line of thinking down.

My body was still tingling from the orgasm that had swept through me like a symphony as I watched him finish undress-ing. His cock was thick and long, leaking pre-cum as he stroked it — tightening his hold as he maneuvered between my thighs. My pussy gave a throb in response at the very thought of how hard he was.

Angelo Santelli was turned on because of *me*. The thought was powerful. His jaw was clenched tight, his cock purple with want and I wanted to lick it like a lollipop — suck him off until he exploded.

"*Piccola*," he groaned right before he thrust into me—no easing in for him. The stretch burned, but only in the best way. It had been a while since I'd indulged in sex, and Angelo wasn't small. "I'd die happy right now buried in your pussy."

I wrapped my legs around his hips as he set up a rhythm that drove him straight up against my cervix. Already, I could feel my next orgasm rising as he pounded into me, his mouth on mine, and his fingers tugging at my nipples, twisting and rubbing in alternating fashions. It felt like he was everywhere, those fingers and lips roving, nipping, sucking as he moved from spot to spot. He felt so good. I had a sense of completeness with him inside me that had been missing, and I could feel those walls that I had built up crumbling.

His hand slid between us rubbing hard on my clit, and that was what I needed to come apart. The orgasm hit me hard, stars exploding behind my eyes as my hips surged against his.

"That's what I like, baby. To feel you come on my cock. Just what I was waiting for, my beautiful girl."

Warmth spread through me as his come jetted into me, and he groaned, his hips jerking against me. I stilled as I watched his release, felt the flood between my thighs.

"That was ..." I trailed off as he looked down at me pensively.

"Amazing." He cupped one of my breasts. "You have glorious tits. Look at these little rosebuds." Bending, he took one of my nipples in his mouth. "I could suck on these all day. Our children will make me jealous."

"Children, huh? More than one?" We hadn't discussed anything concrete, but I'd told him I chose him. To me, that meant I had committed. We hadn't used any protection, and I hadn't wanted to. "How many do you want?"

He pulled me to his side, frowning at the bandage on my shoulder, immediately alert to the wince I gave. He had taken as much care as he could to avoid impacting the wound, but it definitely hurt from the extra 'activity,' though I didn't care.

"How's the shoulder? Did I hurt you?

Maybe you should have a pain pill? Was I too rough?" He was immediately solicitous.

"I'm fine. I promise. Answer my question." This was important to me. It was a secret hope of mine that I'd nurtured. Even when I was young, I'd wanted to be a mother. If we ended up in a situation where Angelo didn't want children because of his fucked up past then I wasn't sure how I'd feel about that. Frankie had felt like that for years, not wanting children. Maybe he wouldn't want them. If that were the case, I suppose we would adapt. Maybe I could volunteer somewhere, but that would be hard for me to accept. I bit my lip while I was waiting for his reply, anxiety swirling.

His hand slipped between my thighs, and he smirked as his fingers slid in and out of my channel. "Lots. A whole house full. I hope you're pregnant right now. I want you knocked up. I'm going to fuck you every chance I get. How do you feel about that?" He captured my mouth and bit down on my lip. "When you're nice and round I'll fuck you even more. These tits. I'll spread my come all over them. I'll fuck you when you're sleeping. Twenty-four-seven."

Oh my God, the dirty talk. Nobody had ever talked to me like that before. I squirmed against his hand, rocking up against his fingers. "Yes. Yes to all of it." The words came out like a moan. Need blazed all over again at the images that he was planting in my mind, and the thought of having his baby inside me. The idea of him taking me when I was most vulnerable. It was unexpectedly hot.

"Yeah? That's what you want. You want me to slide my cock into that greedy pussy while you're dreaming sweet dreams? Or you want my babies, Theo? All of it, my greedy girl?" He latched his mouth to a nipple and sucked hard, so hard that tears sprang to my eyes and he added a third finger pumping into me.

"All of it. Your babies." Rocking my hips up he circled my clit with his thumb working it in tandem as I ground into him turned on by the thought of it all.

"That's it. Come on, *piccola*. You're so close already, aren't you?"

I was embarrassingly close. Just on the edge already. He was stroking his cock while he worked me, his hand moving up and down his shaft while he teased my nipples.

"Not yet. You're going to come on my cock again. I'm right there." Sliding back into me his wet fingers gripped my ass, biting into the flesh as his cock ground into me. This time, he undulated slowly against me so deliciously that my head flopped back against the pillow.

"Just like that. Keep doing that." He was hitting everything as his hips rolled into mine, his forehead leaning against my chin as he focused. "Yes, Angelo." His name came on a scream that I was sure the neighbors could hear. I let go. This man was going to kill me.

"We're going to have to change the sheets," I said as he rolled onto his back, but his smirk was pure satisfaction. "The staff are going to think we are nymphos."

"The staff will keep their mouths shut. I'm going to run you a bath and get you an ibuprofen."

I watched him go. Damn. Even his ass was fine.

CHAPTER 29
ANGELO

THE AIR outside *Fortune* was damp with the threat of rain, the kind that smelled like rust and memory. I lit a cigarette as I stood in the alley beside the club's back entrance, letting the smoke settle into my lungs like an old friend. Quitting was a process. It wasn't so much the nicotine, but the comfort of the cigarette between my lips and lighting the match — that first flare. My thoughts drifted far from here, back to last night with Theo.

It was everything I had dreamed it would be, and didn't that make me a sappy son-of-a-bitch. I'd mastered the art of keeping people at arm's length—especially women. In the mafia, women were plentiful and easy. They threw themselves at you everywhere, but last night had cracked something wide open. And now, I didn't know what to do with the goddamn light pouring in.

She had finally fallen asleep, her hair tangled after the bath, her head tilted against the pillows, exposing the arc of her neck and tempting me. Theo was a blend of a goddess of mischief and heartbreak. Her body curled unconsciously into mine during the night, her hip draped over me as she slept. I couldn't wait to tell her that she talked in her sleep. She mumbled, nothing discernible, but it was cute. Super cute. Her mouth scrunched up into a pout as she talked to herself. I stayed longer than I should have, just watching, listening to her. She seemed to be concentrating on something, and I wondered if she was dreaming of our babies or working on new dress designs. Either way, I was fascinated.

I stubbed the cigarette out against the brick and made my way into the club.

Inside, the private lounge was already buzzing, filled almost to capacity with additional capos and adjacent soldiers from our organizations. It felt like we were hurtling closer to the truth, grasping at each straw coming our way. Squeezing each piece of territory put pressure on whatever operation they hoped to establish here in New York, so what we were doing was working.

Conall leaned against the bar, nursing something dark, probably Irish. Maxim had claimed one of the leather chairs, legs crossed, a folder open on his lap. Ilias was the only one pacing, which meant he was ready to kill something or someone. Possibly both.

I closed the door behind me, sealing the world out. "Gentlemen."

Maxim didn't look up. "You're late."

"You'll survive," I muttered, tugging off my coat and draping it over the back of the nearest chair. "I needed a quick smoke."

Conall lifted his drink. "Theo won't like that too much."

"Probably not," I said. "She'll forgive me, though." The smirk was already growing on my face at how I'd make sure.

Ilias barked a laugh and finally stopped pacing. "You better be treating her right you dick."

"Of course I am. And you're the dick." I frowned at him.

"Let's focus," Maxim added, his voice quieter. "Tell us about Cardoni."

I nodded, dragging a hand through my hair. "Valentino told me something about his father. The old don had an affair with

Carlotta. Years ago. It went on for a while—long enough for her to think it meant something."

That got their attention.

Ilias straightened. "What kind of something?"

"She wanted a seat at the table. Not just a voice. A real seat. She wanted to be Donna of the Five Families. That had been her true goal, according to Val's father. He had kept journals, but Valentino said he'd had a soft spot for her." Just the thought of the whole thing turned my stomach, not because she had the ambition to be head of a mafia, but because she had tried to connive her way there. It was always her game.

A beat of stunned silence followed.

"Insanity," Maxim said flatly. "She wouldn't have gotten that far."

The Five Families in New York City had always represented the traditional Italian mafia: the Santellis, the Cardonis, the Olivetos, the Scarpatos, and the Vanellos. They had never agreed to unite under a single don and scarcely agreed on anything else. Only out of necessity did they meet occasionally to stave off other organized crime groups. This discord was part of the reason other families were so upset when my father signed the blood oath with the Irish, the Bratva, and the Greeks. It had long been an assumed and unwritten law that the Five Families were bound together, so they were unpleasantly surprised by what my father did.

Still, if they united under anyone, I'd be hard pressed to think it would be a woman, especially back then. The mafia world was sexist — even I would admit that. It was unusual to find crews that were run by women.

"No," I agreed. "But she's always been smart. She gets into people's heads. Manipulates. Think about it. Vallone. Cardoni. Santelli. Those are the ones we know of." If I knew her, she had also been in bed with the others. Oliveto and Scarpato. Francesca was Vallone's daughter. Santelli was infertile. It made me wonder if she had gotten pregnant on purpose by two of the other dons to have Remo and me...

"Jesus," Conall said, his eyes narrowing.

"It gets worse," I said, reaching for the file Maxim had brought. I flipped through the pages until I found the property list. "Valentino gave us this. He suspects they've been using some of their remote holdings as meeting points. Private homes, warehouses. Places even he's not regularly in."

I tapped one address near the bottom. "This one's in Long Island. High walls. Private security. No digital footprint. He hasn't been out there in over a year."

Maxim grunted. "Renzetti could be using it to regroup. Or worse—coordinate with others."

Ilias's hands curled into fists. "He's already taken shots at our ports and tried to shake down some of my warehouses in Astoria. And that thing with the Greek trucking company? That wasn't random."

"He's testing our defenses," I said. "Looking for weak spots."

"And you think Carlotta's with him," Maxim said. "Still running the show."

"I know she is. Salvatore doesn't breathe without her say-so. He's too erratic on his own. But with her calling the plays, he's a goddamn scalpel. Precise, ruthless, and patient."

They all looked at me. I exhaled and leaned back in my chair. "We need to search the Cardoni properties. Quietly. We also need to keep an eye on anyone who has ever worked for Carlotta in the past. Housekeepers. Drivers. Her old lawyer. Every name she ever touched."

"She's not just trying to come back," Conall said. "She's trying to rule."

"She's trying to rewrite the hierarchy," Maxim added. The men fell silent again.

I never liked this part of the job, but I had become good at it—cold strategy. I'd done it since I was sixteen. It came easily now. Too easy. What didn't come easily was how my thoughts drifted back to Theo, asleep in bed when I'd left this morning, how her hair had smelled when I bent down to kiss her forehead before I left this morning: lavender and something warm, like sunlight.

I hadn't told the guys about that. I didn't need to. They already knew I was slipping. Or maybe they didn't. Perhaps they just thought I was tired. Distracted. Working too hard.

But I wasn't just tired.

I was fucking terrified.

Because Theo wasn't like any other woman I'd known. She wasn't a liability. She was fire and silk and grief and defiance, all wrapped in her wild, impulsive mind that could turn my world upside down with a look.

And for the first time, I didn't want to win by crushing the opposition. I wanted her to come to me because she *chose* me.

Because even though we'd shared a bed

283

now, even though her body still haunted my sheets... I didn't have her heart.

Not yet.

"You sure this is the right play?" Ilias asked, drawing me back.

"It's the only one," I said. "We find the bitch. We end this."

Maxim gave a sharp nod. "Then let's get to work. We'll get ourselves together and get it done."

———

Hours later, I pulled into the driveway of the brownstone. The windows glowed warmly behind the wrought-iron fencing, and the porch light was still on. Norris kept the place humming like clockwork—meals prepped, sheets changed, security tight. But it wasn't the house I was thinking about. It was her.

I stepped inside, loosening my collar. The scent of roasted vegetables and honeyed tea lingered in the air.

Norris met me in the hallway with a knowing look. "Miss Theo's in her studio. She fell asleep there again." He hesitated, then added, "She looked tired. Quiet today, but she's back at work. Started sketching this afternoon. That's a good sign. She seemed happier. Miss Frankie came over."

That made me feel a little better. I knew that I was happier. Things seemed to be slowly moving towards a resolution. We had a plan in place. Conall's man, Gallagher, was collecting intel on some locations, while we had Kostas and Veronica covering the others. By morning, we should have a few spots to target with multiple teams. They were fishing expeditions at best, but hopefully, we'd catch something in the nets we were casting.

Maxim's contacts with the cartels in Belize and Honduras had yielded nothing. Renzetti wasn't there. He had managed to evade the massive operation we set up to find him. My hunch still suggested he was holed up somewhere with Carlotta. I was banking on it.

My chest tightened. I nodded and made my way toward the studio until I found her collapsed on the chaise with her sketchbook limp in her hand. Gathering her in my arms, I carried her upstairs, tucking her between the covers. Stripping off my jacket, I joined her, savoring the feel of her body next to mine, but I stared at the ceiling as I ran through what was ahead.

Carlotta. Renzetti. War on the horizon. I

didn't know if I could protect Theo from the crossfire.

But God help me, I was going to try.

CHAPTER 30
THEODOSIA

THE DREAM WAS HAZY, like floating as you struggled to consciousness, pulling yourself forward to a reality you weren't sure you wanted when the fantasy was so delicious. That's what this must have been—a fantasy. I spread my legs farther, the ache building to a crescendo as I opened my eyes.

Angelo watched me as he slid his fingers into me. "What were you dreaming about, hmm? You were squirming in your sleep just begging for my cock."

The words sent a shiver of delight through me. "I'm guessing you started already." I looked pointedly at his hand that moved lazily over his engorged shaft that already leaked with evidence of how aroused he was. "Maybe I was dreaming of you."

"I like that, and yes. I started already. I wanted you all day." I squirmed on his fingers.

I liked that, too. The fact that he wanted me, and the fact that the evidence of it was right there. The validation that he found me sexy. I wanted this to be combustible for both of us. The thought of him between my thighs while I slept was somehow taboo, and at the same time a total turn-on.

"Good. Too bad I woke up. Maybe I'll pretend to keep sleeping next time, and you can keep going with your fantasy. Stuff me full." I watched him carefully as his eyes dilated and his lips parted, his breath coming in short pants. *Oh*, he liked that idea. "You could slide your cock inside me and come and I'd never even wake up. You want me to have your baby, don't you? You'll need to try extra hard even if you come home late." He pumped his shaft, squeezing it so hard that pre-cum spilled over the edge. My pussy clenched as I watched him.

"Those are dangerous words, *piccola*."

"I mean them." I had felt better today, stronger. My shoulder felt better, and I had hardly touched him at all. That wasn't fair. Moving to straddle him, I knocked his hands away. "Let me." Bending to kiss him, I inhaled his scent, that familiar combination of his that felt like home to me, even with the smoke and gun oil that constantly swirled around him. Tracing my lips over his earlobes I followed the path of his neck, like he had done to me, learning each spot, taking my time even as my pussy ached.

"Baby," he groaned as I teased his nipples with my tongue. "I need you."

His cock slid between my folds, and I rocked against it as I explored the feeling of his shaft sliding against the sensative skin there. It felt exquisite against my clit. His eyes had fluttered shut, and I ran a hand to the juncture of our thighs where his cock was trapped flat to his belly. He wasn't the only needy one, but I was willing to draw it out a little. The man was beautiful in that dangerous, carved-from-stone, sinner-in-a-suit sort of way. His lashes were absurdly long for someone so capable of murder. He had only one tattoo, right up against his rib cage. Right now, he was vulnerable and all mine.

Not the fancy kind. Not like the dramatic sprawling pieces I always imagined mafia dons got in their twenties after too much tequila and a hit gone wrong. This was clean.

Intentional. Fine-lined. Small, near the curve of his heart, just over his ribcage.

Non serviam

I leaned in, licking the words and letting my fingers ghost over the letters as I continued rocking my pelvis, using his cock to edge closer to an orgasm. The ink was sharp against his warm skin. Black. Not new, but not faded. Old enough to mean something, permanent enough to sting still.

I retraced the edge of a letter, fascinated and aching all at once. "It's Latin."

"Mm. *Piccola*, we can talk about it later." He rocked against me as his fingers dug into my flesh, his shaft peeking between our bodies. "Let me in." I could barely pay attention as he said, "It means, *'I will not serve.'*"

"That's very dramatic of you," I teased softly, but it lacked the usual sharpness. "Even for you." My focus was on how he felt against me, but my fingers splayed over the tattoo and his heart.

He cracked one eye open and looked at me. "It's a reminder."

"Of?"

His jaw flexed. "That no one owns me. Not my blood. Not the Commission. Not the past."

I didn't say anything. Just kept looking at the words, the smooth, warm expanse of his skin, the muscle twitching beneath my fingers. I pressed my lips there, to kiss away the ghosts I knew clung to those words.

"You know," I whispered against his skin, "you could've chosen something more hopeful. Like… *hope*, or *live, laugh, love*."

Unable to wait anymore I slid onto his cock and groaned, savoring the feel of the stretch.

"Hmmm," He gave a rough chuckle and anchored my hips, driving up into me. "Not allowing a tattoo needle anywhere near me again. Conall might say it doesn't hurt, but he's a liar."

Keeping one hand on his chest I put the other on my clit, rubbing it hard. I wasn't sure that I would be able to come like this. I needed more. Needed him powering over me. My shoulder still wasn't a hundred percent. I whined a little as I slid against him, trying to find my rhythm.

"I need more," I whimpered.

Rolling us to my back, he angled back in. "Like this?" He searched my face.

"Yes, but harder. I want it harder."

He obliged, grinning like a maniac as his

shaft hit even deeper as he pulled my knees up. Each strike, his pelvis hit mine, bone to bone, grinding against mine before pulling away and hammering back again over and over in an unforgiving rhythm, even after the first blinding orgasm swept over me, he didn't stop, but kept pistoning into me, watching my face closely, teeth gritted. "Again. Again. Give me another one."

"I can't. I can't." Tears sprang to my eyes as he readjusted my legs and seemed to find his way even deeper.

"You can. You will," he said fiercely. "*Then* I'm going to come."

Amazingly, another orgasm began sweeping over me, the sensations I was chasing that had seemed impossible were right there as he pushed me further until he crashed against me. I fell against the cushions, my legs clasped around him as he came hard, jetting into me until I felt warmth against my thighs.

We were quiet for a while, limbs tangled, hearts syncing. But I couldn't stop thinking about that ink. About what it meant. About who he'd been when he got it—and the fact that I was seeing a piece of him that no one else had. A private rebellion etched into his skin.

Sunlight filtered in like a slow exhale, dappled and golden through the half-closed curtains. I blinked against it, the warmth pulling me from the depths of sleep and into something softer.

Angelo hadn't moved much. Still sprawled on his side, a hand draped lazily across my stomach, his breath steady against the back of my neck.

I stayed still for a long time. Listening. Remembering his explanation of his tattoo.

Non serviam.

The way his voice went low when he said it, like he was speaking to someone long dead.

I couldn't stop thinking about it. About him. About how someone so feared, so ruthlessly *in charge*, could carry a piece of his defiance like a shield over his heart.

I'd seen that side of him last night— unguarded. The man beneath the suits and the silence. There were still remnants of the boy who had once been forced to serve things he hadn't believed in. Who had sworn he never would again.

It rattled around in my ribs, how much that small piece of ink said. How much he hadn't said outright. Because that was Angelo: he didn't *explain* things. He just did them. Quietly. Decisively. With the kind of control that made people afraid and kept his empire intact.

I turned slowly in his arms, careful not to wake him. He looked younger in the light. Still dangerous—always—but less like a wolf on the prowl and more like one resting between battles. His lashes cast faint shadows on his cheeks. His lips were parted, his chest rising in slow, steady beats. My gaze drifted, unbidden, to that tattoo again.

I will not serve.

What would it mean when someone like Angelo Santelli chose to stay? Not because he owed you. Not because of some family deal or obligation, but because he *wanted* to. Last night was more than comfort. More than heat and softness in the dark. It was a shift—a confession without words.

And that scared me more than the bullets or a kidnapping ever did.

Because what if this didn't last? What if I screwed this up? What if *he* pulled away again? Because the reality had hit me last night. I had never stopped loving Angelo, and I wasn't sure my heart could take him not loving me back.

He stirred then, just slightly, his fingers flexing on my hip. "You're staring," he murmured, voice thick with sleep.

"You're dreaming," I retorted.

"Bout you, probably." His eyes opened. "You okay?"

I nodded, then hesitated. "Yeah. Just thinking."

He reached up and tucked a piece of hair behind my ear. "Dangerous habit."

"I know." I stared at his chest again. At the black ink etched into him. "How old were you when you got it?"

He followed my gaze, his mouth twitching. "Fifteen." He shrugged, but it was a tired, weighted thing. "It was the first choice I made that no one else touched. I paid for it with cash I earned. Went alone. No guards. No driver. Just me. In the middle of the night." His gaze slanted towards the windows, as if remembering. "I didn't tell any of the guys about it. It was just for me."

I imagined him—young, raw, hard-eyed and angry, marching into some dingy tattoo parlor like he had something to prove to the world and himself.

"You wanted to take something back," I said softly.

He met my eyes then, something sharp and honest in his. "Exactly."

We fell silent once more. The heaviness enveloped us like another blanket. I reached out and brushed my fingers over the words again. "So what does it mean now?"

Angelo exhaled through his nose. "It means I still choose. Every day. No matter what this life demands of me... I choose." A beat. "And right now, I'm choosing to stay in this bed with you," he added, lips curving as he tugged me closer. "So, unless you're about to get philosophical again, kiss me."

It started light. Sweet. But his hands slid up my back, deliberate and slow, and that familiar tension thrummed to life beneath my skin. He kissed like he did everything else— with purpose. With possession. Yet, it felt different now. He wasn't just taking. He was *giving*. And I felt it everywhere.

When we finally broke apart, breathless and warm, I pressed my forehead to his. "You know, if you keep making it this easy to fall for you, I might stop being mad at you."

He grinned. "That's a tragedy I'm willing to risk." He gave me a wicked smile as he slid inside me. "You did say I needed to work hard." He groaned. "*Piccola*, you're always such a good girl. Spread those thighs."

As I followed his instructions, I thought, If this was how he was going to wake me up, then I would be agreeing to marry him in no time.

CHAPTER 31
ANGELO

A-HOLE *Chat*

> Conall: Gallagher has something on that Long Island property. It looks hot. There's definitely someone staying there. We have at least one person there, accompanied by perimeter guards.

> Maxim: We should hit it.

> Ilias: Agreed. If there is any chance that Renzetti or Carlotta are there, we need to take it.

> Me: Agreed.

> Maxim: One hour?

Conall: One and a half

Me: Done

I texted Bacco and Remo to update them, leaving it to Bacco to assemble a squad. It probably wasn't necessary, but I didn't want to take chances and discover that we didn't have enough men.

———

The property was nestled deep in the woods of Long Island—the kind of place you had to know already existed to find it. No digital footprint. No paper trail. It wasn't listed directly under Valentino Cardoni's name, but it was his. Old money. Old secrets. Valentino had specified that this property had been in his family since his father's days, when Carlotta was still around. The property was under his aunt's maiden name, which was quite clever.

I had given Val a heads-up yesterday that we'd be checking this place out. He replied that we had carte blanche with what we found and how we proceeded. I wouldn't forget that. For all he knew, we were planning to blow the place up. Hell, Remo did bring enough C4 for that.

The house was set back behind twelve-foot stone walls, covered in creeping ivy and flanked by massive iron gates. Private security patrolled the perimeter—not the usual rent-a-cop types, either. These guys wore earpieces and moved with military precision. I clocked at least four snipers in the trees and another six guards at the front and rear entries.

Maxim, Ilias, Conall, and I crouched behind the treeline with our teams. Bacco and Remo had protested that they weren't here, but I'd sent them to another Cardoni property outside of Jersey, which had been a bust. The air was cold, sharp with the tang of pine and damp earth. My gloved hands rested on the grip of my H&K. My pulse was steady.

"Looks like he's been preparing," Ilias muttered beside me, scanning the walls through a scope.

"Preparing to die if that fucker is in there," Maxim growled.

Conall nodded at me. "Your call."

"Let's go." I gave the signal. This was one of my favorite moments— the feeling right before the fight, just before we struck someone who was unaware we lurked nearby. My adrenaline surged, my heartbeat pounding, my friends at my back — it was thrilling every time.

Two of our men fired silencers at men who were stationed near the trees. The snipers were dropped without a sound. Another team took out the rear patrol. Then all hell broke loose.

We swarmed the gates, breaching with small charges that blew them open with a thunderous groan of twisted metal. I was the first through, my boots crunching gravel as we stormed the courtyard.

Gunfire erupted from the second floor. I dove behind a stone fountain, returning fire as Maxim's team flanked left. The bastards were entrenched, utilizing the balcony and upper windows for cover, but it wouldn't save them.

"Suppressing!" Conall shouted, unloading a full clip.

I ran low along the wall, flung a flashbang through the main entrance, then barreled in after it exploded. The front hall was chaos—a guard staggered toward me, half-blinded. I dropped him with a shot to the throat. Another lunged with a knife. I spun, disarmed him, and slammed his head into the marble wall.

Ilias followed behind me, with Kostas and Vaso. They were methodical, cold, and moved like a storm—no wasted motion, delivering clean headshots. The Anthakos brothers were a force I wouldn't want to mess with, but I was glad we were on the same side.

"Clear the upper floor!" I barked into the comms.

We stormed the staircase. Maxim kicked in door after door. We found two more guards and a man who appeared to be a financier, attempting to delete files from a laptop. I shot the floor near him first. Then I turned the barrel to him.

"Where is he?"

"Gone, I don't know, I swear—"

I shot him in the leg. "Wrong answer."

"Basement! There's a panic room—"

"Show me."

He limped down the hall, bleeding onto the wood floors. We followed a tight formation, weapons up. He led us to a nondescript door behind a wine rack in the kitchen. High-end shit. Climate-controlled.

"Biometric lock," he stammered, like that would stop us. This wasn't the fucking movies where we needed some code breaker or a thumb print. Most walls were made just of 2x4s and crappy sheetrock.

Maxim didn't wait. He shot him in the head and planted a charge on the doorframe. We ducked back as it exploded in a fireball of plaster and smoke. It was easy as pie to kick a hole big enough to walk through. Sure enough, Renzetti cowered inside. His toad-like appearance was immediately recognizable.

He was huddled in a corner, armed with a Uzi that it was obvious he didn't know how to use. He opened fire immediately, but the live rounds pinged off the walls. I ducked, rolled, and flanked hard right. Conall tossed a flashbang. We moved in.

I shot him once in the shoulder, then a second time in the thigh to drop him. He screamed, dropped the weapon, and tried to crawl.

"You think you can burn my businesses? You think you can touch my family?" I growled.

He coughed up blood. "Your mother—she lied to you. She used us both."

"Where is she?"

"I don't know. She's always ten steps ahead. She was here, but she's gone." His face was pinched with pain. "I could help you. I could be useful."

I believed him. Too bad Veronica and

Kostas had already broken into his network and accessed the trafficking data. They had enough to shut it down. Most of it had run through a computerized transactional site on the dark web. Kostas would be sifting through names and locations that we might be able to go after, but we didn't need this joker. I shot him once more, right between the eyes—the silence after was deafening.

Conall exhaled. "One down."

"Not the one I want." It made me grumpy.

"Man." Conall kicked the body. "You're so testy. You should be on Cloud Nine looking to have a smoke and a fuck after this, and you're whining." He shot me a wink. "Cheer up."

We swept the rest of the property and found rooms full of maps, blueprints, and burner phones. A wall displayed photos of me, Maxim, Ilias, and Conall. On another board were high-value targets: Cora, Cora holding little Vasily, Francesca, Theodosia, Polina, and another woman turned away from the camera, her hoodie pulled up to cover most of her face. It was chilling to see the detailed photos of the women in our lives, and the focal point that had been put on them.

I didn't need to look at the others to know they were just as pissed as I was. As expected, it only took a moment before Maxim erupted, pointing at one of the pictures of his wife and son. "What the fuck is this?"

"Canvassing their targets most likely," I said sourly. "Looking for weak spots." I rubbed a finger over my lips, thinking, before tapping the woman with the hoodie and turning to the others. "Who's this?"

"Galena. Even they couldn't spot her. Good girl." Ilias began to remove the photos from the board methodically. "Go see what else you fuckers can find."

Maxim gave Ilias a dirty look, but followed me out of the room. "So, your half-sister seems a little wily."

"Yeah, I checked on her years ago. Things seemed good. She was living with her mother and a new stepdad, an all-around good guy. There was no reason to get in contact with her at that point. She knew nothing of the bratva life, and her mother seemed to be keeping it that way. She has been going to school and work. Fuck, she even walks to school. I didn't want to disrupt it. Once we decided to go forward with the blood oath," he hesitated, but I knew immediately what he meant. "I knew it'd have to change, but I thought she could be normal for a while."

He'd hoped somewhere deep down that

maybe Galena would get to skip out on being tied back into the criminal world we inhabited. Maybe she'd be able to breathe free, but that wasn't meant to be. Her fate had been written twenty years ago.

"Look at this." I poked at the walk-in closet. High-end women's clothing. Italian designers. Expensive. Classic. My mother's taste. A half-drunk glass of red wine on the nightstand. A cigarette still smoldering in a crystal ashtray.

She'd been here. Probably less than an hour ago.

Maxim stood beside me, arms crossed. "What now?"

I stared at the clothes. At the wine. "We'll keep looking. We've taken one of her toys. We just need to keep kicking the cans."

"Agreed." He stared glumly at the ashtray. "She had pictures of Cora, and it looks like Galena is on the run, which means she knows something is up." He ran a hand over the back of his neck. "I was stupid to think she could have just a few more years of normal life. I'd thought maybe she'd …"

"She'd what?" I snapped. "She'd get married? Then what? She was already promised. You knew that."

"I know. She was just happy. She was a

happy kid with regular parents living in a little house that seemed normal. Nothing like ours. It was nice. Quiet. Why shouldn't she have that? I thought maybe Ilias would dig his heels in, maybe refuse."

It wasn't a ridiculous fantasy, but it was still a pipedream that made me irrationally angry. "Let's go tell the others what we found. We need to regroup and call in the cleaners." I ground my teeth together and forced myself not to say anything to him about Galena. It wasn't my place anyway.

CHAPTER 32
THEODOSIA

I SAT on the sofa in the studio Angelo had set up for me, limbs stiff from falling asleep in a position not sanctioned by any chiropractor. Naps still seemed to be part of my repertoire these days, but I told myself they were a form of healing. That was my story, and I was sticking to it.

My sketchpad had slid to the floor beside a sprawl of pencils, fabric swatches, and the remnants of a bag of lemon drops that I'd been rationing like wartime supplies. Despite the chaos, something electric hummed in my veins. Design ideas had come flooding back last night like an old friend I'd ghosted and missed terribly.

"Alright, alright, let's get to it," I muttered, tying my curls into a haphazard bun and stretching until my shoulder protested. It still twinged, a dull reminder of the bullet that had torn through it, but it had healed significantly. The wound was puckered and no longer raw. I was stronger now—healing, restless, and ready to claw my way back into the design world.

Mythos Designs, the New York version ... I hummed and called Vivienne on video, hoping she wasn't in the middle of something. Her face popped up immediately, all sleek black bangs and bright green glasses. "Theo! You're alive! Oh, thank God. I was about to start designing mourning veils."

I laughed. "I *was* dead for a minute there, I think." I hadn't shared the details with her, but she had the basics and knew that I had been kidnapped.

She rolled her eyes dramatically. "Well, I assume you called because your fingers have started twitching to sketch again?"

"Girl, I am ready to take over the world. Just need a decent assistant on this side of the ocean. I can't keep texting you at three a.m. your time. You'll start resenting me, and I can't have that."

Vivienne winked. "Already do, love. But it's a sexy resentment."

Narrowing my eyes at the screen, I considered, "Unless you're willing to move over here?"

"Nice try, and I'm flattered - but pass. I'm sticking to my side of the ocean, but you need someone to keep you on track. I agree with that."

We caught up for a bit—she discussed her latest intern disaster, the bizarre fashion trend she was raging against, and a quick analysis of Milan's recent couture week, which we both decided was too beige for our souls.

"I think it's time you rooted yourself in New York," she said, twirling a stylus like a weapon. "Start small. A pop-up or a capsule collection. You've got eyes on you now."

"Yeah," I said softly, my voice hitching slightly. "But I need to know it's safe. That it's *real*."

Vivienne's brow arched, her gaze piercing through the screen. "Is this about what happened in Florence?"

I nodded. "The way those clients pulled out... I've never stopped thinking it was fishy. But I couldn't prove it. And I didn't want to believe—"

My phone buzzed with a notification for a video call. *Veronica Petrova Walters.*

"Hang on," I told Vivienne. "I think I've got a hacker on line two."

Vivienne shrieked with delight. "Oh my God, answer it! Sounds very glamorous. We'll catch up later."

A cool, striking blonde in a deep blue tattered t-shirt that made her eyes pop appeared at a desk piled with papers and multiple monitors glowing behind her as I accepted the call. She was stunning in a petite, waifish way. Designing clothes for her would be so much fun.

"And you're Theo," she said with a smile, with none of the Russian accent I expected.

"That's me," I said, squinting. "And you are?" Although I already knew who she was. She was one of those women who skirted the mafia world. She had their respect, and I respected the hell out of that. Angelo mentioned Veronica, and so did Kostas when I texted him earlier today.

"Veronica Walters. Maxim's cousin. Kostas and Angelo asked me to look into something for you."

I knew Kostas would have contacted her, but my heart skipped a beat when I realized Angelo had taken the time to message her. "Angelo? He didn't tell me."

She smiled faintly. "He likes to protect you. I did tell him I'd need to tell you, since I prefer full disclosure. We'll meet at some point, so things can't be anonymous. After all, Max is family." Her eyes crinkled around the edges, and I searched for a resemblance to the icy Russian that I grew up fearing, but came up short. She looked nothing like him. "I've been digging into the abrupt collapse of your client base in Florence. At first glance, it appeared to be market shifts, personality conflicts, and perhaps some garden-variety envy. But when I peeled back a few layers, I found fingerprints."

My pulse quickened. "Whose?" I asked, but I already knew the answer.

"Exactly who we suspected. Carlotta's." Veronica forked a spoonful of cottage cheese into her mouth, humming a little as she did so, and I had to suppress a little shiver. I hated the stuff.

Hearing it was vindication. At least there wasn't anything I had done wrong. There had been months of anxiety during which impostor syndrome had wreaked havoc on my psyche. Now I knew it was part of what-ever game Carlotta was playing.

"She orchestrated a subtle campaign," Veronica continued, clicking something on her keyboard. "Anonymous reviews. Discreet emails to investors suggesting to buyers that you had connections to certain... controversial figures. And more directly, she threatened two of your early backers. I have logs."

"What a bitch."

"I don't think she intended to ruin you," she said. "She wanted you out of Florence. Off balance. Vulnerable. Initially, it looks like she wanted you back in New York with Angelo. That's what it appears to me. Then she changed tactics with the whole kidnapping scheme — but that looks like it was all a minor distraction."

I laughed, but it came out hollow. "Didn't seem minor to me."

"Of course not. I didn't mean it that way." Veronica's lips twitched. "She's ambitious. Twisted. But intelligent. What she didn't account for is that once you root yourself somewhere new, you bloom."

I ran my fingers over the edge of my sketchpad. "I thought I was paranoid. I told myself I was imagining it. The whole 'someone is out to get you' thing."

She forked more cottage cheese into her mouth and then spoke around it. "Paranoia is just pattern recognition with a bad PR rep."

I barked out a laugh. "God, you're dramatic."

"I'm Russian. It's a birthright."

"True." Tapping a pencil on my sketch

pad, I considered. "I appreciate you taking the time to look into it. It's been something that messed with my head. Now I can think about moving forward and how I want to do that."

"Your work is amazing. I'm sure you'll be able to start fresh, but I have gone through and scrubbed what I could regarding negative reviews or emails. I'd recommend a mini-PR campaign with whatever you do going forward. If you send it to me, I can give it a boost through certain avenues."

"That'd be great. And thank you, really. Hey, you wouldn't model on the side, would you?"

Her eyes widened. "Uh, no. I've ..." Her mouth opened and then closed. "I appreciate it, truly. It's better to keep a low profile in this lifestyle if you know what I mean." I did know exactly what she meant and hadn't thought about having photos out there of myself. I guess I needed to.

We ended the call after she forwarded her findings to me. I sat stunned for a few minutes, reflecting on everything Carlotta had done. It had been calculated just as Veronica had said. Growing up with Frankie, I'd known that her mom harbored deep-seated hatred and was mean, but this seemed next level. Even I couldn't decide if she was being super-villain smart or just crazy. There had to be some kind of endgame here that we were missing. Was she playing chess while we were playing checkers? Why would she want me back in the States? Initially, she wanted me with Angelo, but when he wouldn't comply, she had me kidnapped ... then this thing with Renzetti?

It was making my head spin. I'd talk it over with Angelo when he got home; there must be an explanation. I exhaled deeply, pushed those thoughts aside, and then leaned over to begin sketching again. The lines flowed more easily now, as if I had carved out the blockage in my chest.

This time, the collection wasn't Florence. It wasn't Athens or Milan or any place I'd been before. It was *now.* It was New York, where there were typically raw edges, high collars, and silhouettes that whispered power and rebellion, but I wasn't designing anything like that.

I was halfway through a preliminary design for an adorable christening outfit when Norris poked his head into the studio.

"Miss Theo, dinner in an hour?"

I looked up, grinning. "Only if there's

dessert. Preferably one that comes in the shape of a pie."

He chuckled, eyes twinkling. "You drive a hard bargain."

As he disappeared, I looked back at my sketchpad and smiled. I'd fallen down the rabbit hole of baby clothes: onesies, little overalls, snaps, and bows. I'd need to conduct some research on suitable materials for infants.

Carlotta had wanted to push me off balance, but all she'd done was end up sending me back where I belonged all along.

To the man who'd gone to war to protect me without saying the words aloud.

But I could feel them. I could feel *him*.

And I wasn't running anymore.

CHAPTER 33
THEODOSIA

I WAS elbow-deep in fabric swatches and doodles when I heard the front door click open downstairs.

I froze, pencil hovering midair, as the wonderland of colors, lines, and textures I'd been lost in for the past few hours flickered away like smoke. For a beat, I sat there blinking at the cotton samples scattered around me, as if I'd been building a nest. Then, Angelo's heavy, unmistakable tread echoed through the house, and my heart did that annoying fluttery thing it had started doing lately.

I flopped back onto the floor dramatically, tossing an arm over my face. "Pull it together, Anthakos," I muttered. "He's just a man. A very large, very broody, occasionally stabby man."

A *clang* from the kitchen indicated where he was headed, and I scrambled up, smoothing down the sailor top and shorts I had changed into earlier—something comfy yet still cute. You know, just in case someone broody and stabby happened to notice.

I padded down the hall, following the warm aromas of baked bread and roasted chicken, feeling like a strange hybrid of a nervous teenager and an old married woman. When I peeked into the kitchen, the sight that greeted me nearly short-circuited my brain.

Angelo Santelli, mafia kingpin extraordinaire, leaned against the counter, talking quietly to Norris, the housekeeper-slash-Alfred-the-Second. He was dressed all in black tactical gear, including a black Henley, black cargo pants, and a holstered weapon at his hip. His dark hair was mussed, his sleeves shoved up to his forearms, and he looked—how was this fair—completely edible. Also, a little bit dangerous, like he could murder someone without breaking a sweat if you said the wrong thing.

Norris caught sight of me first and gave a pleased nod. "Ah, Miss Theo. Just in time."

Angelo's head snapped up, and when his

eyes landed on me, the hard lines of his face softened just a hair. Enough that it felt like he was hauling me right into his orbit with nothing but a look.

"You're home early," I said, stupidly, because duh, Captain Obvious.

"Hi, *piccola*." His voice was rough, like gravel coated in smoke.

We just stared at each other for a second, the warm kitchen around us blurring at the edges. He looked wired. There was a buzz coming off him, like a live current. I wanted to reach out and smooth the crease between his brows and maybe climb him like a tree.

Instead, I hugged myself and leaned against the doorframe. "Long day?"

He huffed a low laugh. "You could say that."

Bless his soul, Norris broke the moment by bustling around to set the small kitchen table—just two plates, a bottle of wine breathing next to them, candles already flickering as if this were *a thing*. I flushed.

"Mr. Santelli called ahead," Norris said with a slight smirk. "Said he wanted something...simple and elegant. There is dessert on the counter. I'll leave you to it." He gave a slight bow and left us with a wink.

Simple. Right. Like anything about this man was ever simple.

I perched on one of the chairs while Angelo washed up, rolling my pencil nervously between my fingers. When he finally sat down across from me, a wall of heat, strength, and something distinctly dangerous radiated off him, and I found myself blurting out, "So, how was work?"

He gave me a look like he wasn't sure if he wanted to laugh or flip the table. Instead, he leaned back in his chair, studying me with those almost hazel eyes. "Well, good news. We found Renzetti."

I blinked. "You did? Renzetti? As in, the guy who's been setting fires and trying to murder everyone? The a-hole who almost sold me off? That's great news." They had been tearing apart every location they could, looking for where he might have scurried off to.

"That's the one," he said grimly, reaching for the breadbasket and tearing off a hunk of crusty loaf. "Found him hiding in a Cardoni property on Long Island. The place was locked down tight. Private security. No digital footprint."

That meant they got him. The thought made something in me relax. The idea that he'd been squatting somewhere nearby and plotting hadn't sat well. I leaned forward, utterly hooked. "But you got him. Was it bad?"

He shrugged one massive shoulder. "Could've been worse. He had some resistance—mercenaries, not real soldiers. Paid men. They scattered the second they realized we weren't screwing around."

I shivered at his casual ruthlessness, but not in fear. His tone was similar to how someone else might describe fixing a broken engine or taking out the trash: efficient and unapologetic.

"And Renzetti?"

Angelo's mouth twisted. "Dead. We tried to get him to talk, but he went down swinging. Kind of."

"Good," I whispered, relieved. Dead was good.

He tore another piece of bread, his hands steady even as a storm brewed in his eyes. "Found signs Carlotta had been there too. Clothes in a guest room closet. Even a glass of wine, but otherwise nothing that could help lead us to her."

I set my chin on my hand, heart thudding. "She's slippery."

"She's worse than slippery, but I'll find her

eventually." His voice darkened. "And Renzetti...he wasn't the brains. He was a pawn. Carlotta's pawn. Always was."

I swallowed. "What now?" I wondered what sort of limbo it left us in, with Carlotta still out there.

He gave me a small, grim smile. "We keep looking. And we tighten security—all of us. But we go on with our lives. I have a feeling that Carlotta will continue to do what she does. We'll get her." There was confidence in every line of his body when he spoke.

"I believe you." I did, too. Angelo wouldn't quit until he figured out her game. Now that he knew she had been in the shadows this whole time, he would focus on using every resource he could to find her.

He reached for his wineglass, swirling the deep red liquid thoughtfully. "Speaking of all of us … I was thinking."

"Uh-oh," I teased, but my heart leapt a little. After everything that had happened, I realized I was ready to move forward with Angelo. Earlier, I had been sketching baby clothes, not only for Frankie but also for myself, potentially. A wedding had been on my mind. Maybe he was going to bring it up?

That earned me the ghost of a genuine smile. "Maybe we could have a family dinner? Like your siblings. Frankie. Conall. Maybe Remo, too."

I straightened, excitement sparking through me even though that wasn't the question I had truly hoped for. "Really?" As a teenager, we always had big family dinners, the quintessential loud Greek family with everyone talking over everyone else. My brothers were unbearably protective, but they were awesome.

He nodded. "It's time. We need a real family dinner. Start acting like what we are."

My chest squeezed, a messy mixture of joy, nerves, and something I wasn't ready to name. "I'd love that."

The corners of his mouth lifted slowly, dangerously, and breathtakingly. "Good. I'll talk to Ilias about it and see what day is good. Perhaps you could call his cook? She's pretty great. You want to do Greek?"

Evgenia was a fantastic cook, and she had been with our family for many years. She'd make you cry over her food, and I loved her kataifi. I wondered if I could convince her to make it for me. The honeyed dessert was one of Polina's and my favorites. The thought of my sister brought a poignant pang. I missed her terribly.

After that, we ate in a warm bubble of

almost normalcy, with the candlelight casting golden highlights in his hair and the kitchen feeling cozy around us. I told him about my day, how I'd spent the morning on a call with Vivienne.

"She thinks I should hire a New York assistant," I said, waving my fork, but I watched him cautiously for his reaction. "Someone to help me get set up here." Mafia men had certain views about their wives working, and I knew that was where we were headed: the altar. This was the make-or-break moment for Angelo—how he handled my work.

He nodded, approving. "Smart. What do you think about that?"

"I haven't decided yet how to proceed. If I want to have the same sort of setup, or focus online? I could do a pop-up now and then. That would involve less commitment."

"Whatever makes you happy, *piccola*. You're very talented. I would never want you to stop doing what you love." Taking a sip of wine, he paused briefly before adding, "You know that funding isn't an issue. Whatever you need."

His response was perfect. Open-ended and generous. "Thank you. I'll think about it. And—" I hesitated, biting my lip.

He immediately picked up on it, setting down his fork and giving me his full attention. "And?"

"And I got a call from someone today. Veronica called."

"Right." His brows lifted. "Maxim's cousin. She occasionally works for us. For me. I talked to her about the situation with your business. The suspicions that I had."

"Yeah. She...uh, she said she works with you sometimes. On, you know, intelligence and hacking and super spy stuff."

He chuckled, low and dark. "Sounds about right."

I toyed with the stem of my wineglass. "She looked into everything—my label...back in Florence. I thought I'd just failed, or maybe someone was badmouthing me. But it wasn't that."

After the phone call, I reflected on what she'd said and the undeniable wave of relief that followed. When I was little, I struggled with people's perceptions of me—not just how I looked, but also how I acted. Putting my designs into the world was an internal battle for my art. As I grew older, I made a conscious effort to reclaim my power, navigating the world as if others' opinions didn't affect me. I didn't want to be someone who was impacted by someone else's words. What I thought mattered. However, when everything ground to a halt, it had become hard to maintain that inner calm. This felt like vindication.

His gaze sharpened. "What was it?"

I swallowed. "It was Carlotta. Like you thought." He went utterly still. "She was pulling strings," I said softly. "Threatening clients. Blackmailing. Making sure no one wanted to work with me. It wasn't about the business. It was about...moving me like a chess piece."

The silence stretched heavy and taut between us.

"I'm sorry," he said finally, his voice rough with anger. "You didn't deserve that."

"No." I smiled, sad and small. "But it's over now. And honestly? It just makes me more determined to succeed. Reminds me that I can't let things like that slow me down, or change who I am."

He leaned forward, elbows on the table, those dark eyes burning into mine. "You *will* succeed, Theodosia. I'll help you make damn sure of it."

I believed him in a way that transcended reason, logic, or common sense. Maybe I was insane. Maybe I was falling for a mafia don with blood on his hands and a fortress around his heart. But in that moment, with the candles flickering and his hand reaching across the table to close gently over mine, I didn't care.

I was exactly where I was supposed to be.

With him.

CHAPTER 34
ANGELO

IT STARTED with lamb roasting in the kitchen.

And the scent of oregano, garlic, and lemon was so thick in the air that it practically dragged you by the nose. I stepped into the brownstone and nearly got tackled by the wall of heat and noise. Someone had cracked open the windows to let the scent spill onto the street, and if the entire block didn't show up at our door in the next hour demanding a plate, I'd be shocked.

Norris looked frazzled but determined, manning the stove like a general. He wasn't alone either. Standing beside him, barking orders in rapid-fire Greek, was Evgenia — the Anthakos' family cook. A terrifying five-foot-nothing woman built like a fireplug and capable of feeding an entire army without breaking a sweat.

When I entered the kitchen, she gave me a once-over, as if she were assessing a side of beef. "You're too thin," she declared in heavily accented English. "Sit! Eat! Before you waste away!"

I blinked. Norris smothered a grin behind his apron.

"You let her take over?" I asked him dryly. Norris typically managed our house as if he owned it himself, so I was surprised. He didn't like anyone else in his kitchen.

"I'm not suicidal, sir," Norris muttered under his breath.

Fair enough.

The counters were buried under platters —slow-roasted lamb, crisp-skinned lemon potatoes, grilled vegetables, bowls of tzatziki and hummus, and fresh pita piled high. The centerpiece was a massive moussaka, with layers of eggplant, beef, and golden, bubbling béchamel. There was a cucumber, tomato, and feta salad, as well as olive dishes and fresh shrimp platters with their shells on. I'd eaten at the Anthakos household a few times, and it was exactly what I expected, just on a bigger scale. If push came to shove, I'd even have to admit that Greek food was the absolute bomb. The flavors were out of this world.

Spanakopita big enough to feed an army, wine flowing like we had stock in the vineyard. Norris had even lit a few extra candles and dug out real linen napkins, like we were hosting the Pope and not a bunch of bloodthirsty criminals and the women who loved them.

It was chaos. It was insane.

It was *perfect*.

I spotted Theo darting between the kitchen and the dining nook, laughing as she tried to steal a slice of spanakopita before Evgenia could slap her hand away with a wooden spoon.

My heart squeezed hard. This. Right here. Was the life I hadn't even realized I wanted. Family. Food. Laughter.

The brownstone buzzed with noise and heat, everyone packed into the kitchen and adjoining dining nook like we were just any other big dysfunctional family. Laughter mixed with clinking glasses. Someone—probably Theo—had managed to sneak on music low in the background, something French and flirty that made the whole place feel like a snapshot from a life I didn't know I wanted until recently.

Theo floated through the chaos in one of those dresses she designed herself, some flowy thing that clung to her hips and whispered around her ankles like it had secrets. She laughed at something Vaso said—probably something wildly inappropriate—and bumped her hip against Ilias, who was mock-arguing with Evgenia over a piece of pita bread.

For the first time in a long damn while, my house felt like a home.

Theo caught me staring and grinned, mischief lighting up her whole face. Her hair was pulled up messily into those Princess Leia buns that I liked. I imagined a little girl with those buns, and the thought made my heart explode.

She looked like a painting come to life.

"Don't just stand there, Santelli!" she called. "We need someone to taste test before Evgenia poisons us all!"

Evgenia shot her a scandalized look and muttered something that sounded suspiciously like a threat to turn Theo into stew.

I chuckled low in my chest and made my way to her. "You're trouble," I said under my breath as I passed, brushing my fingers lightly along her lower back, then down towards the cleft of her buttocks.

"Always," she said sweetly, squirming under my touch. "Angelo," she protested, as my fingers slid cupped one cheek and squeezed.

"Hmmm." I kissed her neck, giving it a little lick before pulling away reluctantly. The dinner had been my suggestion, but now I wanted some alone time. "Later then," I promised.

I didn't even pretend to resist, but let myself be pulled into the whirlwind of setting the table, pouring drinks, and stealing bites of food when the women weren't looking.

Frankie and Conall arrived next, with Remo swaggering behind them, arms full of wine bottles and a paper-wrapped package from some bakery he swore was the best in the city. He didn't even blink when Evgenia scolded him for bringing dessert, smacking him with a spoon.

"We are having Theo's favorite! Not some store-bought cardboard dessert from the corner." The woman frowned at him and looked as though she might do him serious harm.

Remo held up his hands in surrender, his eyes laughing. I wasn't sure he knew what kataifi was, but he was in for a treat. If someone pressed me to explain what it was

332

made of, I'd struggle to say, but they resembled little crispy bird nests filled with walnuts. Almost like traditional baklava, except the phyllo dough was shredded. It was delicious at any rate. Theo looked excited about it, and that was all that mattered to me.

It wasn't long before everyone was crammed at the dining room table, balancing plates and glasses, passing dishes over heads, arguing, laughing, and insulting each other as if it were a competitive sport.

Somewhere in the middle of it, I caught Maxim giving me a smug look over his wine glass.

I ignored him.

Mostly.

The smug fucker was probably beside himself with the knowledge that I had come over to the dark side and given up my resentment about this blood oath arrangement. The funniest part—the sickest part of it all—was that I had. Even if the origins of the blood oath still ate at me a little, there was so much of me that was thankful I had ended up here in this place.

Later, after Evgenia had pronounced herself satisfied with our ability to feed ourselves and retreated to the kitchen with

Norris, I grabbed Maxim, Ilias, and Conall for a quick sidebar in my office.

We slipped away without much fanfare, though Theo caught my eye as I passed. Her smile was easy, trusting, and I felt that same bone-deep urge to *protect* her rise up like a tide.

Five minutes. Then I'd be back at her side.

Ilias paced immediately, agitated energy rolling off him. "I've got news."

"About Carlotta?" Maxim asked, lounging against my desk like he didn't have a care in the world.

"Some," Ilias said. "But first—Galena."

Maxim straightened. He'd been on edge since we'd seen the board at the Cardoni property, and I knew that part of that was because his long-lost sister had been on it. I wasn't sure what to make of the fact that there hadn't been a clear shot of her.

My gut tensed. We'd all been dancing around the subject of the blood promise matches lately, too wrapped up in wars and betrayal to think about the future we'd all been chained to before we were even born, but we needed to resolve these matters. Theo and I had told each other we wouldn't hurry, but it would be safer if we finalized the marriage. She'd be better protected that way.

Tonight I had plans to propose. I only hoped she would say yes. Then we needed Ilias to complete his part of the bargain, but that wouldn't work if he couldn't find Galena. Fuck.

Galena... she was a ghost. A question mark. She was supposed to be Ilias's match, but I wasn't even sure that Maxim knew that much about his half-sister. All I knew was that her mother, Maria Yakonova, had been one of Alexei Volkov's mistresses. Maria had taken Galena when she was a toddler and disappeared into New York, new paperwork and everything. Alexei Volkov had been an abusive asshole on the best of days and was known for trafficking women, so her getting as far away as possible with her little girl was the best thing she could have done as a mother.

"It took me a long time to find them," Maxim said, folding his arms. "I checked on her three or four years ago. She was living with her mother and stepfather. Normal neighborhood. He was a schoolteacher. It was obvious Galena didn't know anything about us. I saw no reason to change her circumstances when we hadn't moved on the blood oath. She had been Polina's age. Just finishing up with high school." He looked sheepish. "I meant to contact her after graduation. See if she might have wanted to meet, but she was happy. I wasn't worried about her. Even Maria was different. Nothing like I remembered her. They all seemed very 'Leave it to Beaver.' Normal. You know?"

"Things changed," Ilias said grimly. "Fast."

There was no reason to tell Maxim that he fucked up because it was written all over his face that he knew. Ilias tossed a thin manila folder onto the desk. A handful of surveillance photos spilled out—Galena, but not the carefree girl on her way to college life that Maxim had described.

This Galena looked...haunted. She was a beautiful girl, looking nothing like her broody giant brother, but thin and blond. Very classically Russian.

Tired. Thinner. Her clothes weren't the bright, breezy styles of a student, but muted, functional things. Always always looking over her shoulder, her head covered and face hidden or in profile.

"What the hell happened?" I muttered.

Ilias's mouth was a hard line. "There was some kind of incident on the street with Maria and Galena when they were walking home in the evening about six months ago. They were mugged, and Maria was badly injured." Ilias swallowed before continuing, his throat working. "They had to be transported to the hospital. The records show they were beaten badly. Both of them were assaulted. Maria died."

Maxim swore under his breath. "Was there a police report?" He ground out.

I already knew that we'd be killing some people. Not that I ever minded a little murder.

"Yeah. Already pulled it. Then the stepfather got into debt. He lost his job and had a heart attack." Silence fell like a hammer. Ilias leaned over the desk, fists braced like he wanted to punch a hole through the wood. "She's alone. She was working two jobs. Barely scraping by."

"And she still doesn't know anything?" Conall asked quietly.

"No," Ilias said. His voice cracked on it. "She's clueless, but I can't find her. She must have gotten some kind of hint that people were tailing her because she just vanished."

I stared at the photo of her hurrying through a rain-slicked street, face half-hidden by a scarf. Something cold coiled low in my gut.

My eyes slid over to Maxim, who had his eyes shut as if in pain. "I fucked up. This is totally on me. I should have pulled her out of there and put her in my own home." He scrubbed his hand over his face.

"*Fratello*. You couldn't have known any of this. You aren't a magic eight ball." I tried to comfort him as best I could. How was he supposed to predict what would have happened?

"Angelo is right. You couldn't have known what would happen," Ilias ground out.

There was more he wasn't saying. There was a lot to our lives. It was dangerous. The last month or so was a perfect example. Bringing someone innocent into this mess wasn't something to take lightly. I could see why Maxim had left her in her quiet life for as long as possible, but that wasn't an option anymore. It forced a choice she was never prepared for. I had watched Theo, strong and stubborn as hell, struggle with the knowledge that her path had never been hers to choose. But Theo had grown up in our world, and she'd known that in the end, she'd have no choice because the underworld would come for her family otherwise. This girl didn't have that background knowledge. I wasn't sure how someone like that would react.

"I'll put out feelers. See what we can do

without scaring the fuck out of her, but let's do our best to find her. She isn't safe out there on her own." I clapped a hand on Ilias's shoulder. It went without saying that Carlotta was potentially looking for Galena, which meant we needed to find her first. He nodded, briefly squeezing his hand over mine, and then Maxim dragged us back to business. "We should find out if there is any information on the assault. Maybe see if she's running from the fuckers who were involved?"

"We'll find her," Maxim swore. "There's no way we won't. I'll drag in Veronica to see if she can do some facial recognition shit with traffic cams. Maybe we can get a hit that way."

That was smart. We divided up the people to talk to before addressing our other matter.

"Carlotta," Maxim said, snapping the folder shut. "Let's talk about what we found at the raid." Maxim tossed a slim USB drive onto my desk. "Surveillance photos. Financials."

Ilias leaned in, tension radiating off him. "Carlotta used Renzetti like a shield. Everything he did—the attacks, the hits, the disruptions in the city—was on her orders."

"No real loyalty," Maxim added. "The men he used weren't soldiers. They were mercenaries. Hired guns. And now that he's gone—"

"They're gone too," Ilias finished grimly.

That was interesting. We didn't operate that way in the organized crime world. Our ranks were filled with men we could count on, made men who would die for the *famiglia*. We had assumed that Salvatore (or whoever he was) had been trying to make a bid for the Olivetto mafia. I frowned, picking up the drive and rolling it between my fingers. "Meaning she's exposed. This is an opportunity."

Ilias nodded. "The clothes in the closet weren't just a stopover. There were records hidden in a safe under the floorboards. Coded transactions. Shell companies."

"She's been moving money for years," Maxim said darkly. "Using Renzetti as a shield. Many of the records we've found we haven't cracked ... *yet*."

"Without him..." I said slowly, the pieces clicking together, "She's exposed."

Maxim nodded. "For now. But she's smart. She'll vanish if we don't move fast."

I glanced between them, reading the unspoken weight in their faces. We all had a stake in finding Carlotta now that we'd seen the board that had been up. She had it out for our women, which was odd. I hadn't been sure what to make of it yet. Had she been planning hits? Or kidnappings for ransom?

"Exactly." Ilias grinned, all teeth and menace. "And we have the trail now. It's just a matter of following it."

"She's running scared," Maxim added. "For the first time."

I wasn't sure that Maxim was correct, but it was good news that we had a lead. I couldn't shake the feeling that cornering Carlotta would be like trapping a wounded animal. Blood was coming.

I just hoped it wasn't ours.

———

By the time we rejoined the others, Theo had somehow convinced everyone to play a Greek trivia game she invented on the spot.

(There were no rules. Only yelling.)

I slipped into a chair at the edge of the group, content to watch for a moment.

Theo perched cross-legged on the couch, barefoot, animatedly explaining why souvlaki was superior to gyro. Frankie argued passionately. Conall seemed to be questioning every life choice that had led him to this point. Remo was gleefully stirring the pot. Maxim went straight to his wife to snatch up baby Vasily, who had been passed around more times than I could count but seemed to be content anyway. I loved seeing Theo snuggling the baby, burying her nose in his neck where that sweet baby smell lingered. Most of all, I could picture her with our own baby in her arms.

Theo caught my eye and smiled, slow, sweet, and a little shy, like she still couldn't quite believe we were allowed to have this.

Neither could I.

Later, after the others trickled out, leaving only remnants of food and wine and the lingering hum of laughter, I found Theo in the kitchen, perched on the counter, swinging her legs.

I walked straight to her, fitting myself between her knees.

"This was a good night," she said, voice soft.

I pressed a kiss to the corner of her mouth, saying, "The best."

She looped her arms around my neck. "How was your day, by the way? Before all the lamb-induced madness?"

I hesitated. Then, because she deserved the truth, I told her how close we were to ending it. I explained how Remo and I had worked on some of our back business, including laundering some of the money we managed for the Commission. Amid all this madness, I had relied heavily on my under-boss, Carlo. He had done a great job, but he still needed guidance. He was too soft for my liking, especially when Bacco and I were out of the office. I even mentioned the warehouses hit in Red Hook and the other in Yonkers. They'd been hit by Scarpato's men last week.

She smiled a little. "I'll be happy when we can close the book on that chapter with Carlotta, but I'm glad that we've found our peace together."

I raised a brow. "Does that mean you'll agree to be my wife?" I gripped the counter beside her hips, desperate for her answer. She was strong, brilliant, and mine — if she'd agree. "I don't deserve you," I muttered.

Theo grinned wickedly. "Probably not, but you're stuck with me anyway. Yes, I'll be your wife even if that's a crappy proposal."

I laughed, low and hoarse, and kissed her like a drowning man finding air.

CHAPTER 35
THEODOSIA

I WAS STILL FLOATING from the night downstairs.

And maybe because Angelo's hand had found the small of my back and remained there the entire walk up the stairs. Steady. Warm. Possessive.

I liked it far too much, this feeling of normalcy and home. We'd had a wonderful evening with family and friends. The only person missing was Polina, who was away at school. I doubted that my brothers would allow her to come over for an evening like this with so many crime bosses, but I needed to start working on them. They needed to start seeing that they couldn't keep excluding her from everything. This was our life, and it

344

couldn't stop just because they were worried for her.

For the first time, Angelo and I had entertained like a couple, and I couldn't get enough. Then there was the proposal. It didn't bother me that there hadn't been flowers or something elaborate. He had waited for me to be ready, and boy, was I prepared to be Mrs. Santelli.

We barely reached the landing before he tugged me closer, his mouth finding that sensitive spot just below my ear, which made my toes curl.

I laughed, breathless, and leaned into him. "Someone's in a mood," I teased, my voice slightly shaky. My mood matched his exactly, and I guessed he knew it.

"Someone's got plans," he murmured. "You told me that I had work to do."

Before I could ask him what he meant, he grabbed my hand and led me to the bedroom. He turned to face me, his dark eyes steady in the dim light. He looked… nervous. *Angelo Santelli*: King of the Bronx, mafia don, slayer of enemies, wielder of terrifying silences — nervous.

I blinked. "What?" I said, a little wary. "Is there a body hidden under the bed?"

He huffed out a laugh. "Not tonight."

"Good. I just cleaned under there."

He pulled a small velvet box from the nightstand drawer, thumbing it open with one big hand. Inside, nestled against black velvet, was the most beautiful and unique ring I had ever seen. It wasn't traditional—no fluffy diamond halo or safe, boring solitaire.

Instead, it was bold—a rectangular step-cut black sapphire glittered in the center—stunning, like the clearest night sky. Tiny baguette diamonds fanned out around it in sharp, clean lines, creating a sunburst pattern that screamed Art Deco in the most delicious, dramatic way. The band was platinum, slim, and detailed with a delicate engraving of tiny repeating fans, like a whisper of old New York glamour.

It was stunning.

Elegant and eccentric at the same time.

Exactly the kind of ring that made people lean in and say, "Tell me the story behind that."

I pressed my hand over my heart. I could see it already. The black sapphire would *pop* against a dramatic tulle gown — something *draped*, not stiff, with bias cuts that whispered instead of shouted. Maybe a low back. Tiny pearl buttons. A faux fur stole thrown over my shoulders if it was chilly. My bouquet would be dahlias, or perhaps black bat flow-ers, sprays of silver eucalyptus, and a few moody, deep-blue thistles tucked in for a touch of chaos. No tiara. No glitter. Just a sweep of soft waves pinned to one side, and these art deco details glinting at my ears and wrists — tiny echoes of the ring that started it all.

The kind of wedding that didn't feel like a performance, but a story — a crazy, fierce, reckless, beautiful story only we could tell.

"I had it restored," Angelo said quietly, watching my face like a hawk. "It's from the Depression, but it reminded me there is still light even when everything feels dark. It reminds me of you."

My throat went tight, too full of words I couldn't form. "It's perfect," I whispered. "Guess you're stuck with me now, Santelli," I murmured against his mouth.

"*You're* perfect," he said, voice rough. "I love you."

"I've *always* loved you." It was the truth. I never stopped loving him, even in the dark. My love for him spanned years full of heartache, but that didn't mean it had ended. It was a full-circle sort of love.

I stared at him — this complicated, brutal, beautiful man — holding the ring against my finger as if he didn't already own every piece of my battered heart.

It looked... old.

Loved.

Story-soaked.

Just like something I would have designed myself if I had been given the brief: *whimsical, stubborn, romantic, slightly mischievous, likely to prick her fingers with a sewing needle.*

My throat closed up.

"Theo Anthakos," he said, voice low but steady. "Marry me." I nodded so hard I nearly fell over.

"Yes," I said, half-laughing, half-sobbing. "Of course, yes. A million times, yes."

His shoulders relaxed, and for a moment, the fierce mafia don disappeared, revealing just Angelo.

My Angelo.

He slid the ring onto my finger, his touch reverent. It fit perfectly, like it had been waiting for me all along. When I looked back at him, he was already standing, invading my space, his hands cradling my face, tilting it upward. I barely had time to gasp before he kissed me. Not a polite, chaste kiss.

Like he was writing his name across my soul in invisible ink.

Pulling him closer, I wrapped my arms

around his neck, feeling the tension rippling through his muscles. I realized he was holding back. Barely. I wasn't interested in holding anything back.

I kissed him harder, lightly scraping my nails against his scalp, and he made a low, vicious sound that did terrible, wonderful things to my insides.

"*Piccola*," he growled against my mouth. "*Amore mio*."

I pulled back just enough to meet his eyes. "Give me everything."

He grinned then—that rare, dangerous flash of white teeth that always made my knees weak. "You asked for it," he said, voice dark with promise.

He came down over me, mouth hot and desperate, hands greedy as he stripped away my dress in one rough pull. The cool air hit my skin, and I gasped, but it was swallowed by his mouth. He kissed me like he wanted to memorize every sound I made.

I clawed at his shirt, frustrated by the buttons, and he chuckled against my throat, low and dirty, before yanking it off over his head. I let my hands roam — broad shoulders, scarred ribs, the sharp planes of his hips. My fingertips brushed the tattoo by his heart — the line of script.

This wasn't tender lovemaking. This was desperate and rough. Our teeth clashed as we struggled to kiss harder, my fingers scrabbling against him as he battered into me. I was slick with want, but he wasn't small. Still, the stretch and pinch of his cock drove the orgasm through me so brilliantly that I screamed wordlessly into his shoulder as I came, my nails scraping along his skin as his hips drove into me.

"That's it, *piccola*, give it to me. Again. Damnit. Again." He ground out as he tweaked my nipples. "I want it all."

"Don't hold back. I want you to come." I clamped around his cock, enjoying the ecstasy that took over his face as he pistoned in and out of my body, that feeling of him gliding in and out making my eyes roll back.

He narrowed his eyes at me, and pulled out his cock glistening. "Not yet. I want to savor it. Roll over, *piccola*. Lay flat."

He stroked himself while I did as he said, and even as I laughed, he adjusted a pillow under my hips. "You look so pretty like this. That ass of yours wants me to do naughty things to it." Calloused fingers caressed my skin before they dipped down to slide into my pussy. He leaned over me, his lips nipping at the skin on my spine, sucking the tender flesh into his mouth while his fingers continued to thrust and and tease. "I love your skin. Have I told you that?"

I squirmed, trying to thrust against his fingers, only to whine when they disappeared. "Wait," I protested.

"Don't you worry, baby." The velvety tip of his cock notched to my slit. "I'm going to take care of you right now. Take care of both of us. I'm going to come in this pretty pussy of yours, and then I'm going to start all over again. You're going to stay just like this."

"I will?"

"Yes. I'm going to fill you up." He gave me a light slap on the thigh as he shoved into me. His fingers moved to my clit. The sheets on my nipples and the sting against my skin made sensations bloom through my body. "That's it, *piccola*. Do you like that? You seem extra wet." He pulled back out and then rammed in again. "Are you my naughty girl?"

My voice was muffled against the sheets, but I managed to whimper out a barely audible. "God. Please." He gave me another slap, harder this time, enhancing everything, and I wanted to rub myself against the sheet to give even more friction.

"Not God. *Angelo*. Say it." He gave my ass cheek another small slap and I came apart on a cry, desperate and needy just before he jerked and came hard, pumping into me, gripping my hips hard as liquid heat spread into me.

Collapsing in a messy heap, he pressed one hand over my belly as he rolled me over before he kissed my temple. "Give me a minute of recovery."

"That's right, you're getting old," I teased.

———

Later, tangled together under the soft, rumpled sheets, Angelo brushed his thumb over the ring on my finger.

"You sure you want this?" he murmured, voice rough with exhaustion and something heavier underneath.

I twisted to face him completely, my heart overflowing. "You're an overprotective, infuriating, brooding mafia boss who ruins my plans and steals all the covers," I said solemnly. "And I love you more than anyone or anything. Yes, I want it all."

He blinked. Then, slowly, a genuine smile

blossomed across his face. "You're trouble," he said, brushing my hair back. "I'm so glad you're mine."

"Always," I whispered.

He kissed me again, slow and deep, like a vow.

And somewhere deep inside, I made my own vow back.

No matter what came next — wars, betrayals, ghosts from the past — we were a team now.

And God help anyone who tried to get between us.

CHAPTER 36
ANGELO

THE NIGHT AIR in Naples was heavy with the scent of salt and diesel, a thick balm that clung to my skin as we stepped off the private jet. Lights glittered along the harbor, but beneath the postcard perfection was a rot we'd all tasted.

Unfortunately, we weren't here for the pizza, and we weren't here to play tourist.

Ilias, Conall, Maxim, and I had followed the trail from the blood-stained floorboards of Renzetti's hideout to this ancient city teeming with ghosts and secrets. The USB drive we'd pried from his safe was a treasure chest—full surveillance logs, old contacts, bank account routing numbers, and, most importantly, receipts. Carlotta may have thought Salvatore was just a patsy, but he had been hoarding information on her. He'd been suspicious enough to start paying close attention, and that was enough of a trail for Veronica and Kostas to begin picking up threads.

Carlotta wasn't just hiding. She was thriving. The entire sojourn with Renzetti had been a minor blip on her radar, and we were uncovering the layers. It had only been one move in her game. We still had difficulties figuring out her plans or why she had come to New York to involve us. Initially, I'd wondered if her whole play had involved the Santellis and the blood oath. Her comments to Theo suggested that maybe she was angling for a power dimension that would leverage a play within the Commission or her role as my mother, but it all jangled like an off-key note. There was no love lost between us, and we both knew it. I would never do her any favors.

When Valentino mentioned that she wanted to be a Donna, that made sense to me, too, but now? I was still lost. I'd even floated the idea to Remo that maybe we were related to the Cardonis. Since Frankie's biological father had been revealed to be Don Vanello, we'd both been ruminating more about who our bio-dads could be. It was clear she'd been strategic, just as she was with everything. I hadn't told Remo, but I went so far as to have a DNA test done with Val's consent for both Remo and me. It was more about understanding Carlotta's mind and potentially her next move than finding answers to who my father was. I didn't care about that. In my mind, I was an orphan in more ways than one. My parents didn't exist to me. Val had the grace to look disappointed when the results were negative, as if he'd like to have me or Remo as a sibling, but we both knew that wasn't true. He had his own little *famiglia* and wanted to distance himself from our drama as much as possible. He'd been more than accommodating, so I couldn't fault him.

We knew Carlotta had money and means, but the scale we uncovered was shocking: shell companies tied to arms dealers, mercenaries bought and paid for, and a black-market syndicate operating under her command. She'd been getting money from somewhere, and all of the information we'd uncovered cemented the fact that she'd been operating in the shadows beyond our reach in a startling fashion for longer than we knew. Renzetti was just a public face, a sacrificial pawn. When I shot him, it hadn't ended anything; it had only peeled back the first layer.

And now her web had spread to Ilias's global shipping empire. Our suspicions led us to believe that her New York antics had all been a distraction—a flashy show to keep Ilias and his brothers from seeing what was happening. Already, Ilias's enterprises had been hit multiple times. Ilias and his brothers ran smuggling operations worldwide that would be clutch for the sort of shady operations that Carlotta was involved in.

We stopped outside a compound nestled into a cliffside overlooking the sea. We had decided to take this the whole way, regardless of how far we had to go. It seemed as if Carlotta was skipping town, but with a few recent hits on Ilias's properties lately that we were sure she was responsible for, we knew we couldn't just let it lie that she was out of New York.

"You guys ready for this?" Maxim grinned over at me. He elbowed Lev and wiggled his eyebrows, thumbing off the safety of his Glock.

He had been manic about tracking down my mother after he'd found the photos of his wife, son, and sister on the board at the house where Salvatore was staying, not that we blamed him. The others had been on board before, but they were extra motivated now that they knew that the evil bitch had been monitoring people they cared about. We could have compartmentalized it if it had just been us, but adding the women and little Vasily kicked everything up into overdrive.

Conall narrowed his eyes, spinning a knife around his knuckles before slamming it into its sheath. "We're ready, fecker."

The property we were at belonged to Nino Barone, an arms broker whose loyalty was known to be swayed by the highest bidder. He was a punk and a low-level dealer who couldn't have navigated the vast waters of the volume of weapons we dealt with, but we knew he had intel about the mercenaries hired for Carlotta, if not organized them himself. We weren't here to chat.

The wrought-iron gate loomed as we approached, one of those old things with pillars every eight feet you see on estates. It was impressive if you liked that sort of thing. If I could get away with a fence like that in New York, I'd totally build one. Two guards, dressed in black and carrying rifles, barely had time to lift them before I fired. One down. Conall shot the other in the knee. The security here was weak to say the least, especially for an arms broker. The guard scrambled for his radio, but he was too slow as we swept forward.

"Keep him breathing," I snapped even as Ilias rolled his eyes at me. "We'll need him to talk." Turning to face the guard, I gripped my brass knuckles and grinned at him as Maxim and Ilias hauled him to his feet and Conall kicked away his weapon. "So, what's it going to be? You going to tell us what we need to know?" Sending a brutal punch to his ribs, I paused before sending another into his gut.

"What do you want to know?" he grunted out. He was already looking pretty rough, and he didn't seem as if he were interested in holding out any information, but I still wanted to punch him again. Looked like loyalty was a little scarce in these parts. That's what you got when you paid for it. Geez, this guy was a pussy. For fun, I nailed him again, rolling my eyes at Conall. "What's the rest of the security layout?"

The guard's head lolled on his shoulders, and for a minute I thought he'd spit up blood. "I need a hospital. My knee." The knee was leaking pretty badly, but he rambled when he didn't get a response. "Just six guys at the house. Just the two of us at the front. Two at the back. Two at the office door. I won't say anything. I don't give a fuck about Barone. *Please.*"

Ilias shrugged. "I believe him."

Spinning my brass knuckles on my thumb, I nodded, "Yeah, I believe him, too." I gave Ilias a wink. I recognized the look on Ilias's face. "Let him go." A flash of relief crossed the guard's face. Dumb fucker. Maxim gave a dark chuckle and released him as the man stumbled on the bum leg, just as Ilias tightened his grip ruthlessly, bringing up a knife and swiping it across his throat.

"Can't ever be too sure," he said, stepping away as the body fell.

"Agreed," Conall chuckled darkly. "Never know. He could have run. I mean ... not far."

Sometimes Conall was a funny fucker. "Wow, security sucks. Maybe he's broke."

"I don't know. Either way. Big mistake." Maxim's grin echoed ours as we prowled forward. "Let's split and meet inside." It was an easy choice. Four of them left and four of us — perfect. We could split them and take Barone without issue. Maxim and Ilias split off to deal with the ones in the back, while Conall and I handled the ones by the office door.

The villa sprawled with marble and old money, showcasing classic European architecture that took your breath away and made you question your mortality and place in history. Paintings of saints hung on the walls, who wouldn't save anyone tonight, no matter how hard anyone prayed. The interior was vast, illuminated by low-light wall sconces that provided just enough light as we moved from room to room. True to his word, we weren't seeing any other guards as we traversed the villa. Before our arrival, we had received a blueprint from Kostas, who was still on the ground in New York, so we had a good idea where we were going.

We moved quickly and efficiently, clearing each room as we went, ensuring they were empty. It seemed unlikely there were no staff, but it was late. By the time we reached the office, Maxim and Ilias had already caught up like the greedy fuckers they were, but it wasn't as if we needed any help. The two guards were focused on a television playing what appeared to be an Italian dub of *Die Hard*. The two certainly seemed to be into it. It was almost a shame to murder them to such a classic. Almost.

We found Barone in the study, snorting coke off a leather-bound ledger like it was just another Friday, and we hadn't just slaughtered six of his men. He barely had time to blink before I slammed him into the wall.

"Tell us about New York," I growled, pressing the barrel of my Glock beneath his chin.

"I don't—" He blinked blearily at us, as if we were apparitions that had materialized out of thin air.

I pistol-whipped him across the mouth. Blood splattered the white plaster behind him. "You hired out men to disrupt our operations in New York. Paid killers. Mercs. To Carlotta Santelli. Ring a bell?"

"Who are you?" he asked, struggling to his feet.

Conall sneered. "How about telling us the truth? Nobody for miles out here. We can do anything to you that we want. We've taken out all your security. Which was shit, by the way."

"Yeah, pathetic. Come on, Barone. We've come all this way." Maxim prodded Barone's ribcage with his gun barrel. "You know who we are. You had pictures of us."

Barone whimpered, hands shaking. "She paid me." He shrugged. "I don't ask questions." Shoving the gun back under his chin, he babbled. "She asked for more on this side of the ocean. Asked me to arrange logistics. IDs. Transportation."

"Details. Transportation to where?" I demanded.

"She said Trieste. But it was only a waypoint. There's something—something else. Romania. Border town. Săcueni. A factory. That's all I know." He spat out the facts like bullet points.

I stepped back. "Good."

And then I shot him in the leg. He howled, collapsing.

"That's for your future memory. You'll be compensated every time she sends a message." I followed him to the floor, whipping out my knife and pinning it under one eyeball, pricking it just under the tender inner lid. He cringed away from me, snot running from his nose. "We'll pay double what she's offering. She texts, you do what she asks. Then …" I pressed.

Ilias leaned against the desk. "Come on, you're a smart guy. A businessman."

"Then I call. I'll let you know what she says." His head was thrown back against the wall, as far as he could get from me, his eyes wide with panic. "I will, man. I swear it. You don't even have to pay."

"We will pay. If you don't do what we

363

say." I clucked my tongue. "Let's just say." I turned to Maxim. "You don't want to find out. Open the safe." I gestured to the wall-mounted safe where we cleaned out the associated files, leaving the stacks of cash and gold behind.

We left him bleeding. He didn't know it yet, but he was a dead man walking. As soon as we got Carlotta, he'd be a dead man.

Back in the SUV, the gravity of what we had uncovered began to sink in. Carlotta wasn't just operating a shadow network; she was building something—something big enough to strike at the Commission from every angle. However, it was how dangerous she was that posed the biggest problem.

"Renzetti was a show. Her real plays are still on the board," I muttered, watching the coastline slide by.

"She hit the Anthakos fleet in the Adriatic last month," Ilias said, voice low. "Two ships burned. No survivors. They were small, but …" he left it hanging.

"I thought that was pirates," Conall said. "You didn't mention that it was Carlotta."

"She made it look like pirates, and it wasn't her personally," Ilias replied. "But the timing… the intel… it was too clean. It was definitely her. And now Galena is gone." His jaw clenched. "That bitch."

Maxim didn't speak, but I could feel the weight of it crushing him. He was beating himself up after Ilias revealed information about Galena. He'd thought he was doing the right thing by leaving her to her normal little life away from the Volkov Bratva, but now it seemed that it had been a mistake. Of course, we could talk until we were blue in the face, telling him he did the right thing by letting her have a sense of normalcy. Even now, we didn't know anything about why Galena ran. It could have something to do with my mother, or it could have been something else entirely.

We drove in silence from the villa. Ilias sat with his forearms resting on his knees, jaw locked tight, his phone gripped in his hand as if it owed him answers. I caught him glancing at a photograph—one of Galena. In this one, her face was still turned away, unaware of the camera, her hair wind-swept as she hurried down a side street.

Back at our safehouse, a restored monastery turned base of operations, I poured a stiff drink. The room was stone and candlelit, rustic with heavy tapestries and the faint scent of incense that had lingered for centuries. I preferred it to sterile modernity.

Ilias approached quietly. "If she hurts Galena—"

"She won't," I said. "We don't even know what's going on with her. Who she's running from — or why she's running. If it has anything to do with this whole scene." That was the truth. Galena was somewhat of an anomaly. Granted, it probably did have to do with Carlotta, but maybe it'd make him feel better to think otherwise. "We'll find her."

"You don't know that we will." His face was set in a worried frown that I hadn't seen from him in a decade. "And what if …"

"Here's what I know," I replied, clapping Ilias on the shoulder. "Carlotta doesn't act without purpose. She sees people as tools. If Carlotta has her, then she's not dead. We would know if she had her because she would have let us know. Galena would have been trotted out as a pawn. That's how she operates. If she doesn't have her, then Galena is hiding from something else."

He nodded tightly. "Which is a problem we can solve."

"Exactly." Whatever happened to Galena. Whatever she was running from, we'd figure it out. Later.

Maxim joined us, holding an old leather portfolio we'd pulled from the safe. "Found this. Shipping manifests. Trieste to Săcueni. But the real gem is this—"

He pulled out a photograph. It showed a warehouse in Romania, fenced and heavily guarded. Men in tactical gear. One wore a patch we'd seen before—on the mercenaries at the Cardoni house.

"She's there," I said.

"Or was," Maxim corrected. "The photo is a week old."

We'd have to move fast.

Still, I couldn't help but think of Theo. The way her hands trembled in mine when I slipped the ring on her finger. The way her laughter lit up the brownstone during dinner. I hated being away. There was no place I'd rather be than at home with her.

"Well, let's roll it up here then. Call the pilot." Conall began gathering the files as he spoke. "The sooner we get in the air the sooner we can get this shite over with. I want to get home to Frankie." He gave us a shy smile. "She's agreed to a baby."

"Are you serious? That's exciting news." I clapped him into a hug. "I can't wait to be an uncle." Most of all, I was glad that Frankie had come to terms with whatever had been holding her back. She had never told me, but I think she'd been worried that she'd be like our parents. She hadn't wanted a life like that for a child. We'd always wondered if we were defective somehow.

Together, we cleaned up and gathered ourselves before I stepped away to call Theo. She answered on the second ring. Her voice was warm and sleepy.

"Hey," she said. "Still alive?"

"Barely. How's my fiancée?"

She laughed. "Sketching my wedding dress. Drinking tea. Missing you."

That last part settled in my chest like fire. "I'll be home soon," I promised.

"You better be. I have design ideas to show you."

I smiled, even as my hand curled tighter around the photograph of the Romanian compound. The war wasn't over, but we were close.

For Theo, I'd burn the world down.

And for Carlotta? I'd start with her empire.

Brick by bloody brick, so my family would finally be free.

CHAPTER 37
THEODOSIA

I SHOULD'VE KNOWN. Anytime Frankie Santelli-O'Kelly got that edge in her voice—the hinted at, *I have a plan*—something deliciously chaotic was about to happen. Although she usually said that about me.

The brownstone was suspiciously quiet when I padded down to the kitchen in fuzzy leopard-print slippers, one of Angelo's over-sized black T-shirts, and a pair of boxer shorts. I had been in a design fugue since sunrise, sketching ideas for my bridal gown that ranged from Grecian goddess to 1930s flapper. There had been an idea in my head when Angelo slipped the ring on my finger, but now I had so many wayward thoughts sliding away from me that I finally had to call for reinforcements.

I had barely poured myself a cup of coffee when the front bell rang like a death knell of calm. "I've brought backup!" Frankie's voice boomed from the doorway.

Behind her trailed Cora, radiant as ever despite holding a very opinionated infant with a fluffy lion pacifier clipped to his onesie.

"I thought this was a *casual* brainstorm," I muttered as one of the guards pulled the door open wider, ushering them inside, looking apologetic. Maybe I should have gotten dressed? It was Norris's morning off, so I figured I could get away with it.

Frankie breezed past me like she still lived here. "Casual? Theo, please. You're marrying my brother, and you're my best friend. I've seen you naked."

"True. We'll probably traumatize Cora."

"Nah," Cora grinned. "And we've brought snacks." She inclined her head towards her guard, Finn, who was toting around not only what looked like scrumptious trays of three kinds of hummus, warm pita triangles stacked like Jenga, a cheese board that could fund a semester at FIT, and little phyllo cups filled with spiced feta and honey. Was that olive tapenade? "Where should Finn put those? Living room?"

"Yeah, let's set up there." Frankie clapped her hands together, gesturing to Finn, who looked all kinds of fed up.

"Sure, lead the way. I'm just here to carry everything," he mumbled. "God help us if we got attacked in the street. My hands would be full."

"You could always throw a rosemary sprig at them," I suggested.

"That'd always do it." Cora winked at him even as he rolled his eyes.

Finn was one of Conall's top guys and had been assigned to Frankie for a while now. Given the upheaval involving Carlotta and Salvatore, it was understandable that she still required protection. Seeing her make him schlepp appetizers and baby gear made me laugh, although it was a legitimate concern that he couldn't reach his weapon if needed. However, if I knew Conall O'Kelly, two other men were outside. Finn was just close protection.

"I figured we deserved proper provisions for plotting," Cora added, setting baby Vasily into a padded portable rocker that had appeared in the living room. Evidently, Norris had unearthed it just for the occasion. Even on his morning off, the guy was omniscient.

"I love Norris," I whispered, bending to

coo at Vasily. He was adorable, and the urge to snatch him up was almost unbearable, but he was still fast asleep. "Look how prepared he is."

Finn motioned to get Frankie's attention as he sidled towards the doorway. "I'll just be over in the kitchen, ladies."

"Norris?" Frankie understood me perfectly. She snatched up a slice of manchego. "Same. He's a wizard. I'm not sure what my brother would have done without him, and he cooks like a dream."

"How is Vasily still asleep?" I asked. I was making mental baby notes.

"Practice. He's been conditioned not to mind a lot of noise." Cora laughed. "I swear he'll sleep through anything. Maxim insists on taking him everywhere, so the poor thing has to endure being passed around, riding in the car, and the noise. If he doesn't sleep where he can, then it's just too bad. So, he's adapted."

We all cracked up as we plopped onto stools. I grabbed my sketchbook and clicked my pen. "Okay," I said, "wedding ideas. Frankie, you're the newlywed. Thoughts?"

Frankie lifted her hand like a politician mid-press conference. "I mean, was my wedding a wedding? Conall basically kidnapped me and gave me no choice." She was nothing but happy, but we all frowned. All of it was true, and I was a little mad about not getting to at least design a dress for her. It was all kinds of messed up that she got married in scrubs. "But—avoid rayon. It attracts static, cats, and regrets. Second, don't do a ten-tier cake. Nobody needs that many tiers."

"Noted," I said, scribbling. "No rayon … because I use so much rayon." I laughed. "And Cora?" I turned to her, raising a brow. "You looked like a literal goddess at your wedding. Spill."

"I did love my dress," she admitted sheepishly. "Maxim picked it out. I was so nervous throughout the whole thing. The service and reception are a blur, but the dress was my favorite part."

"Well, it was beautiful. It does seem like a common theme. Everything is a blur, and in the end, you can't remember anything. I should probably focus on what's important to me. The dress. Everything else will fall into place."

We were laughing when a low *yawn* came from the rocker. Baby Vasily had opinions.

"His timing is impeccable," I said, reaching for a piece of pita.

Frankie leaned over, as he settled back into the rocker and went back to sleep sucking on the pacifier. "He's the Commission's cutest member."

"I don't know," I said, "Maxim gets weirdly soft around babies. I think it's the scruff."

Cora's smile faded a little, and she glanced toward the window, her fingers brushing Vasily's tuft of hair, seeming to take comfort in the softness of her baby. I didn't blame her. He was an angel. "He's been... tense. Since the raid."

I sobered, too. The air shifted just slightly —less hummus, more heaviness. Bringing up Carlotta was almost like one of those folk-tales, like saying Bloody Mary out loud. The atmosphere immediately changed. She was an absolute stain.

"Carlotta," I said, definitively. They both nodded.

"She's a ghost," Frankie murmured. "Every time they think they're close, she slithers away. It's like she's five steps ahead. My mother is evil." She glanced over at me. "Nobody is sure what she's doing or why she's doing it—the whole thing. The kidnapping," she clarified. "It seems like it was all a diversion."

Cora rested her chin on her palm. "And it's more than that. Maxim's been trying to find Galena again. He's worried. Really worried. I'm not sure how much Ilias has told you, Theo ..." she trailed off.

I looked between them. "I haven't heard anything. Honestly, I don't know anything about her at all." That made me feel a bit like a monster. The only thing I knew about her was that she was matched with my brother, but I hadn't given it a second thought. My plate had been kind of full.

"Her mother was Alexei Volkov's mistress. She took off when Galena was around three years old—just vanished—literally. Maxim hadn't taken over yet, so things were still under Alexei's control, but he didn't care that much to look for her or couldn't find her. Not too long ago, Maxim decided to find Galena," Cora hesitated.

"Because of the blood oath?" Frankie asked. "I mean, they had to be thinking in advance, right? The four of them they'd known about it for years."

Cora bit her lip. She was pretty adorable, I had to admit. She had her funky style. I'd love it if she'd let me dress her, but I doubted she'd wear anything but jeans and a t-shirt. Even now, she wore a tattered zombie t-shirt and even more tattered jeans with holes in them. Gardening shoes rounded out her ensemble. You'd never peg her for a mafia wife in a million years. The only expensive item she wore was her wedding ring, but even that looked effortless.

"I'm sure that was most of why he looked for her," she admitted. "But he didn't tell her about the Volkov Bratva because she was happy. She had a normal life. Her mother had married a normal guy. Maxim just wanted her to be happy." Her fingers went to one of the holes in her jeans, picking at a frayed thread. "Then, I guess things went to shit for her."

"She and her mother got mugged or some-thing. Maxim didn't tell me much about it, but it was bad enough that her mother died. Then her stepdad had a heart attack a few months ago. Then she went off-grid. Conall said she's on the run." Frankie looked to Cora for confirmation.

"Yeah. It sounds bad. They haven't been able to find her." Cora nodded, looking grim.

Frankie crossed her arms. "And she doesn't know who Ilias is, does she?"

"No," Cora said softly. "She's never been in this world. Not like us."

I swallowed. There it was again. That divide. The one that used to terrify me but now just made me... fiercely protective. Of Frankie. Of Cora. Of baby Vasily. Of all of us who'd been stitched into this bloodstained tapestry through fate and family. My heart went out to Galena, the thought of her being hurt, seeing her mother injured, and losing the family she had. At the same time, I could respect Maxim for trying to keep her away from the underworld. What he had chosen made sense at the time. Still, wasn't it the same thing? Other people deciding what was right for us?

"Do you think Carlotta's trying to get to her?" I asked quietly.

"It's possible." Frankie nodded. "Or at the very least... keep her hidden. It would gut Ilias. She knows how to strike deep."

I leaned back on the stool, exhaling. "It's like everything is a web she's spun."

"And we're the flies," Cora said.

I looked at Vasily, asleep now, his tiny chest rising and falling like a whisper. "No," I said, voice firm. "We're not flies. We're wasps. Beautiful, terrifying, and unafraid to sting the ever-living hell out of anyone who comes for our nest."

Both women grinned.

"Well, we can leave Galena to the boys for right now. Once they find her, we'll show her that she has more family than she ever knew about. We'll show her all about this world. Help her fit in." Frankie's face was resolute. "For now, let's focus on planning a wedding so glorious that Carlotta will spontaneously combust from jealousy," Frankie said. "Something ethereal. Gothic. Decadent. Like if Chanel and Morticia Addams had a lovechild."

"I *knew* I invited the right people," I said. "I could get behind this idea. I want it to be a storybook." I closed my eyes, trying to picture it.

We spent the next two hours plotting aesthetics, discussing venue ideas, and arguing over whether an all-black bridal party would be dramatic or just confusing. As the day passed, Norris popped in occasionally with new offerings, declaring his time off officially over. He brought apricot scones, rose tea, and, at one point, hot honey drizzled over salty halloumi.

"I'm marrying Angelo just to get access to Norris," I whispered to Frankie, who nodded solemnly.

Later, when the sun began to set and shadows stretched long across the kitchen tiles, I leaned back in my chair and just... watched them. Cora, with her baby, her eyes soft, and Frankie, who was waving her hands as she described how Conall danced like a mafia robot. I had my sketchbook open, ideas flowing like I'd just refilled the tank.

Life was good.

CHAPTER 38
ANGELO

THERE WAS something brutal about the Romanian sky in April. Not stormy. Not serene. Just blank — like God turned his face away.

We landed under fake names with burner phones and adrenaline stitching our plan together like a half-healed wound. No greetings, no customs, on a runway that was hidden from the tourist traps of Bucharest. Just a convoy of black vehicles waiting like vultures, engines rumbling low.

The warehouse on the outskirts appeared to have been ravaged by time and left behind. A rusted monolith with broken windows and concertina wire strung like barbed lace along the fence. The kind of place nightmares grew teeth and mercenaries were bred.

But someone had been here recently. Tire tracks. Fresh gravel. A crooked security camera blinked like a drunk eye above the east gate.

"Too sloppy," I muttered.

"Or bait," Maxim said beside me, arms crossed. The wind ruffled his coat, but he didn't flinch.

Ilias was glassy-eyed, binoculars pressed to his face. "She's here," he said, voice grave. "She has to be."

"She's careful," Maxim added. "But this? This would be arrogance. She'd have to think we're slower than we are."

"Or she wants us to come," Conall said, cocking his rifle like he was cracking his knuckles. The edge of Irish in his voice was sharper here, which had been added in by his father through sheer violence, not by any exposure to the actual beauty of Ireland. I wondered if Conall knew that the colloquialisms he used in his speech sometimes echoed the father he hated.

I stood with them on the overlook, wrapped in black, pistol heavy on my hip. *Santelli*. That name used to be a shield. Lately, it felt more like a brand that had been ironed onto my soul. Carlotta would hear it in the silence before we shattered her doors. If the others thought I would hold back, they thought wrong.

She was close. I felt it—like a splinter buried deep. Or at least... she'd been here recently enough to poison the air.

———

We split into teams.

I took Ilias. He moved like a man who'd forgotten how to walk without rage. The kind of fury that didn't roar anymore — it simmered, low and slow, under the skin.

The side entrance was chained, but the lock had been tampered with — not professionally. Sloppy. Someone in a hurry, or someone cocky.

"Camera's looping," I whispered. Veronica's tech team, all the way in New York, had hijacked the feed. The glitch was subtle—just enough to buy us time.

"Got ninety seconds before it resets," I said, crouched beneath the rusted frame of a side door. My gloved fingers brushed the rusted hinge. "This place is wrong."

"Feels like a shell," Ilias said. "Like something used to be here, but it's been gutted."

He was right. The inside was hollow. Too clean in places, too abandoned in others. Like someone had scrubbed the crime scene but forgot to take the bodies, we moved in.

The corridors were narrow, lit by emergency strips that buzzed like insects. Shadows warped and shifted, distorting the crates and busted machinery into jagged silhouettes. My eyes adjusted, but the unease stayed.

Ahead — voices. Slavic.

I tapped Ilias on the shoulder, and we flanked. Four men. Complacent. Young, or maybe just stupid. Not mafia — no tattoos. Mercs. I hated mercenaries. They fought for paychecks, not blood. There was no soul behind that, and I couldn't respect it.

Ilias's silencer hissed. The rest flinched a little too late, jerking around to see their comrade fall. Ilias was a shadow — rifle butt to the throat, one clean break as I moved through the space like a blade. One shot to the chest. One to the head. No hesitation.

Thirty seconds. Four bodies.

"They're not mafia," Ilias said quietly, scanning the room. "Mercs. Same as before."

"Carlotta doesn't trust anyone she doesn't buy." I crouched, rifling through one of their vests. No insignia. No dog tags. "NATO gear. Black market. High-grade."

"Too bad she can't buy better quality

mercs." He gave a dark chuckle, looking over the pile of bodies.

"No shit," I agreed.

———

We discovered the nerve center buried deep beneath the concrete, with lights flickering overhead in dull strobes, the kind that turned time syrupy and strange. Screens covered one wall, displaying ports, shipping manifests, customs data — not just from Romania, but also Dubai, Trieste, and Piraeus.

"She's not just siphoning Ilias's trade routes," I said. "She's building an empire."

Veronica's voice crackled through our comms. "These routes were activated three weeks ago. Coordinated across four continents. This was planned long before Barone."

"Trace them," I said. "Every route, every transaction, every fake identity she's tied to these ports."

"I already started," Veronica said. "But you won't like it."

"I don't need to like it," I whispered. "I need to end it." This just solidified for me that while I'd been living my life away in New York, forgetting that my mother existed, she had been plotting, planning, and thriving.

Not only that, but she had been doing so in the one industry that I had been trying to eradicate from the Santelli name — trafficking. She must have been laughing at me the entire time. I ground my teeth together. I'd been a fool for not seeing the bigger picture.

———

The basement reeked of damp concrete and burnt circuits. It was a surveillance hub cobbled together from stolen parts and black-market dreams. Cables coiled like snakes. Screens flickered. There was a low hum that vibrated through my bones.

"Plug into port three," Veronica's voice crackled in my ear. "Top left. I've got you."

I slotted the USB and waited.

She worked fast. "Encrypted drives, multiple archives—wait. I'm in."

One screen lit up. Surveillance stills. There were ports, shipping lanes, and container yards.

Ilias stepped closer, tension rising. "She's moving goods across borders and using my shipping lanes. That's why she studied the Anthakos network. It was always about logistics. That's why she was in New York. It had all been a little bit of a magic show. A diversion. She wanted us looking in one direction while she was focused here in Europe."

"She's been piggybacking on every legal channel you built. Not just goods," Veronica said. "Weapons. Personnel. High-value transfers masked through dummy cargo."

The truth shattered through me. Of course, she had. The old ways weren't enough for her. She wanted something global. Untouchable. We had been thinking small. She'd just used us.

"Trace every line. Every transaction. Every hidden dock and shell company," I said. "We unravel her like a thread. Let's start buying our own mercs. I want a location. Next time we fly out. Let's make it count. I have an idea. Let me percolate on it a little, " I said, toeing a cable. It might be insane, but if we want to catch her in person, then maybe we need to be a little crazy. Ilias might not like it much, but it might be the only way.

CHAPTER 39
ANGELO

THE ADRENALINE that had driven me for the last forty-eight hours had curdled into something colder. Something precise. Carlotta wasn't just a ghost anymore. She was an *operator*—a strategist. And we'd been reacting while she orchestrated from the shadows. That was ending *now*. We needed to change our game.

I stood at the head of the table — cheap plywood warped from humidity. A map of the Black Sea was spread open like a wound. Our knives were stabbed into ports and cities like sutures, trying to keep the thing from splitting further.

"She wants Ilias," I said flatly. "Specifically, his shipping routes. She's been circling them like a shark for months."

Ilias sat back, arms crossed, expression unreadable. He hadn't spoken much since the surveillance room discovery, but I knew the look on his face. I'd worn it before, the flat look that said everything was fine while his eyes were banked with hate.

Conall leaned forward. "You want to give her the Anathakos shipping network?"

"No," I said, voice sharp. "I want her to *think* we are."

Maxim's brow furrowed. "Explain."

"She's too smart to walk into a trap unless the prize is irresistible," I said. "We give her what she wants: Ilias. A solo meeting. On his turf. On one of his ships. Something... quiet. Off-grid. She'll believe he's breaking ranks. That he's ready to deal her in."

"Why would she believe that?" Conall asked. "Ilias wouldn't do that."

"She doesn't *know* him. She only knows what she wants to believe, and what she wants is power. We'll make her think that Ilias is interested in the business. That he's willing to cut us out, and cut her in. We can make her think that Ilias is willing to do what he needs in order to keep his company in the black."

"Give her a lie wrapped in desperation," Ilias murmured, finally catching on. "Make her think I'm bleeding out."

I nodded once. "And let her come in for the kill."

Silence stretched. The plan was insane — bold. It had to be. She wouldn't take a risk unless she thought the reward outweighed it. But it wasn't just about her empire. It was personal. She needed to *win*. And winning meant turning one of us against the other. That was what made it crazy, but part of it hinged on the idea that she still had one step rooted in taking us down. That there was still a piece of her that would enjoy that.

I lit a cigarette I didn't want and stared out over the city. This place — Săcueni, Bucharest, the whole damn Eastern Bloc — felt like the rotting teeth of the empire my mother wanted to build. Maybe I was just in a shitty mood.

"You good?" Maxim's voice behind me was low. Tired.

"No," I said.

He came to stand beside me, arms crossed, gaze fixed on the horizon. "You think she'll bite?"

"I know she will," I said. "The question is how close I need to let her get before I pull the trigger."

Maxim didn't speak for a while. "You know she'll bring backup."

"I want her to bring it. I want her to think

she has the upper hand," I said viciously. Just the thought of her coming to the meeting tantalized me.

"She'll sniff out anything that smells like a trap." Maxim tried to be reasonable. He and Conall had been trying to reason with me for the past few days, as if I were actually being unreasonable about this plan.

"We're not baiting her into a setup," I said. "We're baiting her into a *conversation*. One where Ilias is supposedly defecting. Where I've stepped away. Where the Commission is fracturing from the inside."

Maxim frowned. "We're going to need to sell this so hard." He rubbed a hand over his neck, looking over the map.

I met his eyes. "She'll believe it if we leak that I have already splintered from the group."

Maxim's face darkened. "That's a line."

"Not if it's for show. Not if it gets her in arm's reach." I flicked the cigarette off the rooftop, watching the ember spiral. "Let her think I'm angry that I don't trust any of you anymore. That I've lost control in my anger over Theo. That Ilias offered me a new future. Ilias will be my brother-in-law after all. It's believable. We need her to come to the meeting. That's it."

Conall grinned in the gloom. "It could work. She remembers you as the boy who was all teeth and claws, who let his anger get the best of him. She doesn't know the man you've become." He nodded. "This could work."

Veronica patched into the encrypted call, her voice clear despite the lag. "I've laid the digital breadcrumbs. Rumors that you and Ilias met secretly in Sorrento. That you've pulled funding from the Commission's larger pipeline. Will that work?"

Ilias, seated next to me, snorted softly. "Yeah, I think that'll be enough to get her interested."

"She needs to think I'm ready to betray everyone for the sake of survival." I'd thought this through and talked it over with Bacco and Carlo before I brought it up. I wanted to ensure that our lines of communication didn't have any holes that she could see through.

Veronica continued, "She'll do one of two things: retaliate, or try to co-opt you."

"She'll co-opt," I said. "It's what she's best at. Manipulation."

"And when she does?"

I looked at Ilias. "We give her a meeting. One of your deepwater cargo ships. Greek registry. No crew. Just her... and us. I want it rigged to blow. Something you can sacrifice."

Ilias nodded slowly. "Good. We're not fucking around." His grin widened. "She'll think she's cutting a new deal. We make her think she's carving up the Commission with a new partner."

"And then?" Veronica asked.

I didn't blink. "Then I'll either put a bullet in her skull and drop her body into the fucking Black Sea or I'll blow her sky high, or both just to be sure."

———

The sea outside the port of Trieste glittered like spilled oil, dark and rippling under the weight of the coming storm. I stood on the deck of Ilias's freighter—*Nykte*—a steel beast usually tasked with hauling legitimate cargo for Anthakos Enterprises. Tonight, it had a different job: to become a tomb.

The air carried the tang of salt and diesel. Below deck, our men moved silently, checking gear, sweeping every inch of the ship for bugs or last-minute surprises. This plan had no room for error. Carlotta had eluded us for months, her fingerprints found on black-market deals, data leaks, and targeted hits. Now, we'd drawn her out—not with threats, but with ambition. The only thing she loved more than control was winning.

And we were about to give her both, or the illusion.

"She took the bait," Ilias confirmed, joining me at the railing, suit jacket flapping in the sea breeze. "Private meeting. One-on-one. She thinks I'm going rogue."

"Arrogant. Good," I said, voice flat.

Maxim joined us next, his expression unreadable, with the moonlight accentuating the harsh angles of his face. Conall lit a cigarette behind him, squinting at the horizon. "She's still using Renzetti's encryption patterns," Maxim murmured. "She thinks she's clever. This whole plan she's building hinges on Ilias's shipping lines. She must really want them. This is a huge risk."

Ilias didn't respond. He didn't need to.

We had all seen what Carlotta left in her wake: the soldiers she'd corrupted, the lieutenants who turned up dead, the girls trafficked under fake medical licenses, and the poison she'd poured into every corner of the world we built.

The conference room had been transformed into a high-stakes boardroom.

Chrome fixtures adorned a sleek Greek marble table, accompanied by coffee, Turkish delights, and imported wine—a theater of civility.

Behind the fake wall, I had a weapons locker, a kill switch for the doors, and a live feed to the upper deck. Like we'd planned, the ship was rigged to blow. Everyone would be escorted off the ship except for a small squad of Ilias's men. The detonator would be held on a small shipping vessel by Maxim and Conall. It would be a second option for us, just in case. I was pretty sure that we wouldn't need it, but you never knew.

Frankie had sent me a photo of Theo earlier. She was laughing at something baby Vasily had done, arms full of fabric swatches. That girl made me think of sunlight even in places like this.

"Thirty minutes out," Conall called from the comms. "We need to get ourselves over to that fishing boat or we'll blow this whole op," he chuckled darkly. "And not in the way we talked about."

I flexed my gloved hands, leather creaking. "Positions."

Ilias would meet her first. Alone. Play the part of the ambitious younger crime boss looking to break from the Commission. He'd offer her access to his shipping lines. That was her weakness—legitimacy. With Anthakos Enterprises, she could move anything under the radar.

"She won't expect me," I said. "That's the bait. Just enough truth to make her feel safe."

"She'll want assurances," Ilias said. "Documents. Trade access."

"Hand her that USB full of mock manifests just like we planned."

Ilias looked at me then, really looked. "You ready?"

"No," I said honestly, but when the mother who raised you to be a weapon turns that weapon on your family—

You *reload*.

And you aim for the heart.

———

The transport boat moored easily alongside us, despite the rocking swell. She emerged like a wraith in a white trench coat, her eyes concealed behind oversized sunglasses. Two guards, Eastern European muscle, flanked her. She appeared older than I remembered, more brittle.

But her smile was the same. Sharp and cruel.

I watched her through the feed as she stepped onto the deck, her heels clicking sharply against the steel. Ilias greeted her with a disarming air of casual confidence, like it was every day that you had a meeting with a super villain.

"Ilias," she purred. "Your message surprised me. All of these developments have surprised me."

"I figured it was time to stop playing second fiddle," he said, walking beside her into the conference room. "The others have become... possessive." She arched a brow. "I believe in partnerships." He continued. "Partnerships that are beneficial." He gave her a wink that was so blatantly suggestive that it made me throw up a little in my mouth. Wow, he was really taking one for the team.

I watched every movement through the security camera: her posture, the twitch of her fingers. Was she buying this?

"Let's get to business, shall we?" She opened a tablet. "I am interested in a ... beneficial partnership." She gave him a coy smile. Gross. "With your logistics pipeline." Her hand traced over his, and I was astounded to see that he was relaxed as she pawed him. She even leaned into him. Eww.

"Of course," he hummed as if he were unconcerned about her wandering fingers.

"I'd provide incentives. Monetary and others," she cooed. "I have product I'd like to move."

Ilias nodded, leaning into her thoughtfully, going so far as to drag a finger over her cheek. "We can do that, but if I turn on the Commission and dip into trafficking, I'm going to need protection."

She leaned back in her chair. "You'd have it."

That was my signal.

———

The door slid shut with a mechanical hiss. Carlotta barely had time to react before I stepped through the secondary entrance with my weapon drawn.

She froze. "You," she breathed.

"Me," I said, pistol steady. "Did you think you could rebuild the empire on our ashes? Or that Ilias would work with you?" I couldn't hold back the sneer.

"Angelo," she started as she stood slowly, defiance crackling in her voice. "I built an empire."

"You built nothing but trash. We rooted it

out. It might have taken a while, but we did it."

Her guards lunged. Two shots rang out as Ilias's guards took them out. It was almost too easy.

Carlotta didn't flinch. She stared at me like I was still the boy who wanted her approval. "Angelo," she said, softer now. "Don't make this mistake. I know things. I know who your father is. I could—"

"I don't care. No speeches. No last words." This was not the sort of evil villain moment where someone talked their way out of their death. This was the end. I hoped Remo would forgive me for not discovering the truth about his parentage, but I wouldn't play games with her.

The shot echoed.

She crumpled.

Now she was just another ghost.

———

The sea swallowed her body silently. No funeral. No fanfare.

Only the wind and the creak of the ship.

"She would've torn us apart," Ilias said quietly.

"She almost did," Conall added.

"But not anymore," I said. "We rebuild. Tighter. Meaner. Smarter."

Maxim passed me a bottle of whiskey after taking a swallow. "To brotherhood."

Taking the bottle, I swallowed and then passed it to Conall. I thought of Theo and the life I had waiting for me back home while I looked out over the water.

Now it was done.

There were always more devils in the dark, but I was ready for them all.

CHAPTER 40
THEODOSIA

THE SKY WAS a soft peach blush when the call came through.

I was in the middle of sketching an elaborate embroidery concept for the wedding table runners (which sounds excessive, but hello, you don't just marry the don of the Santelli mafia with a few white roses and a shrug). The idea had hit me in the middle of the night like most of my good ones—bold, whimsical, and a little chaotic. I'd already spilled two cups of tea, pricked my thumb, and ruined a perfectly good silk scarf I was using for the spilled tea.

Norris was humming something vaguely operatic in the kitchen downstairs. The scent of lemon and garlic floated up from the oven like an invitation to heaven.

Then my phone buzzed.

It was a message from Angelo.

> Future Hubs: It's done. She's
> dead. I'm coming home.

I froze. My stylus hung in mid-air like my brain couldn't quite catch up. Carlotta. Dead. The woman who had nearly orchestrated the unraveling of everything—gone.

I stood slowly, knees trembling like I'd run a mile in heels, and walked to the window. The brownstone street below was quiet, unbothered. The world hadn't exploded, no bells rang, no celestial choir sang.

There had been whispers and smoke signals, the kind of silence that meant danger. When he left for Romania, I knew what he meant to do, but the knowledge had curled inside me like a warm but unpredictable sleeping cat. Part of me hadn't believed she could be ended. Part of me had been waiting for another chess move.

I stared at the message again, reread it five times, and then turned on my heel, the hem of my kaftan fluttering like a cape. The house was quiet except for Norris and the rhythmic tick of the antique clock in the foyer.

I descended the stairs barefoot, my mind spinning. Norris turned from the stove, face crinkling into a smile. "Miss Theodosia. You look like you've seen the archangel himself."

"Close," I murmured, and grabbed the back of a kitchen chair to steady myself. "I came to make myself some tea."

Norris blinked. "Something happen?"

I looked him square in the eye. "Nothing bad. Something wonderful. Carlotta Santelli is dead."

He stilled. No questions. Just one solemn nod. "I'll put the kettle on and get us some scones." He gave me a wink. "I think there's a fresh batch."

Angelo didn't walk through the front door that evening. He prowled.

The moment I heard his boots on the steps, something electric raced down my spine. I was curled up in the armchair, a blanket over my knees, my sketches tossed aside, watching a rom-com. I didn't move until the door opened.

And there he was.

My dark prince. My war-torn king.

His coat was damp at the edges, and his eyes were shadowed but bright—the kind of brightness that came after blood. His hands were bare and clean, but I saw it in his posture. Something terrible had unraveled inside him and taken shape as something new.

"You're home," I said. "I missed you."

He didn't speak at first. Just crossed the room, wrapped his arms around me, and buried his face in my hair. We stayed like that. No clock ticking. No words.

Just breathing each other in.

And then, he whispered, "It's finally over." He pulled back enough to look at me. "I didn't want you to hear it from anyone else. I had to do it myself," he murmured. "She fell for the whole thing. Thought Ilias turned on us. She wanted his ships so badly that she stepped right into the trap we had."

"And you sprang it," I answered. He'd told me about it, explained the whole thing the day before. It had been bold. Frankie and I had wondered whether Carlotta would buy it.

His mouth twitched. "We burned the whole goddamn thing." He looked older. Sharper. Like the edge of him had been honed in fire. "Blew that ship up to kingdom come afterwards. It was glorious."

"Are you okay?" I asked gently.

He pulled me into his lap, arms around my waist. "I will be. Now."

CHAPTER 41
ANGELO

PEOPLE WHO CLAIM that jet lag isn't real are lying. After a shower and a hot meal, I curled up with Theo. She smelled like sunshine and charcoal pencils, in that order, her dark hair wrapping its tendrils around me. I tucked her against me before collapsing into a sleep filled with boats on fire and bodies floating down to Davy Jones's locker.

When I woke Theo had a leg thrown over my hip and one of those luscious thighs pressed against my cock which was already at attention. Rolling away, I watched as she fell back against her pillow, her eyes fluttering as she settled again into sleep, mumbling a little to herself. The cami that she wore to bed had shifted, exposing her nipples, pink and soft in the daylight.

Unable to help myself, I leaned forward, pulling down the rest of the cami. Her tits were luscious and ripe. Touching each one softly, I watched her face as I trailed fingers along the sides of each one, weighing them in my hands until I circled her nipples. I even went so far as to give each one a gentle suck, so they glistened in the morning light, looking like juicy berries, wet and ripe.

I didn't want her to wake. I remembered she'd said that I had her permission. The thought made me even harder, and I had to take my cock in my hand encircling it in a vice grip collapsing against the pillows as I watched her. Maybe I'd lie here and jerk off while she slept. My balls tightened. Perhaps I'd do both. Jerk off and then fuck her. Indulging for a moment, I worked my length lazily with the pre-cum that had already gathered, watching Theo the whole time. I was close. Moving my hand faster along my shaft I let myself go, my cock jerking as I came. Fighting to catch my breath, I fell back against the pillows. I could clean myself up, but instead I scooped up my come and parted Theo's thighs so I could spread it over her pussy.

She was soft and warm. I went back for more come and repeated the pattern until she was slick, opening like a flower. Already I could sense that she was aroused, her body flushing, her pussy beginning to weep. Kneeling between her thighs, I watched her face for signs she was awake. She looked asleep, but I remembered what she'd said … she'd told me she would pretend while I stuffed her full. Working my fingers into her channel, I teased back and forth circling in and out, around her clit and back inside just shallowly. She was soaked already, dripping over my hand.

My dirty girl.

My cock was hard as iron again as I eased inside a tiny bit, just the tip. My thighs trembled with the effort. If she was asleep, I was going to keep her that way. Her face was still relaxed, but there were signs of restlessness. Maybe she thought she was dreaming? Leveraging myself over her, I thrust shallowly, so slowly that I thought I might die of pleasure as the tip dove in and out. Whispering to her quietly, *"Who's my dirty girl? Look how naughty you are."*

I worked a little further, my pelvis pumping languidly back and forth. This was heaven, I thought. Fucking my pretty little angel. There was no way I could hold back anymore, though, against all that white hot heat. She was dripping all over my cock, and that was all it took for me to blow my load even with my cock only partially inside her and my hand gripping the base.

Jesus.

Leaning back on my knees, I took in the sight of her. Rumpled with come dripping out of her. Perfection. When she opened her eyes and gave me a sleepy smile, I couldn't help but be pleased.

She wiggled her bottom a little and eased a hand between her dripping thighs. "Having fun?"

"Very much so. About to have more." No way would I be leaving her wanting, not to mention I had every intention of making up these last few days that we'd missed. If I could spend every day in bed with her, I would.

Flipping her over, I arranged her on her knees. "Push that ass out, *piccola*. Let me see that pretty pussy of yours. I want to see it dripping." I gave her ass an experimental smack watching her moan and wiggle. "Were you pretending, little girl?"

She moaned as she did as I asked, even as I smacked her other cheek, watching the red bloom over her flesh. I knew she liked it when I gave her a light spanking, and I was going to comply at every opportunity. Her pussy was pink and swollen and dripped now as she did as I asked.

"That's it, baby. Just like that." I covered her body with mine rubbing myself against her, my semi-hard cock against the crack of her ass as I moved back and forth. Snaking a hand around to her clit I darted my fingers through her slippery folds to flick her clit.

"I'm so close," she whimpered. Her greedy pussy latched onto my fingers as I pumped them into her in time with my thrusts.

"What were you dreaming about, beautiful. Be truthful?" My fingers pinched her clit.

"Uh," she stammered as she squirmed.

My cock was at attention now and I stilled my fingers as she tried to gain purchase. "Or were you pretending? Just wanting me to fill you up, hmm?"

"Angelo, please. I can't remember."

Her body was pliant under mine, her folds slippery with fluid. I had only one thought. I was going to fill her with more. Make her come. Put a baby inside her. Today. My cock slid against her skin as I flattened the palm of my hand making it impossible for Theo to get any gratification. "You want my cock you greedy girl?"

"Yes, yes, yes." She pressed against my hand as I pushed hard against her.

"How do you want it, Theo? I could put it here?" I pulled back and held my cock against her tiny forbidden hole. "Do you want it there?" She whimpered so delicately that I was tempted to try it, but she wasn't ready for that. Slapping her on her ass my cock jumped as the red raised underneath the skin. "Use your voice. Where should I put it?"

"My pussy. Put it in my pussy. *Please.*"

"That's my good girl." Notching to that pretty pussy of hers I rammed into her, curving over her body so that I could capture that kernel of nerves at the same time as I pistoned in and out of her desperately until she fluttered around me with a scream. "Fuck yes. Milk me dry. This is what I meant when I said I'd fill you up, *piccola*. Every day."

It felt like she was dragging every drop from me as I came, the ropes of come jetting into her over and over again as I jerked against her. When I collapsed next to her I set a lazy hand over her pussy to push the come back inside her.

"You're crazy. You know that?" she said, giving me a lazy smile. "I love it."

It was a good thing she did, because I loved her. So much that my heart hurt.

———

I rolled my shoulders, glancing at the passenger seat. Theo was half-asleep, curled up in oversized white overalls, black Converse high-tops, and a long-sleeved black-and-white striped t-shirt. I had already teased her that she was in her mime costume and gotten a smack for it. She had her hair piled high today, lanced through with glittering sticks that she said were vintage. Sunlight poured through the windshield in soft golden stripes as we coasted down the Hudson, on our way to a place she didn't know existed. Not really.

A surprise.

She deserved one after being cooped up in the brownstone all this time.

I found the space the week after I returned from Romania. Nestled on a quiet street in the Meatpacking District, it was a high-ceilinged, light-soaked corner unit with raw brick walls, industrial beams, and floor-to-ceiling windows. It was the kind of place where dreams would get sewn into fabric, the kind of place where the very soon-to-be Theo Anthakos-Santelli would build an empire of her own.

She stirred beside me, groaning. "Where are we going again?"

I smirked. "You'll see."

"If this is a bait-and-switch brunch situation, Angelo, I swear to God—although I'm not unhappy to be out of the house," she added.

"No bait. No switch." I reached over and laced my fingers through hers. "Just trust me."

She huffed, but I saw the smile tug at her lips. She'd been glowing since I came home. And louder. Busier. Her entire brain was firing on all cylinders as wedding planning consumed every spare thought. It was infectious.

"Frankie thinks we should do a garden theme," she said, quickly picking up the thread. "But Cora wants old-world glamour. You should've seen her Pinterest boards. It's like Versailles and the Met Gala had a baby. Both are pretty funny since Cora didn't plan her wedding, and Frankie didn't even get one." She frowned. "Maybe that's why they're so invested."

I chuckled. "And what do you want?" It seemed like she was struggling with that, trying to balance what everyone else wanted. Someone needed to ensure that Theo got what she wanted.

Theo leaned her head against the window. "Color. Texture. Layers. Nothing boring. And I want there to be food stations, not a sit-down dinner. People should graze and dance, not be stuck beside someone's drunk uncle."

"You realize we're still probably inviting that drunk uncle."

"Sure, but he can wander."

She turned to me, eyes sparkling. "You don't mind me going crazy with this, right? I know you probably pictured something quieter. Classier."

"Theo," I said, slowing as we pulled up to the curb, "I pictured *you,* which means chaos. Glitter. And a string quartet playing AC/DC. I love you. Whatever you want for a wedding. Whatever that looks like is what I want."

"I love you, too, babe." She laughed as I parked, then frowned. "Wait... why are we stopping here?"

I got out and walked around to open her door. "Come on. You'll see."

The building appeared unremarkable from the outside—an old warehouse with faded signage and worn concrete steps. However, the interior had been completely renovated into something breathtaking. I unlocked the door and stepped aside to let her enter first.

The moment the light hit her face as she stepped inside, it was worth every second of keeping the secret.

She froze. "Oh my God."

The studio was massive, sunlight spilling across the warm hardwood floors. Exposed brick walls framed the room, and tall windows overlooked the street. Empty rolling racks stood, and the central table was bare—but it radiated promise. I'd had a couple of industrial sewing machines brought in, embroidery machines, and so much fabric that there were racks filled with it. There was even a private nook at the back, partially walled off, featuring a vintage drafting desk and a moodboard already pinned with swatches I'd stolen from her sketchbooks.

She walked in a slow circle, mouth slightly open. "Angelo... what is this?"

"It's yours."

She blinked at me. "What do you mean?"

I leaned in the doorway, arms crossed. "You wanted to start *Mythos Designs* here in New York. This will give you space to work. Professional. If you wanted. No pressure."

Looking around the space, I tried to organize my thoughts. I thought I had prepared the speech, but I had been wrong. "When this whole thing started, you left New York to pursue something. I don't want you to ever feel cheated or that you made a bad bargain. In Florence, you had started something great. My mother messed that up for you." I still wasn't saying it right.

She moved slowly, reverently, touching the beams, running her hand along the windowsill. "This is insane. I …."

"You deserve everything." I reached for her, wrapping my arms around her, pressing my face to her shoulder. "I'm going to make sure you have it."

She tilted her face to mine, eyes glassy. "You know you aren't responsible for what your mother did."

The words hit like a hammer. But I didn't flinch. "I know, but I'm still connected to that woman and what she did." I hadn't confessed to Remo yet that I'd had a chance to find out who his father was, and I'd turned it down. I wasn't sure it'd do him any good to know that information. "The studio isn't about her. I want you to be happy here."

"This is gorgeous. I love it." She leaned in

for a kiss, letting me bend her back so I could nip at her throat.

There were still calls I needed to make—loose ends in Naples and Singapore, and a few men who needed reminding that the Commission was neither weak nor fractured, but that could wait.

CHAPTER 42
THEODOSIA

THE AFTERNOON of my wedding began with a cup of decaf tea and a sense of panic that only a designer-turned-bride could feel when she realized her hand-embroidered gloves had gone missing. I had been running full steam to finalize the details for the last two weeks. Deciding to make my own dress, as well as Frankie and Cora's, had proven to be a bit more than I could handle. I had barely made it.

"Norris!" I called out, darting around Angelo's brownstone in a silk robe printed with black-and-white stripes and tiny embroidered hearts. "My gloves! Have you seen my gloves?" The gloves with the pearl skull buttons! The gloves that took me a week and a ruined manicure to finish!

Norris, unfazed, looked up from his task of carefully arranging trays of lavender macarons and dark chocolate tartlets shaped like playing cards. "Check under the cat."

We didn't even have a cat. But there *was* a suspiciously lumped throw blanket on the chaise in my studio. I flung it back to find my gloves nestled there like misbehaving children, clearly moved by no one but my absent-minded self.

Crisis averted. I pressed them to my chest and exhaled dramatically. "Ok, we're in the clear. We may proceed."

My wedding day. My *wedding night*. It still felt like I was starring in a very elaborate fever dream—one where I'd fallen in love with the brooding don of the Santelli mafia, gotten engaged in his fortress of a bedroom, and was now preparing to marry him in a gothic garden wonderland.

Was it too on-the-nose that I'd chosen an Alice in Wonderland-esque/Through the Looking Glass theme? Probably. Did I care? Absolutely not.

The small garden had been transformed for the evening ceremony, with the massive weeping willow serving as the ceremony's centerpiece. We had to expand slightly into the former parking area and convert it into a chessboard, which increased our square footage; however, everything worked seamlessly. Antique mirrors hung from the trees, mismatched velvet chairs were provided for guests, tables were shaped like oversized playing cards, and candelabras perched on top of them. Fairy lights and canopies would drape over everything, making it look even more magical. Guests were invited to wear themed masks if they chose to.

I'd gone full Theo. No regrets.

I stood before the full-length mirror as Frankie zipped me into my gown.

"You look like a haunted porcelain doll," she said with genuine admiration.

"I was going for 'Victorian ghost who murdered her husband on their honeymoon and still haunts the grounds in couture.'"

"Well, nailed it," Frankie said, drily.

My dress was custom—obviously. It featured layers of sheer black tulle embroidered with crimson roses, tiny hidden thorns, a high collar, and fitted sleeves. My veil was cathedral-length, scattered with hand-sewn pearls. I wore the gloves, of course.

I'd even made gowns for Frankie and Cora, unique and whimsical, that matched their personalities and the theme. Both were simpler versions of mine, with lower cuts and shorter sleeves, but full tulle skirts. Frankie's had the Alice theme—a deeper blue with a white sash and puffed sleeves that looked innocent. I'd embroidered white rabbits throughout. Cora's dress was in shades of emerald green, featuring a deep V-neck bodice that matched her eyes, and was embroidered with tiny caterpillars that made her laugh. Luckily, one of the machines Angelo had purchased for my new business space was a commercial embroidery machine. It had taken a few online tutorials and a visit from a representative to get the basics down, but it had made some magic happen.

"You nervous?" Cora asked, holding baby Vasily on her hip as he gurgled and tried to eat the edge of her chiffon shawl.

I paused, heart thudding. "No. Just… It's a big day, and he's not just any man. He's *Angelo*."

"You mean the man who stares at you like he wants to fight the Devil himself?" Cora smirked. "Who looks like he's about to ravish you any second?"

I flushed. "Yes. That one." The one who had ravished me this morning, driving into me until we collapsed onto the sheets, sated and happy.

The bridal suite door opened, and Maxim

419

stepped in, flanked by Ilias and Conall. "They're ready," he said, accentuating the wolf in his smile. Maxim cradled Vasily protectively in one arm, holding him comfortably as if it were just another Tuesday.

Ilias offered me his arm. "You look amazing. In the best possible way." He had been stressed over the last few weeks, and I could see the lines around his eyes. He had been spending all his time and considerable resources trying to locate Galena without success, which was driving him crazy. Today, he was trying to put it aside, but we were all concerned for him and hoping Galena was alright.

Smiling at him, I said, "Coming from you, that's a compliment I'll cherish forever." He didn't miss the sarcasm.

We filed out. The garden hummed with soft music, *"Turning Page"* by Sleeping At Last. Valentino Cardoni sat in the second row, his young daughter asleep against his shoulder. Remo gave me a wink and muttered, "You're gonna give my brother a damn heart attack."

Perfect. Everything looked gorgeous. Well, almost perfect. I had hoped my sister could be here. Polina had finals, and Ilias had forbidden it despite the tears we'd both shed.

He was being an overbearing ass about the whole thing. Not about her having to stay for finals — if it had just been over that, I would have set a new date, but about her not being around our 'lifestyle.' If he wasn't careful, Polina was going to full-on revolt. However, family drama would have to wait. Tightening my hold on Ilias's arm, I set my sights on the aisle in front of me.

Angelo stood at the end of the garden path, beneath a wrought-iron arch blooming with blood-red roses. He wore a black-on-black three-piece suit. His eyes, those soul-punching eyes, were locked on mine like he'd been waiting his whole life for me.

I walked towards him and everything else disappeared. We had intended to keep the ceremony brief, but each of us had something small we wanted to share. Angelo took my hand as if he were claiming it forever. The judge that Angelo had wrangled into being our officiant looked slightly uncomfortable, but rambled through the ceremony while we watched each other.

When it came time for our additions, Angelo added gently, "I vow to build you a world that is safe. That's ours. No matter the cost. To love you deeply as you deserve. To honor you and our children. To never let any harm come to you, and to strike down our enemies."

The judge looked at him askance, and I wondered if it had been wise to bring him here to witness Angelo vowing to potentially commit crimes even if it made my panties wet.

My voice trembled only once. "And I vow to be your chaos, your calm, your home. I vow to love you unconditionally as you are. To take you, Angelo Santelli, as my husband."

When the judge pronounced us man and wife, we kissed to thunderous applause.

The reception was just as I envisioned. Kostas and Vaso reenacted our childhood dances with an embarrassing flair. My brothers gave toasts that made me smile.

"Here's to Theo," Ilias said, raising his glass. "Remember the time you took Nonna's curtains and turned them into a dress? You've always had a vision, Thea. It just usually involved breaking things or stealing fabric from somewhere you shouldn't."

Everyone chuckles and glances over at us. "Really, curtains?" Remo asks.

"But look at you now. Gorgeous. Glowing. Married. To a man I once swore I'd strangle with my bare hands." I looked askance at

Ilias, who still had his glass raised and that serious expression on his face.

"Did he really swear he'd strangle you?" I asked Angelo in a stage whisper.

"Well, when we were like twelve," he whispered back. "Pretty sure he got over it." He kissed my shoulder. "Pretty sure."

The audience was in rapt attention, particularly those we had invited who are 'mafia-adjacent'. Most of the people here were *famiglia*, but there were a few guests who had been invited due to other connections they had that were potentially useful. The wedding was still intimate, but some people couldn't just be ignored.

"Don't worry, Santelli. I've evolved. Now I'd use piano wire. I'm classy like that."

Angelo smirked even though a lady next to me looked over nervously. Those who weren't familiar with our situation might wonder if Ilias was serious, but it was hard to believe when Conall was snorting in his whiskey like he was.

"Seriously though…You two are disgustingly in love. Like, 'burn the house down but call it foreplay' kind of in love, it's terrifying and inspiring. Mostly terrifying. And Angelo —credit where it's due, man. You didn't just show up. You stayed. You protected her, made her laugh, provided her with a dream space for her business, and managed to survive several dinners with our family without anyone getting hurt. That's love. Or masochism. Either way—respect." He raised his glass. "So here's to Theo—my brilliant, feral sister, and to Angelo—who now belongs to her, body and soul, good luck with that. May your life be filled with beautiful things, good wine, and no FBI raids. And if there *are* FBI raids, may your security footage always mysteriously glitch." He grinned. "To chaos and couture. To murder and matrimony. To Theo and Angelo—may you always be each other's favorite felony."

Geez, my brother was going to make me cry with that speech. I raised my glass as Ilias polished off his glass. "Yamas!"

Later, Angelo pulled me aside while I was making the rounds. I'd swapped my heels for a pair of flip-flops. "You made this..." he looked around the garden, now glowing with fairy lights and candlelit shadows, "...a dream. A fairytale."

"You gave me the space to make it. That's love, right? Letting the other person be exactly who they are. Crazy and all." When I asked people to come in costume, I wasn't sure they'd deliver, but they did. We had a

Cheshire Cat, a Mad Hatter, a White Rabbit, and even someone with a teapot mask. Anyone who knew me knew I loved a masquerade.

He pressed his forehead to mine. "And I love exactly who you are."

We danced our first dance beneath the willow tree to a rendition of "A Forest" by The Cure. It was very us. Later, as the guests drifted off, I stole one last moment with Cora and Frankie, watching the lights flicker across the garden.

"You did it," Frankie whispered. "You're Mrs. Santelli now."

I grinned, touching the wedding set on my finger. "I'm officially part of your family, which is somehow scarier."

We all laughed, and behind me, Angelo waited—my future wrapped in a suit, bloodlines, and something tender neither of us ever expected.

Our wonderland was real. It had thorns, but that was the way I liked it.

———

Looking over at Angelo as he took off his jacket, the evening played out in my mind like a movie reel. It had been exactly as I imagined: absolute perfection, from Lev arriving with his Mad Hatter mask to the impromptu game of charades we played after most of the guests had left.

One of the things I loved most was the sense of family that being with Angelo gave me. I cherished every facet of our relationship. That feeling of being under the stars with his friends, laughing together amidst the remnants of costumes and scattered cheeseboards around us, was incredible. The love on everyone's faces surrounded me so tightly that it almost burned. I gripped Angelo's hand so hard that he turned, caught the look on my face, and told everyone to get out.

"What are you thinking about so hard over there, *piccola*? Naughty thoughts?"

He stripped off his shirt, exposing all those planes of muscles, making my mouth water. I hadn't even moved, still parked on the edge of the bed in my gown, but I moved now, collapsing on my knees and fumbling with the front of his slacks.

"I like what you're thinking, wife," he growled as he rushed to help.

He was hard before my mouth closed around the tip, my tongue swirling over the smooth skin, tasting the saltiness that was distinctly his. My other hand gathered his balls and rolled them just the way he liked. I'd found that the savage edge he rode in the mafia world bled out into every part of his life. He could be gentle, but he liked a bite as well.

"Theo," he groaned, as I ran my tongue along the slit at his tip. "That feels so good, baby." He stared down at me his eyes dilated as I flattened my tongue and relaxed my throat to let him thrust deeper as I sucked.

He groaned as he thrust gently forward into the cavity of my mouth. He was thick and long which made sucking his cock challenging, but I'd adapted into a hand-job/sucking version that he seemed very fond of. I was working on my gag reflex, but he seemed to be more than satisfied with what was happening, so I wasn't going to second-guess myself.

"That's my dirty girl. Are you wet?"

Angelo knew me well. I was soaked through my thong, my thighs slick, but I didn't want to touch myself. I knew I'd go off like a rocket. What I wanted was between my lips right now. He pulled out with a pop as if he could read my mind.

"That's enough of that, *piccola*. I know where my come needs to be—no wasting it. I want it between your thighs. Deep inside you." His current obsession seemed to be fixated on getting me pregnant, and I couldn't say I minded at all. Either the idea or the activity. He picked me up and planted me on the bed before shucking off his slacks. "Let's get you up and out of that gown before I ruin it."

Standing, I let him undo the clasps on the back of the dress until it fell onto the floor in a pool of fabric. "You're so beautiful, wife. Up on the bed. Spread those thighs so I can see what's mine," he growled as he fisted his cock.

Doing as he asked, I let my legs fall open, watching his face as he bit his lip in anticipation. There was never any doubt in my mind that I turned him on when we came together. Every glance, every line of his body consistently showed me that I did. He had helped me make significant progress in my confidence.

Crouching between my thighs he ran his fingers up against the silk gusset that covered my pussy. "You *are* wet," he groaned. "Dripping." Even his words were coated with approval.

My corset pushed my breasts to new heights so they spilled over the top, but I made no move to stop him as he pushed the thong aside and shoved into me. It was exactly what I wanted—Angelo raw and unfiltered. Angelo had varied moods when it came to sex, but he always made sure I was ready first and always left me satisfied. I'd learned that I would take him anyway he wanted me. We were already starting to splinter on the second thrust, my head thrown back, my nails raking a path down his back as he pounded his release into me.

"I got you a wedding present," I said as he cupped a hand over my pussy sliding his fingers into his come and pushing it back into me. The habit always made me hornier than ever, making me want to go another round even when I was tender and sore.

"This seems like a very satisfactory present. I'd give it five stars, " he smiled at me.

"You'll like this present too." In fact, he'd love the present I got. "It's in the bathroom. Go look."

He gave me another lazy squeeze, those calloused fingertips swirling around my clit. "Okay. I'll be right back, but I have plans for you." He leaned in for a kiss.

Wiggling out of the corset and the soaking panties, I slipped beneath the sheet before he came back, standing stunned in the doorway holding the pregnancy test in one hand.

"*Piccola?* Does this mean what I think it means?"

"If you think it means we're going to be parents, then you're right."

He threw the stick onto the bed and cradled my face, staring hard at me. "I'm going to make you happy. I swear it. I'll be the best father I can be. One that our children deserve. The man *you* deserve."

Finally, Angelo Santelli was mine.

CHAPTER 43
ANGELO

SIX MONTHS LATER

THE HUM of *Fortune* was different after hours. No music pulsed through the walls, no bodies pressed against the bar. Just the low hum of electricity and the distant clang of a glass being shelved somewhere in the back. The bar was closed, but we'd taken over the lounge like old times.

The city outside pulsed with life, but in here, it was the five of us again.

"I miss when we had an enemy," Conall said dryly. "At least you could put a bullet in that. All this hunting for someone who doesn't want to be found, and doesn't know who we are, is ..." He threw up his hands.

I let out a humorless laugh. We were all grappling with intense emotions about Galena. Still, I couldn't disagree with Conall.

It was easier when there was an enemy to confront. That was more up our alley than searching for a girl who was hiding from the world.

Maxim didn't speak. He stared at the table as if it might crack under the weight of his thoughts. "Galena is just afraid," he muttered with irritation.

"She didn't leave because of anything to do with our world," Ilias said finally, as if that made anything better or told us anything we didn't know.

"No," Maxim agreed, voice tight. "I should have been there for her. She doesn't even know she's a Volkov."

"You would have told her," I said. Her not knowing she was a Volkov had ultimately become an issue. If she had known she had a brother, she could have come to Maxim for help.

"I would have," Maxim admitted. "I should have." Regret tinged his words. Maxim was having a hard time moving past the knowledge that he had missed the fact that his sister's circumstances had changed. She had been injured, and he hadn't even known.

Kostas had dug deep. Veronica had chased signals, burned through her usual arsenal of tracing tools and dark web tactics, but Galena had left nothing behind—no pings, no purchases, no footprints. It was like she had ghosted her way into another life.

"She knows how to vanish," Ilias said. "Or she has just watched a lot of TV."

"She's scared," Maxim said, his voice raw. "And she's smart. She thought disappearing was the right thing to do."

"Six months," Conall said. "She hasn't even sent a message to a friend?"

Maxim shook his head once. "Nothing we can find."

"Dead?" Conall asked quietly.

"No," Ilias and Maxim said in unison.

They knew. We all shared the same stubborn gut feeling. She was out there. Somewhere. Hiding from a past we didn't create, but sure as hell could burn down if we found it.

"She might resurface eventually," I said. "When the heat's low. When she thinks no one's watching."

"I won't stop looking," Ilias muttered. He'd developed a stubborn interest in Galena that I wasn't sure I understood. There hadn't been any pressure from anyone recently regarding Galena, not that it meant he was off the hook ...

Maxim's hands were clenched into fists, knuckles white. He didn't say it aloud, but I could feel it: he was torn between hunting down every shadow and letting her have peace.

"Maybe that's the point," he said, voice low. "Maybe she doesn't want to be found. Not yet."

"What about the police report about the assault?" Remo asked.

"Haven't been able to narrow anything down on that." Maxim shrugged, his thoughts far away. "We worked through the intel they had, but Galena didn't identify anyone."

Even as we canvassed the neighborhoods and shook the trees, it seemed like the small-time crooks scattered. It felt like we did more harm than good by asking questions about her, and in the end, we decided we weren't helping anything and were bringing more attention than anything else. The report had turned out to be a dead end so far, but I had a sneaking suspicion that Ilias was still pursuing his own leads.

"We'd better wrap this up," Maxim tapped an unlit cigarette on the bar. "The women are going to be pissed if we're late."

Ilias glanced at his phone with a frown. "You're not wrong."

We had family night tonight, and we were already pushing it to make it back on time. Our wives had been understanding about the meeting and had worked around it, but expected us to arrive in a timely fashion. After everything that happened with Carlotta, we decided it'd be nice to have a rotating weekly dinner. Tonight it was at Conall and Frankie's, and I'd already received pictures earlier from Theo of her and my sister making funny faces as they made cupcakes.

We'd driven separately, which I didn't mind. It meant I had a chance to drive my Lamborghini Miura. I babied it as I drove over to Conall's Vinegar Hill building that he owned. Coaxing it down the alley behind the building, I flashed the headlights until the bay doors opened, allowing me to drive into the back entrance and let the doors seal behind me so I could park.

Conall had completely renovated the entire building to accommodate all of his soldiers. There were floors of meeting rooms, bunk rooms, and apartments for his right-hand men. At the top of the building, over-looking the Brooklyn Bridge, were his and Frankie's apartments. It was a cool place, but

435

I wouldn't want to live with my mafia so directly.

Giving Finn a nod as he opened the door to the penthouse for me, I ducked inside. It was already noisy and crowded, filled with laughter that only the chaos of our combined families could bring. My eyes were on Theo holding up a tiny pair of ruffled violet baby bloomers to show Frankie. She glowed now, her hand often resting on her stomach to feel our daughter kicking.

I moved forward, pushing past the obnoxious O'Kelly brothers, ignoring their jibes that they tossed my way. They loved to tease me about my singular focus. Wrapping Theo up from behind, I slid a hand over her belly as I bent a kiss to her neck. "Hello, wife. How are my girls?" She leaned back against me, relaxing.

"Husband," she purred. "We're good. I brought Frankie the rest of the outfit I was making for my niece."

Frankie rolled her eyes. "It could be a boy. We don't know yet."

Just this month, Frankie found out she was pregnant. We were thrilled for her and Conall, not to mention how happy we were that our children would be growing up together.

"Sure, but it could be a girl," Theo said reasonably. "Can't hurt to have a few starter outfits."

"That's right, piccola. You're so smart," I praised. I'd stopped listening and was focusing on pulling her against me. For some reason, her increase in libido had just amped mine up. I wondered if I could pull her into Conall's office and fuck her before dinner.

Frankie was giving us a knowing look. "You know, you could put that in the guest room for me. It'd be a *huge* help. I need to get a few things in order before dinner, and I don't want it to get dirty."

"What?" Theo started and then caught on. "Oh? Right. Thanks bestie. Angelo will help." She shoved it into my hands and hurried towards the guest room.

Giving my sister a wink, I followed my wife. Conall's penthouse was gorgeous, but it only had two spare rooms, an office, and the guest room, which was going to be designated as the nursery. Before I even pulled the door shut, Theo threw herself at me.

"What took you so long?" She fumbled with my belt.

"Oh, my naughty girl is needy …" I teased as Theo cut off the rest of my words, slamming her mouth against mine. I knew this

437

would be fast and furious. Ever since the pregnancy, Theo went off like a rocket as soon as we started, but I wasn't complaining. Getting the message, I let my wife take control as she dropped my slacks and pushed me onto an office chair before shimmying out of her panties. "Take what you need, *piccola*."

Fuck, she was so hot. Anchoring her back to my front I helped her sink onto my cock. "Just lie back, baby. Make yourself come while I fill up that pussy of yours. I'm going to make you feel so good. I can't get enough of you."

She slid her hand between us, her fingers feathering over me as I thrust in and out of her channel before going back to flick at her clit. I loved being close to her like this, feeling her tightening around me. Keeping up the pace while I pumped into her, I whispered, "That's my dirty girl. You've been waiting to be fucked all day haven't you?"

"Yes," Theo moaned, as I bit down on the flesh of her neck. I put my hand over hers, pinching that kernel of nerves. That was the magic trick. My wife came apart in a blaze, her pussy fluttering around me, finally allowing me to give in and surge one final time before I emptied into her.

Later, when we gathered around the table,

my hand in Theo's, I looked over at the crazy family to which we belonged and felt blessed. As an eleven-year-old so long ago, this image would never even have crossed my mind as a dream or a wish. Damn — I was so lucky. My gaze caught Ilias's for a heartbeat. His was somber and filled with worry. I wanted so badly for all of my family to find what I had. Vowing to redouble my efforts to help in the search to locate Galena, I refocused on Theo.

She was my happily ever after.

————

The End

THANKS FOR READING

Thank you <u>very much</u> for reading *Angelo's Vengeance*! If you enjoyed the book, I would greatly appreciate it if you could take a moment to leave a review.

As you can guess, the Haven Fox universe continues with Ilias's story in *Belonging to Ilias*. You can also get a glimpse of some of the other characters mentioned in this book in earlier novels of the Commission series, starting with *Maxim's Promise* and continuing to *Conall's Reign*.

If you're hungry for even more, you can check out my previous series, *The Iron Brotherhood*. You'll find novels with open-door spice, alpha men, stalking, and MC/Bratva Crossovers.

You can find complete book lists on my website: https://havenfoxauthor.com/

If you'd like to be notified of upcoming releases, you can follow my Amazon author account. You'll be kept up-to-date. 🤍

Get ready for Galena & Ilias's story next.